HOT MESS

BOOK ONE IN THE LOVE IS MESSY SERIES

EMILY GOODWIN

HOT MESS
Love is Messy Duet: Book One
©2017 Emily Goodwin
www.emilygoodwinbooks.com
www.facebook.com/emilygoodwin

Cover Photography: Sara Eirew
Models: Nick Bennett and Paméla Brisson
Editing: Love N Books
Proofreading: Contagious Edits

To all the single parents out there...you're doing a great job.

LEXI

Someday, I'll get my shit together. Today, however, is not that day. I bring my coffee to my lips and whirl around, tripping over the dog. The mug hits my teeth, and hot coffee sloshes down the front of my ivory blouse.

"Really, Pluto? You have to lay in the middle of the kitchen during rush hour?" I glare at the little mutt who looks at me, and then at his empty bowl. "I didn't forget to feed you," I say and grab a towel from the kitchen counter. It's damp from drying last night's dishes, but it'll work. I rub the front of my shirt, swearing under my breath. I'm going to have to change, and I'm already running late.

I take a sip of my coffee and fly to the pantry. "Son of a bitch," I say when I stick my hand into the big bag of dog food. I only feel crumbs.

"Mom, you said a bad word," Grace points out, little feet slapping on the cold tile as she comes up behind me.

I let out a breath. "That's a mommy word. Only mommies can say those words." I grab the dog food bag and look at my six-year-old. "Did you feed Pluto last night?"

"I did," she says proudly.

"How much did you feed him?"

She shrugs and looks away, a move she mastered years ago. "I don't know."

"You fed him all of it," I say with a shake of my head, closing my eyes in a long blink. I had it mentally planned out to give him the last of his food this morning and pick up a bag on the way home from work. "He's on a diet, remember? We have to only give him one scoop in the evening."

"But he was hungry!" Grace says, and her shoulders sag. "I'm sorry."

"It's okay, baby," I say and smile. She's as sweet as she is sassy. "Thank you for helping last night. You take good care of your puppy."

That brings a smile to her face. "Can you do my hair?" she asks, holding out a brush.

"Yes, let me find something for Pluto first. Did you brush your teeth?"

She nods and pulls out a bar stool, climbing up to wait for me. I get three-day-old chicken and rice from the fridge and stick it in the microwave. While the food is heating up, I fly over to Grace, taking another drink of coffee as I walk. I set the mug down and pick up her brush, running it through her brunette locks.

"Your hair is getting so long," I tell her, carefully brushing through her tangled curls. "And so pretty."

The compliment makes her sit up a little straighter, and I can tell without looking that she's smiling. "I want a bun like you," she says and I internally cringe. My own dark blonde hair — a shade or two lighter than hers — is up in the usual messy bun. I'm not talking the cute and stylish kind. I'm talking the if-I-put-on-a-hoodie-I'll-look-like-adrug-dealer kind of messy bun. But hey, at least my hair is clean.

"What about a braid?" I ask and lean back, looking into the living room for my three-year-old. Paige is curled up on the couch watching cartoons. A wave of sadness and guilt hits me when I see her. Like her mother and older sister, she's naturally not a morning person. Yet she's up, dressed and fed before seven a.m. so I can drop her off at daycare before work.

"Okay," Grace says to the braid. I turn my attention back to her, heart aching. I worked part-time when Grace was little and did the majority of my work from home. She didn't have to go to daycare or get up early. I spent my mornings and afternoons with her, playing and snuggling, living out the life I always imagined.

And then I got divorced, and everything changed.

I carefully braid Grace's hair and then grab the leftovers from the microwave, taking them to Pluto's dish.

"I'll get you dog food tonight," I promise him. "But don't act like you don't prefer this."

He gets up and trots over to his bowl, scarfing down breakfast. I pat him on the head, glad I got to keep him. Russell, my ex, and I adopted him for Grace's birthday three years ago.

"Okay, girls," I say. "Coats and shoes, please!"

Grace hops off the stool and goes to the hall tree by the back door. Paige needs a little more coaxing and asks me to sit and snuggle her for a minute. I can't resist. I sit on the couch, turning off the TV, and pull her into my arms.

"I love you to the moon and back, sweet pea," I whisper in her ear. She looks up at me, golden brown hair falling into her eyes.

"I love you too, Mama," she says back and hugs me. "Can I stay home with you? Please, Mama?"

My heart breaks. "What about your friends? Don't you want to see them?"

"Oh, yeah. Friends!" She perks up and climbs off the couch, jibber-jabbering away about her friend Olivia from school. That's my saving grace about this whole thing. The girl is a social butterfly, though I don't know where she gets it from. I'm not exactly what you'd call a "people person" most days.

I let Pluto out into our small fenced-in backyard while we go through the process of dressing for the cool spring weather, putting on shoes and loading backpacks and lunches into the car. The girls start fighting over who gets to hold the stuffed monkey that was discarded on the floor of the car and forgotten about for weeks. Well, until now.

"Take turns," I say, putting the monkey in Paige's hands. "When Paige gets to school, you can hold it," I tell Grace, too tired to tell her kindergarteners shouldn't be bickering like this over a plush monkey.

I glance at the clock, cringing when I see that we should have left ten minutes ago. Dammit. I snap Paige in her carseat and check Grace's seatbelt. Then I fly back into the house, let the dog in, grab my shit, and slide into the driver's seat.

"You smell like coffee," Grace says after we've backed out of the driveway and made it two miles down the street.

Dammit. I look down, tears threatening to form, and see the caramel-colored stain on my blouse. I can't go into work like this, and I don't want this stain to set in and ruin the shirt. I don't have a choice, seeing there isn't time to turn around. How the hell did I forget to change? An even better question might be how the hell did I forget my shirt was sopping wet? Am I that much of a hot mess having some sort of food or beverage spilled on me is the norm? This is going to be a long day. Hell, it's already been a long week. And it's only fucking Monday.

"Mommy?" Grace asks, leaning forward in her booster seat. "Are you okay?"

"Yeah, honey," I say and blink back tears. "I'm okay." I flick my gaze to the rearview mirror and see both of my precious daughters.

And I really do feel okay.

~

"Long night?" Jillian asks me as I rush into the office.

"You could say that again." I set my purse down at my desk and hesitate before taking my coat off. I had left a black cardigan in the car at least a month ago. It was a little wrinkled and smelled like the stale Cheerios it was piled on, but it was better than my stained blouse. I buttoned it up the top and hoped no one would notice I didn't have a cami on underneath. "Paige has been having nightmares again." I sink into the rolling chair and fire up my computer, looking up at Jillian, who's perched on the edge of my desk.

Her hair is brushed to perfection, falling over her shoulders in a wave of blonde curls, and her makeup is flawless. She's been at Black Ink Press almost as long as I have, and we've become good friends as we bonded over books.

"I was up late reading my last submission. The book is great, by the way, a little slow in pacing, but nothing I can't fix. As soon as I laid down, Paige woke up screaming about the man in her doorway. I know they say it's a phase, but this is starting to creep me out."

I unzip my coat and brace for Jillian to say something. Books are her first passion, and fashion is a close second. She's always put together and doesn't hesitate to point out those who aren't. But in the year since my life fell apart, she's gone soft on me. I kind of hate her for it...as much as I love her for it.

"You need to get that place blessed. I swear Russ is sending voodoo vibes your way to make you want to leave."

I shake my head. "I wouldn't put it past him." Who got the house after we split caused more grief than anything. Well, other than who got the kids. He fought tooth and nail for them at first, and swore he'd be in their lives as much as possible. He did great for the first six months, and then he started dating again.

If only he acted like a deadbeat dad *before* the divorce, we might have ended things sooner and spared the heartache. Though, if I left the first time I thought we were broken beyond repair, I might not have Paige. Or Grace. Or have gotten married in the first place.

Having hope that things will work themselves out is my biggest flaw. Live and learn and all, right?

"I don't know how you take care of your kids and work full-time," Jillian says, as we walk to the break room. I can't start the day without a bagel and some coffee. "It's just me, my cat, and sometimes my boyfriend at my house. And I don't have to commute from the suburbs. Seriously, I don't know how you do it."

I shrug and fill a paper cup with coffee. "I don't either. But I just do. I have no choice but to keep going, and it's only by the sheer grace of God I've gotten this far." I spread cream cheese on a bagel and shake my head. "And to be honest, I don't feel like I'm doing a very good job. I'm struggling so much, Jill."

She puts her hand on my arm. "Besides that rat nest on your head and your interesting choice of clothing, it doesn't look that way. I don't know if that's helpful or not, but know the rest of the world can't tell."

"Thanks."

"You're doing great, Lexi. Don't be so hard on yourself, and don't forget to take care of yourself either. You deserve some happiness."

"Are you talking about masturbating again?"

"Not this time, but don't forget to do that either. I know how long it's been since you've had sex. What I meant was you should go out and have fun. Maybe think about dating again."

I pour creamer into my coffee, shaking my head as I stir. A million arguments rush into my head, listing out reasons why I'm not ready to start dating. I open my mouth to spit them out but stop. Because I do want to date again. I wanted to date again before the divorce was official. I spent the majority of my last pregnancy avoiding my husband, the father of my unborn child, because being around him was more painful than being alone.

No one warns you how painful falling out of love is.

"You're right," I say.

"Now I knew you'd—wait, did you just agree with me?" Jillian flips her hair over her shoulder, long lashes coming together as she blinks.

"I did. You're right. I think it is time. I'm ready." We snap lids on our coffee cups and slowly make our way back to our offices. "I'm lonely," I admit. "I've been lonely for a long time."

"I know," she says softly. "Let's go out on Saturday, just for fun. You can practice your flirting skills and let off some steam. Russ has the kids this weekend, right?"

I carefully sip my hot coffee. "He does."

She smiles, blue eyes going wide with excitement. "I got a new top that's too long for me—the curse of being five-foot-two strikes again—but it will look *killer* on you. Come over Saturday, let me do your hair and makeup, and you'll be turning down hotties left and right."

I laugh, snorting into my coffee. "Sure I will."

"You're a MILF, Lex. Don't sell yourself short."

"So, when I meet these hotties, do I tell them I have kids or not? Because they need to know I'm a mom to be one they'd like to fuck, right?"

"Yes. But make sure to tell them you had your vagina stitched shut extra tight each time you pushed a baby out."

Gerry, one of the assistant editors, raises his eyebrows as he walks past. I sigh. As much as I want to find a partner again, the thought of dating scares me. Russell and I met in college, were married at twenty-two, and got pregnant just months after the wedding. Flash forward to now, and it's been a while since I've been on the market.

"Don't stress," Jillian says, reading my mind. "This is just for fun. Find a hot guy to go home with and use him as practice."

"I've never had a one-night stand before."

"I'm well aware."

"If I did, would you think I'm slutty?"

She stares at me, unblinking. "No, and you know how I feel about that. You're a grown-ass woman. If you *want* to sleep with a different man every night, more power to you. You own your body and your sexuality. Do what you want."

"I love it when you talk feminism to me."

She smiles. "I'll text Lori and Erin and see if they want to come too. The four of us haven't been out like this in a long time. It's so overdue."

I can't dispute that. Lori and Erin were also involved in the book world, like us. Lori works in marketing for Black Ink Press, and Erin recently made the move from being an editor like me to a literary agent. She has kids as well, and though they're in high school, it's nice to have another mom to hang out with.

We go into our small offices and get to work. I pick at my bagel while I open my email, shuddering when I see my growing inbox. I skim through, flagging the important ones, move them into a folder, and then check Twitter and Facebook as I finish my coffee. I get sucked into a public temper tantrum between two agents from rival agencies, wasting fifteen precious minutes of my morning.

Then it's back to the emails, replying to authors and agents about the projects I'm working on. I open a document from Quinn Harlow, an author I've worked with since my start at Black Ink Press, happily surprised she sent over changes to her novel already. I lean back in my chair and start reading through them, getting pulled into her romance novel about a billionaire heiress and an ex-convict all over again.

Before I know it, it's time for lunch, and the number of emails in my inbox has doubled. Again. I stretch my arms over my head, refusing to let it stress me out. I'm going to stay on top of things this week, so much I'll be able to either leave early on Friday or take the whole day off and spend it with my favorite three-year-old.

I load Quinn's book onto my Kindle so I can read while I eat, and after checking Twitter and Facebook again, head out, meeting Jillian in the lobby.

"Erin's in the area," she says, not looking away from her phone. "She's at The Salad Bar. Want to go?"

"Sure," I say but feel guilty. The food is good, but I hate

paying over twenty bucks for a bowl of lettuce with light toppings. It's healthy for your body but not for your wallet. I didn't bring a lunch for myself today, anyway. I had time to make the girls' lunches or mine, but not both. They trump me every time.

The bright sun has warmed up the day enough that we get a table outside, soaking up the cloudless day. Erin hugs us when we see her, and I can't help but smile at the sight of my friend. We order our food and swear we won't talk about work, but just minutes later, Erin is telling us about a new author she signed.

"She has a few self-published books that did really well," she tells us. "And has a decent fan base already, but..." She shakes her head and pulls up the author's Facebook fan page. "She'll be a hard sell to marketing. She posts a lot of drunk videos on her fan page." She holds up the phone so we can see a video of the author talking to the camera, waving a drink around. "And she doesn't play nice with the other indies in her genre. I found a lot of other authors posting that she uses them to get ahead, then throws them aside like garbage."

"Ugh," I say. "No one likes a bully."

"She'd have to have a fucking amazing book to make me take her on," Jillian admits. "Have you tried talking to her?"

"Yes, and it's gone nowhere. Like I said, great writer, but an asshole of a person." Erin sighs and sets her phone down. "Enough about work. How's life. Did Aaron propose yet?"

"Not yet," Jillian says, shrugging. She acts like it doesn't bother her, but after five years together, the lack of commitment gets under her skin. "How are your kids?" Her deflection only proves how much it upsets her.

"Driving me fucking insane," Erin admits. Her eyes meet mine. "People say it gets easier as the kids get older.

It's a lie. Don't buy it. They just get moody and mean, and Mom is the last person they want to be seen with. I'll trade you."

"There's no way I'm giving up my babies. They're hardly even babies anymore."

"It goes fast," Erin says. "Savor it. Before you know it, you have two teenagers who only care about what you're making for dinner and how much money they can con out of you."

We laugh and the subject changes to books and publishing again. We say our goodbyes, and go back to work. Back in my office, I answer a few more emails and lean back in my chair to hopefully read through the rest of Quinn's changes. One of those changes is an added sex scene, and oh my God, it's hot. I don't realize I'm biting my lip and leaning closer and closer to my Kindle screen until someone knocks at my office door.

I blink, feeling a bit disoriented—Quinn will be happy to know that—and look up, expecting to see Gavin or even Jillian. The smile on my lips freezes in place and my cheeks flush even more than before. My stomach flutters and I momentarily panic that I have lettuce stuck in my teeth. I didn't check, after all, so it's entirely possible.

"Cole," I finally say, still smiling like an idiot to my boss. "Hi." Getting caught reading a naughty sex scene is one thing. Getting caught reading a naughty sex scene by someone you've fantasized about acting out those naughty sex scenes with is another.

Especially when that person happens to be your boss.

"Hi, Alexis," he says, smiling right back at me, his brown eyes shining in the afternoon sunlight. He's one of the few people who always calls me by my full name. It annoys me when others do, but it's sexy when it's coming off his lips. "How are you?"

"Good. I'm just going through what I think are the last changes for Quinn Harlow's latest book."

"Perfect," he says and comes into the office, leaving the door open. "That's actually what I wanted to talk to you about. I just got out of a meeting with the marketing team and they wanted to bump the release date up." He leans over the desk, staring down at my Kindle. Black Ink is one of the biggest publishers in the business and is no stranger to erotic or taboo novels, but I suddenly feel shy that my Kindle is open to a page—the entire page—devoted to oral sex. Maybe it's because I've wondered what Cole's head would look like between my legs?

Stop it.

He's right fucking in front of me. I'm already hot and bothered from the sex scene. I don't need the image of Cole's handsome face slowly trailing down my body as he kisses my neck, my breasts, the soft skin on my—*stop!*

"How soon?" I ask and clear my throat. "When do they want to release, I mean. And how has that changed the marketing plan? Quinn will want to know."

"They want to move the release date up by a month, and the marketing has already started."

"I think we can do that, then."

He smiles at me, and my panties melt right off. "I knew you'd be able to handle this. And between you and me, I'm glad it's you working on her book. You're one of the best we have here."

I shake my head. "You're too kind."

"Really," he says and moves in a little closer. "Do I need to bring up *The Fake Wife*?" he asks with a laugh. I blush and shake my head. I took a gamble on a debut author's thriller not long ago, and the book blew up. The movie came out over the summer and was a hit. "You've yet to advocate for a bad book. How do you do it?"

I shrug, looking up at him. "I just know what I like and go for it." I don't mean for it to sound as flirty as it does. I'm about to divert my eyes and blurt out something random to take the tension away, but Cole speaks before I have the chance.

"I like that about you," he says coyly, giving me a sexy-as-hell smile. "You'll talk to Quinn Harlow or her agent today?"

"Yeah. I'll email them both right away."

He goes on to tell me the details of everything, and I do my best to listen. I even jot down notes so I can explain everything in perfect detail when I talk to Quinn's agent.

My mind starts to drift to Cole's perfect cheekbones and the alluring way he smells. Cole Winchester is the Editor-in-Chief at Black Ink Press, and is the subject of many office fantasies. The moment you meet him, it's obvious as to why. Besides his looks—tall, athletic, handsome-yet-rugged face that's covered in a perfect five o'clock shadow all day—Cole is a diamond in the rough. He's respectful of his employees. He's responsible and always has his shit together. He's an overall nice guy but can still command the room without even trying. Cole meets all the criteria on my to-date list.

Yet, he's made it abundantly clear that he'll never date anyone from work. Don't shit were you eat and all, I guess. Though I like to think I could be his exception, like one of the leading ladies in the romance novels. And there's that hope again rising in my chest. I've been told that not all is lost when you have hope. But enough of that optimistic bullshit. Having hope only prolongs the heartache.

LUKE

Is murder always a crime? I push my shoulders back into the leather behind me and grit my teeth. I push the buttons on the controller in my hands, taking satisfaction in pummeling virtual zombies to death with a splintered piece of wood. That's the only murder that's happening today.

"Luke, I know you can hear me," my brother says again. He stands to the side, arms crossed over his chest. "Luke," he repeats. "You were home all fucking day. Why are there dishes in the sink?"

It's taking effort to maintain the guise that these headphones cancel out all noise. I didn't do the dishes because I'm not his fucking maid. I cleaned up after myself, but I draw the line at doing his dirty work.

"Luke." Cole moves in front of me, blocking my line of vision. I'm half tempted to keep staring forward, pretending he's not there. I did go three weeks pretending he was invisible when we were kids. Ten years later, and nothing has changed. But I'm close to leveling up on my game. I hit pause, and look up, blood boiling.

Inhale. Hold it. Let it out slowly. I can't lose it, not completely. Cole might be older than me, but I can take him in a fight. Easily. And he knows it.

"I'm not washing your dishes," I say calmly, proud of my level tone.

"I work all day. You don't. Pick up the slack around here if you want to live here."

The controller clatters to the ground. I leap up. So much for keeping my cool. "Did you forget I work at night? You wanna play this game? Really?"

I stare him down, wondering where the hell we went wrong. Cole is two years older than me, and he's always hated me. Chalking his behavior up to typical sibling rivalry doesn't begin to cover it. I don't get it either. Cole and I are as different as brothers can be.

Physically, we share a slight resemblance. His hair is lighter and his eyes are darker. I'm taller by several inches, with pounds of more muscle. Cole excelled academically and I was good at sports. We went our separate ways at college and he was tolerable for several years.

Yet here we are, together again. Fuck my life.

Cole takes a step back. "You came here. To my house. You have to follow my rules."

"You've got to be fucking kidding me!" My nostrils flare as anger pulses through me. "This isn't *your* house." It had to be some sort of a sick joke for our grandmother to leave this ostentatious Manhattan house to us.

Us.

Mom says it was Grandma's final attempt to do what she couldn't: make Cole and I get the fuck along. Unlike my brother, knowing the discord between us caused our mother —and grandmother—angst, upset me. I never wanted to hurt either of them, but I'm not one to sit idly by while my narcissistic brother thinks his shit don't stink. Though I do regret shoving him four Thanksgivings ago. But only because he knocked over a bottle of red wine on Mom's antique armchair.

"You're such an asshole," I hiss, picking my controller up off the ground. I readjust the headphones and sit down. *Keep your cool.* It's not worth it. Not anymore. "After everything that happened, you'd think you'd cut me a little slack." I look right into my brother's eyes. "You're just like Dad."

"Take that back!" he snaps. "I'm nothing like him!"

I ignore Cole, taking satisfaction in the insult. Our father was not a good man. I resume the game, and eventually Cole leaves the room, muttering on and on about how he can't stand living with me.

A wave of sadness goes through me, not uncommon as of late, and I wish for just a second Cole and I got along. I've been in New York City for only weeks, and after all the shit that happened just months ago, I could use a friend.

Whatever. This is temporary. I'll go back to Chicago eventually. My life is—was—there. Someday I'll be ready to go back. Problem is, I have no idea when. The fire was still ablaze when I left, burning every aspect of my life, taking everything I held dear to me, and turning it into ash.

chapter three

LEXI

I wake up with a foot pressing into my ribs. I roll over, carefully moving away from Paige. The girl sleeps like an octopus and has already flipped upside down in bed. I get up, stretching my stiff back, and tuck her under her covers once more.

"Love you to the moon and back," I whisper, kissing her forehead. I tiptoe out of her room and check on Grace, whose room is right across the hall. I turn off the audio book she fell asleep listening to, and check the time. Great. I slept for nearly three hours. It was much needed, but now I'm going to be up even later finishing the read-through of Quinn's novel. Though I can't deny that I'm a little excited to get back to it, despite my exhaustion. While the work is never-ending, I really do love my job.

I take a quick shower, dress in PJs, put my long hair into a braid over my shoulder, and go downstairs to reheat the cup of coffee I poured after dinner and forgot about. I set my stuff up at the kitchen table, purposely seeking out a workspace that's not comfortable. It's less tempting to close my eyes and fall asleep—again.

I left Quinn's characters mid-fuck, in a rooftop pool in Manhattan, no less. I go back and re-read the page before, instantly getting sucked back into the story. I run my hand over the page in front of me, feeling a familiar longing tug at my heart. My eyes close and I exhale, wishing so much I could slip between the lines and disappear into the book.

I finish my coffee, uncap my red pen, and dive back in to the story. No matter how hard I try not to, I imagine the love interest—the bad boy so extreme he's been in jail—as Cole. Each word turns me on, and I'm right there along with the characters getting so worked up I can hardly stand it.

Then I find an error in Quinn's rewrites, putting the brakes on mentally fucking my boss. Which is probably a good thing, since I have to see him bright and early tomorrow to go over a new project I want to take on. I take a deep breath, and power through the next two chapters. I've already read the ending, and Quinn assured me she left the final chapter untouched. I intend to just skim through it, but end up soaking up every single word. That woman is a poet without trying. Every word, every line speaks to me, awakening some part of my soul.

With a smile on my face, I flip the last page over and write a little note for Quinn, telling her how proud I am of how far she's come. She was a brand new author when I accepted her first novel. Being along with her for the ride of total newbie to regularly making the *New York Times* Bestseller List has been fun. She's actually several years older than me, but the nature of our relationship makes me feel a bit like a proud mother.

The smile disappears from my face when I look away from the book and take in the sight of my messy kitchen. Dishes piled up in the sink, the dishwasher is full but hasn't yet been run, and I forgot to put the leftover spaghetti and meatballs away after dinner and now it's wasted.

"Fuck," I mumble, shaking my head. And I need to make the girls' lunches. Why did I stay up so late again? Oh yeah. Work. It's kind of important and all. I'm an editor, but I don't get time to actually edit at the office that often. My days are filled answering emails, talking to agents and authors, and approving artwork for covers. Sitting down and getting into a story while at work is a luxury few editors get to experience.

I let Pluto out and open the dishwasher. It should have been run yesterday, and stinks to the high heavens. I cram a few more dishes in, start it, then pile everything else in one side of the sink. I fill the other side with soapy water, telling myself that I'm letting the dishes soak overnight so it'll be easier to wash them in the morning before work. It's a lie, but if I don't think about it too hard, I believe it and it makes me feel better about leaving the house a mess. I toss the meatballs in Pluto's bowl, throw out the noodles, which hardened from sitting out for hours, and pile more crap in the sink.

Debating on drinking more coffee or not, I get started on the girls' lunches for tomorrow. I'm big on making sure they get a healthy and balanced meal, which is kinda funny since I forget to feed myself more times than not. I draw a heart and a smiley face on a white napkin and put it inside Paige's lunchbox. I write Grace a little note (*I love you! Have a good day and learn something new!*) that goes inside hers. Both lunch boxes slip into the fridge, and I let Pluto back in. I do the quickest job ever wiping down the counters, brush crumbs from the bottoms of my feet—I'll vacuum tomorrow —and rush to crash into my bed, pulling my down comforter up to my chin.

Once the divorce was official, I had to rearrange the master bedroom and get new bedding. If I had the time and money, I'd repaint, even though I love the light purple walls. It was a struggle to get Russell to let me paint the room a "girl" color, though the purple was so light it looks almost gray in dim light. The biggest and best change was being able to line the wall across from me with bookshelves. I own enough books to stock at least three bookstores, and for some reason that bothered Russell. He hated the books and tried multiple times to throw them away.

Throw. Books. Away. He might as well have stabbed me right in the heart.

I had to do everything I could to make the room feel different. This was our room, and while it still harbored the few good memories I have from my marriage, it held onto a lot of bad ones.

I stretch out in bed, trying not to think about how lonely I feel. I'm not lonely because Russ isn't in bed with me anymore. The house felt ten degrees better once he packed up and left. I was lonely long before that, back when we shared this bed, back when we'd see each other for hours every day, and my husband did everything he could to avoid me.

Watching my marriage fall apart was the hardest thing I've ever done. You can only bend so much before you break, and I was constantly reaching down, picking up the pieces and scrambling like mad to put them back together.

Crawling into bed next to a man who no longer loved me, no longer thought of me as desirable, and a man who told me more than once I was no longer good enough, hurt worse than crawling into the empty bed. Seeing my husband every day was a reminder that I had failed, through no fault of my own, on being the wife he wanted. And nothing I did could change that.

My husband fell out of love with me. Though, I was the one who had fallen, landing painfully at the bottom without a clue how to get myself back up. But you know what they say: fall seven times, get up eight. It wasn't until I realized I was clinging onto nothing that I was able to get back up.

I was so scared of being alone. Of starting over. Of raising the girls by myself. The thought of splitting custody hurt. I didn't want to not have my babies on Christmas. And as much as I detested Russ for the way he made me feel in the end, I didn't want him to sit alone on the holidays because the girls were with me.

So, I tried. Again, and again. I tried so damn hard. The pieces of our marriage started to fall faster than I could pick them up, and I began to get buried in the rubble. I'd claw my way out, battered and bruised, but with a brave face, hiding how broken I was inside.

Russ was so unhappy he started getting mean: calling me names, picking apart everything I did. Dinner was overcooked or undercooked. I could spend the whole day cleaning the house and he'd find one thing that wasn't perfect, and flip out over it. I was up too late editing. I didn't work as many hours as I should.

I couldn't win.

Yet, I held onto hope that somehow I'd put in that last piece and things would click into place. We loved each other once. Enough to get engaged. Enough to plan a wedding and start our family. There were bumps along the way, but everyone fights from time to time.

We were happy. We could be happy again, right?

Deep down, I knew Russ loved me. He had to. He was my husband. Yet day after day, he'd ignore me, tell me he couldn't stand to be around me, say the sight of me alone made him angry, and find any way he could to belittle me while making himself sound good. He saw how much it hurt me. He heard me crying.

And didn't do a damn thing about it.

He didn't love me, and as much as I feared being alone, it hurt more to be in a relationship where I already was alone. Paige wasn't even a year old when we separated. That hope was back again, that living apart and away from his children would send Russ into a shock and he'd realize what an asshole he'd been.

It didn't.

He had a new girlfriend before the divorce papers were signed. So here I am, alone, stressed, tighter on cash than I'd like to be. But I'm much happier now. The pain of walking away was nothing compared to the pain of staying. And I have two little girls who will live by my example. The thought of one of them marrying someone like their father was the final straw.

I close my eyes, mind drifting to Cole and his kind, brown eyes. I've known him for several years, and while he's careful to stay professional at work, I've gotten glimpses of his inner personality on more than one occasion. A man who reads is sexy enough on its own. A responsible man with a steady job is sexy as well. Pair those together and Cole Winchester, editor extraordinaire at Black Ink ,is what every bookworm woman wants.

Plus, simply put, he's hot. And, as Jillian and I discovered one fateful causal Friday when Cole wore athletic pants to work, he has a monster cock. It took us both a full week to be able to look him in the eye with a straight face after that. There were dares going around the office—some people even bet money—to get someone to tell him that an outline of The Beast was visible, but no one was brave enough to. Or stupid enough to ruin our visual pleasure for the day.

I start to relax and fall to sleep, thinking of Cole and how kind he was to me during the divorce, and how excited he was when I finally accepted moving from part-time to full-time. Men like Cole Winchester don't come around too often. I'm in no rush to settle, or even date anyone, and I won't bring home a man until I'm sure he's got some serious potential. I can't help but see it already there when I look at Cole.

He might not date anyone from work, but I'll be damned if I don't try.

I'M RUNNING on two and a half hours of sleep, which is okay, because it enabled me to stay home from the office today and spend this sunny Friday with Paige. We went out for breakfast, took Pluto for a walk, played on the neighborhood playground, and snuggled on the couch while watching a movie.

"We have to go pick up your sister soon," I tell her, taking a quick break from playing Barbies to answer a few emails. My inbox is close to exploding it's so full, but I can get to it tomorrow morning. I don't normally like to work on the weekends, but when the kids are at Russ's house, I like to stay busy.

"No. Stay home!" Paige pouts and hangs her head. "Play with me, Mama!"

"We have half an hour," I tell her, and type up a quick reply to an agent who sent me a proposal. The book is for an adult paranormal romance about a demon hunter and a witch, which is way different than the books I usually edit. I tend to avoid anything remotely creepy, but I got sucked in from the little sample I read, and requested the full book. I press send and think about the author, wondering how excited or nervous she'll be to hear she got a request for the full manuscript. I don't request the full book very often. I have to be really into the proposal for the novel, which has gotten me a reputation of being a hard-ass editor. But I'd rather not accept everything that sounds a tad interesting. I have to send out fewer rejections that way, and I hate doing that.

Though since I've come back full time, I have an assistant and can forward the emails to Gavin. He's the one who actually has to type the words and send them. Still, it hurts and I hope the rejection doesn't kill the dreams of the hopeful writer.

"Play knock-knock with Anna," Paige says, holding up her Princess Anna doll for me. I set my phone down, and take the Barbie, moving around to the other side of the plastic ice-castle to have the doll knock on the doors. We play for twenty more minutes, then go into her room to put her favorite stuffed animals in her overnight bag. I do the same for Grace, and stash clean undies, PJs, and an extra outfit in each girl's bag too. Just in case.

They have stuff at their dad's house. Not as much as here, but enough to get them through the weekend. Still, it's hard for me to let go and trust him to be as attentive as I am. It's nothing personal. I don't trust anyone to be as attentive as I am.

"Ready, baby?" I ask Paige.

"Can Pluto come?"

"That's up to your father," I tell her. Russell still likes the dog, and has let him come before. He has a bigger fenced-in yard than we do—and never fails to remind me—that is perfect for the girls and the dog. "I'll text him." Having Pluto helps me not feel so alone when the girls are away, but how can I say no to Paige?

Quite easily, really, but I'm a bit soft now and then.

$\sim$

GREAT, Miss Plastic Tits is here. She stands in the corner of the living room, watching the girls run to Russell shouting "Daddy!" in a chorus of happiness. Sometimes I wish they didn't love their father as much as they do, and that makes me feel like the shittiest mother in the entire world. I have to remind myself that Russ isn't a bad person. He was a bad husband. He might make a great husband if he married someone else, someone who could keep up with his ridiculous standards, that is.

I sigh and put on a smile. This isn't helping. We've been out of love for so long that the feelings of indifference come easily. We've split and gone our separate ways. There is no need to harbor negativity and waste my time being miserable because of him.

Not anymore.

"You look tired," Russ says, eyeballing me. I'm standing in the foyer, holding both girls' overnight bags and Pluto's leash. That dog still gets excited to see Russell as well. "Up late working?"

"Always am," I reply flatly. It's weird that despite all the shit we went through, it still feels natural to launch into a conversation with him about books.

"Get some rest," he says softly, which takes me off guard.

"I plan to." I close the door behind me and let go of Pluto. He runs over, wiggling his way between Russell and the girls. "What are your plans for the weekend?"

Russell picks up Grace with one arm and Paige in the other. Seeing them with their father—all smiles, hearts full of love and happiness—always pulls on my heart. I wish so badly things could have worked out between us, that the four of us could have stayed together.

Miss Plastic Tits tentatively comes closer, offering me a polite smile. Her name is Maggie, and she's been nothing but nice and polite to me, that bitch. She's several years younger than Russell and works in his office. I almost feel bad for her, because I know she's way more serious about this relationship than Russell is.

"My sister just got a boat," she says shyly. "We were going to take the girls out on the lake, if that's okay with you."

"Of course, it's okay," Russell hisses.

I blink and look at Russell. "Isn't it kind of cold for that?"

"We're not going in the water, and if you bothered to look at the weather, you'd know it's going to hit seventy tomorrow with no clouds."

"Make sure they wear life-vests, please."

"They have to. It's the law. Don't act like I'm too stupid to take care of my own children."

And now I'm reminded why I left again. I say goodbye to my girls and leave. Walking down the sidewalk without them hasn't gotten any easier. Will it ever? I let out a breath and drive over half an hour back to my home in the suburbs.

The house is entirely too quiet. I turn on the TV, pour myself a glass of wine, and spend the next three hours cleaning, cursing myself the whole time for letting things get this messy. I don't attempt to tackle the girls' rooms. Or mine. Or the master bathroom.

Giving up, I shower and change into PJs. I crash early and sleep until ten the next day. I wake up feeling refreshed but instantly miss my girls. I get up and start cleaning again until Jillian texts me in the afternoon, saying she made dinner reservations for seven in the city, and to meet at her downtown apartment before then to get ready.

I reply that I'll be there around five, and then start to get nervous. It takes me a while to figure out why. Tonight, I'm supposed to go out and flirt. Tonight, I might get some for the first time in well over a year. Tonight, I'm finally moving on.

chapter four

LEXI

"*I* feel like we should make a toast," Jillian starts, holding up her shot glass full of whiskey. "To friendship."

"To friendship," Erin, Lori, and I all say together, raising our shots in the air. Erin's glass hits mine and booze spills out, rolling down my arm. We both laugh and take our shots. I set my glass down and lick the whiskey off my wrist, still laughing.

It's nearing midnight and I have a good buzz going on. I've spent the last several hours talking, laughing, and drinking with friends. I feel good, and for the first time in quite a while, I think I look good. It only took one glass of wine to get me to agree that Jillian was right to suggest I wear tight jeans, a low-cut tank top, and heels. She curled my hair to perfection and helped lay on black eyeliner that was just thick enough to outline my green eyes.

"That bartender has been eye-fucking you all night," Erin says, elbowing me and pointing across the room.

I grab her wrist and pull her hand down. "No way, and you are so obvious."

She bursts into giggles again, which of course makes me laugh. The bartender just happens to be gorgeous, by the way. Sky-blue pupils outlined in a rim of navy, dark brown hair that is styled in that I-just-had-sex messy look that only he could pull off. Colorful tattoos covered his muscular arms peeking out from his black t-shirt.

Not that I was looking.

But I did have to flag him down to order these shots.

"He so is!" Jillian says, leaning across the table. "He's hot. Go for it."

I shake my head and turn to look again, being just as obvious as Erin but too tipsy to realize it. "Please. He's a hard ten and I'm a...a..."

"A ten," all three of my friends say.

"At least you are tonight," Jillian adds with a wink. "Ya know, since I did your hair and makeup and all."

"He's looking over here again," Lori says. "Go flirt with him and try to get us free drinks."

I smile and start to stand, looking through the crowd at the bar. Hottie McBartender catches my eye and gives me a half smile. I shrink back down in the seat. "What do I say?"

My friends laugh and Jillian pushes her pomegranate martini in front of me. "Here," she says. "Finish this, take a pee break, then go talk to him before someone else moves in on that fine piece of ass."

I roll my eyes at her and bring the glass to my lips. "He's working. He can't just step away and come sit with us."

"Well, he gets off at some point. Then he can get *you* off."

"That would be nice," I mumble, and then shake my head.

"Just go," Jillian says. "You need to get back out there. It's been over a year since your divorce and you haven't so much as gotten a number. It's time to move on."

"I was married for five years. It's not something I can easily get over."

"I know," Jillian says softly. "That's why you need to put on your big girl panties—well, put them on only to take them off, that is—and find a rebound guy, so to speak. No pressure, no strings, just get some experience with men again, and then you can move on to something more serious. Just go have fun. Do it for me. Because I would have so much fun with him."

I take another sip of her drink and look for the bartender again, but can't find him through the crowd around the bar. We continue talking and laughing, and someone on the stage reminds us all that it's open mic-night and that the line-ups are dwindling and pretty much begs people to perform. I turn my attention from trying to find the bartender to the stage.

"Let's sing something!" Erin says, following my gaze. I like to sing, and can play the piano, which was the result of my mother-in-law paying in advance for several months of piano lessons for Grace last year. Of course, she lost interest and instead of fighting her to go, I took the lessons instead. I know some basics, and memorized exactly one song.

"You know I get stage fright," I confess.

"Face two fears tonight," Erin encourages. "Flirting and performing. Which, I guess could be the same thing since flirting leads to—never mind. Don't want to freak you out even more."

I raise an eyebrow and glare at her before taking a deep breath, eyes going back to the stage. I spent so many years letting fear rule my life. Fear of being alone. Fear of losing my children. Fear of making a mistake in filing for divorce, that I'd regret being single, that Russ would move on and I'd be left in the dust... In return, I spent too much time being miserable. It was a hard lesson to learn, but I know now that life is far too short to waste a second letting fear hold you back. In the end, regret haunts you more anyway.

"Fuck it," I say and stand up. "Let's do this. But I need a drink first."

"That'll hit you hard in a minute," Jillian says, eyeballing her empty martini.

"I meant water," I tell her. I slide out of the booth and wait for Erin to follow. We put our names in for open mic night, use the bathroom, then fight through a sea of bodies to get to the bar.

"Shit." Erin looks down at her phone, frowning. She puts it to her ear, wrinkling her nose as she tries to hear the voicemail over the music. "It's David. Something about Stephen sneaking over to a girl's house," she tells me. "I swear to God that boy is going to be the death of me. I'll be right back." She rushes out of the bar to call her husband. I can see her standing by the door, face twisting into anger as she talks on the phone. I'm so busy watching her, I don't realize it's my time to order drinks until the bartender leans across the wooden bar.

"Did you want something?" he asks. I whip around and my eyes lock with his. He parts his lips and tips his head down, smiling playfully. "Something I can get you, I mean."

Suddenly my mouth runs dry. "Water."

He arches an eyebrow. "Giving up already?"

"How is asking for water giving up?" I snap.

"People typically ask for water when they've had too much and are desperately trying to regain control. It doesn't work, by the way. It's already in your system. You just gotta wait for it to pass."

It takes everything I have not to cross my arms and stare him down. I don't, but mostly because I don't trust myself not to check him out. I'm reacting to him physically, though anyone who saw him wouldn't blame me.

"Do I look desperate?"

He straightens up and slowly runs his eyes over my entire body. We're feet apart, and yet it feels like his fingertips are sweeping over my flesh as his gaze moves. I shiver.

"Not at all. So, I'm guessing you're getting water for one of your friends. The one that sped away just a minute ago." He smiles and damn he looks good when he does. The perfect amount of stubble covers his jaw. "She was running to the bathroom to puke, I'd guess."

"Nope. You're wrong. Now can I have my water, please? I'm thirsty."

"You're sassy. I like that."

I take a deep breath, feeling that martini hit me all at once. I roll my eyes. "Yeah, it's so sassy to expect to get a drink I ordered."

He grabs a plastic cup and fills it with water. "On the house," he says with a smile, making me smile back without even realizing it. He's still looking at me, lips parting like he wants to say something else.

Then my name is called.

I take another drink of water and suddenly feel terrified. I turn back to the hot bartender. "Give me a shot."

"A shot of what?"

"I don't care. Just hurry."

"You're a curious thing, you know?"

"Yeah, yeah. Tell me about it later. Hurry!"

He raises his eyebrows and laughs, and then turns away, coming back seconds later with a shot glass filled with amber-colored liquid. I take it, shudder, and wash away the taste with water.

"Put it on my tab," I call to him as I rush away. Erin is nowhere to be seen. I practically give myself whiplash looking for her, finally finding her huddled near the door, still on the phone. She has on her "mom face" and I know she's in a heated verbal exchange with her eldest son. Shit. She can't walk away now, and they just called our names again. I can't do this. I'm not the type of person who sings in public. I'm also not the type of person who takes shit and waits for things to get better anymore.

Now or never.

My fingers tremble as I reach for the worn wooden railing. I grab it, pick one foot up, and unsteadily climb the three stairs that take me to the stage. A few people have stopped what they are doing to look at me, but most are going about their night. Talking, drinking, and not caring that some random girl is wobbling across the stage.

I spot my friends in the crowd. Jillian flashes a big smile and give me a thumbs up, and Lori gives me an encouraging nod. Erin is still in the back, one step away from full on Hulking out, mom-style.

I sit at the piano, fingers hovering over the keys. My brain threatens to shut down, pretending to forget how to play and even the tune of the song I'm about to sing. I close my eyes, take a deep breath, and feel better. It might be the shot of whiskey I just took, but who's keeping track.

My fingers sweep across the sleek ivory keys and I inch forward, straightening my shoulders. The second that first note rings out, something comes over me, and I get sucked into the music. My fingers move effortlessly and the words spill from me, freeing a part of my soul I didn't know was trapped.

The bar erupts in cheers when I'm done, the loudest being from my friends...and the bartender. Our eyes meet and he raises his hands above his head, clapping. I smile back at him and go back to my table.

"You killed it, girl!" Jillian says. "I'm forever jealous of that voice. I can't carry a tune to save my life."

I put my hand on my hip and purse my lips. "It's just one of my many talents," I joke, then sit down next to her. "That was fun. Really fun. I don't know why I was so scared before."

"You have nothing to be scared of," Lori says and flicks her eyes to the stage. A group of girls are up now, belting out Dixie Chicks, all off-key. "You're one of the better, if not the best, singers tonight."

I wave my hand at her. "I'm not the best. Not by far. But thanks."

Erin comes back and grabs her coat. "Gotta bail. Apparently, my son can't keep it in his pants and his girlfriend's father is not happy right now. Wish me luck."

I wrinkle my nose. "Good luck."

She lets out a heavy sign. "The offer still stands to trade your sweet little girls for my boys."

"I'll pass. Again," I say with a laugh. She hugs us all goodbye then rushes out the door. "Want another round?"

"One more then I should go too," Lori says. "Not to be a buzzkill or anything. Chad's all sad I'm not home. I can't decide if it's annoying or cute."

"It's annoying as fuck," Jillian spits out. "Just because he doesn't have friends doesn't mean you can't."

Lori's eyes widen. "He has friends, and he has no problem with me going out! You'd understand what it's like to be away from your husband if you had one."

"I'm getting drinks," I say and slip away. I do not want to get involved in that drama. A barstool opens up at the end of the bar. I take it and pull my phone from my purse, checking for any missed messages or calls. Grace FaceTimed me before bed, needing to hear me tell her goodnight before she could fall asleep. Paige had already crashed, but I at least got to see her sleeping soundly.

Russell takes good care of the girls. He always has. But I wouldn't be their mother if I didn't worry.

"I feel like I own you an apology."

I don't have to look up to know who that deep, sultry voice belongs to. I lock my screen and let the phone fall back into my purse. A rush goes through me the second I look up, finding his face close to mine.

"For what?"

"For judging you."

This time I do cross my arms and glare. "How could you possibly judge me? You don't know me."

"Exactly," he says as he puts two glasses on the counter. "I assumed you were drunk, first of all." He grabs a bottle of whiskey and pours some into each glass. "And I didn't think you had the balls to get up and sing like that."

"You thought about my balls?" I ask and watch the liquid inside the glass slosh as he pushes it in front of me.

"I did. I'm thinking about them now," he says and downs the booze without so much as a flinch. He sets the glass down and bites his lip. It's a deliberate move, I'm sure, one made to look innocent and unplanned. And fuck, it's working for him.

I lean forward, trying to sneak a glance down at the amount of cleavage I'm showing without looking obvious, and run my finger around the lip of the cup. "Maybe my balls are full of surprises."

"I think your balls are full of surprises."

"And what are yours full of?" Wait, what? Did I really just say that out loud? Oh, God. It's not possible to actually die of embarrassment, right? I close my eyes in a long blink, thankful for the extra layer of foundation Jillian put on my skin. It's helping to mask the fire engine red my cheeks are burning right now.

I can't look up, can't meet his eyes. Instead, I bring the cup to my lips and almost choke on the harsh taste of alcohol.

Smooth, Lexi. Real smooth. This is why I will be single until the day I die.

"So, are you a singer?"

"What?" I ask, still trying to recover from the burn of whiskey. Who the hell drinks it straight?

"Are you a singer? Trying to make it on Broadway?"

"Uh," I sputter, mind whirling with what to say. I have no reason to lie. But I have no reason to tell the truth either. This is supposed to be practice, right? My own life isn't that exciting. I bet I can keep him talking longer if I make something up. "No, I'm not."

"You have a great voice."

"Thanks. I was scared to get up there and sing, to be honest. And now I don't know why. It wasn't scary at all. It was far from the hardest thing I've ever done."

He leans forward, piercing blue eyes searing into mine. "What is the hardest thing you've ever done?"

I inhale and close my eyes in a long blink. "The hardest thing I've ever done was accept an apology I was never given."

I open my eyes to find him staring at me, expression softened. The moment passes soon, and the cocky grin is back. He ignores the guy next to me, who's asking for a Jack and Coke, and keeps his eyes trained on mine. "What made you get up and sing tonight?"

I shake my head. "Some weird stuff happened a while

ago that made me realize life is too short to not take chances. I'd rather go to bed at night thinking *I can't believe I did that* than wishing I had. You tend to regret what you don't do more, after all."

"If you say so. I wouldn't know. I don't know the last time I *didn't* do something I wanted to do."

"That's bullshit," I say. "Everyone regrets something."

"Not in the sense you're talking about."

I resist the urge to roll my eyes, smiling and admiring the way his ass looks in those dark jeans. He fills the Jack and Coke guy's order and is back to me.

"Well, aren't you lucky."

He laughs and flashes that smile again. I'm pretty sure my panties have melted into a fabric puddle by now. "I know what I want and go for it."

"You say that like you always get what you want."

Suddenly, he's inching closer to me, bottle in hand. "I do."

Holy shit. How can two words be so intense? I slowly take a breath, wrapping my fingers around the empty glass. "And what do you want right now?"

He pours more whiskey into my glass. "I think you know the answer to that."

Tingles run down my spine, and I feel like a virginal girl again, laying my eyes on the Holy Grail of teenage crushes for the first time. My mind flashes to his flesh against mine, and I find myself very curious about the rest of his tattoos.

I shake my head and loose curls fall over my face, hiding my flushed cheeks. "I...I...uh...I don't know," I sputter, squeezing the glass so hard it might crack and break.

"I'll give you a hint," he says and puts his elbows on the counter, leaning in close. A smile plays on those full lips, and I can smell his cologne over the heavy scent of alcohol coming from the bar. Then he shifts his gaze over my shoulder. "Looks like you got trouble."

I turn and see Lori storming away from the table, lips pressed together in a thin line. She comes right up to me, eyebrows furrowed with anger. "Jillian's pissing me off, so I'm leaving," she says. "Bye, Lexi."

"How are you getting home?" I ask as she gives me a hug goodbye. Lori is always a bit dramatic, and that gets amplified times a million when she drinks.

"I already got an Uber. Then Chad is meeting me."

"Okay. Be safe. Thanks for coming out, Lori!"

She squeezes me tight, and then weaves her way to the door of the bar.

"And then there were two," the bartender says. I turn back around, color immediately coming back to my cheeks. "Are you calling it a night too, Lexi?" he says, having heard Lori call me by name.

"I don't really want to go home yet," I confess and bring the glass to my lips. It doesn't burn as much going down this time. I must be drunk. No more after this. I know my limits, having pushed them a time or two in the past. "You know, I didn't want to even go out tonight. Putting on a bra and pants is just such a commitment these days."

The bartender laughs. "You could take them off."

I shake my head at him, hoping he can't see that I would like to take my clothes off with him. He steps away, filling more drink orders. I pull my phone from my purse again as if I'm on autopilot. Sit here and do nothing? Psshh. I can't do that. I might look like a loser. At least Siri can keep me company and make it seem like I have so many friends I can't keep up with their messaging and emails.

I log into Facebook instead, mindlessly scrolling through my newsfeed.

"Hey girl," Jillian says, coming up behind me. "Trying to talk sense into Lori gave me a headache. Want to go back to my place? I have wine and we can binge watch *Gossip Girl*."

"Actually," I start, "I kinda want to stay."

Jillian tips her head, looks at the empty glass in front of me, and then at the bartender. "No fucking way!"

"We're just talking, but I'm enjoying it."

"That's my girl."

I shake my head. "I need practice, right? It's just for fun. He's not my type."

She looks at me incredulously. "He's not your type? Are we talking about the same bartender? I'd dip him in chocolate and lick him clean if I could." She puts her hand on mine. "Just be safe, okay? Make sure he's not a mass murderer or anything before you go home with him."

"Reassuring, Jillian. That's why I can't do one-night stands. There's too many freaks out there."

She chews on her lip, looking at the bartender. "He might be into some freaky shit, but I'd roll with it. Just no butt stuff. Unless you're into that."

"No. I'm not. How do I know if he's a murderer?"

Jillian laughs. "I'm joking, Lex. I already asked that cocktail waitress about him for you. She said he's new in town and is a nice guy. Maybe a player, but not a murderer. Have fun. Fuck his brains out. And call me if you need anything. I'm only a cab ride away." She hugs me goodbye, goes out the door, and I'm left at the bar alone, waiting for Mr. Hottie to come back.

A while later, he's still pouring drinks and talking to other customers. The crowd is thinning and no one is singing anymore. I check the time on my phone, realizing the bar closes in twenty minutes, and suddenly feel stupid.

What the hell am I doing? I grab a twenty from my wallet and put it on the counter, and then get up to leave.

"Leaving already? I was hoping I could buy you a drink."

I turn around. Fast. Too fast. I stumble in these damn heels and catch myself on a barstool, looking into the bartender's blue eyes. "A drink?"

He laughs. "That's totally unoriginal coming from me, I know."

There's something about his smile that makes my own lips curve into one too. "Just a bit. And I suppose I can allow that." He holds my gaze as I walk back to the bar, taking the same seat I just had.

"I'm Luke, by the way," he says.

"Nice to meet you, Luke."

"You have incredible eyes," he says, making me flustered.

"Green is the rarest eye color," I blurt, cursing my compulsion to make everything awkward.

"I've heard that." He puts his hand on mine, fingertips brushing against my skin. I never thought such a small gesture could be described as erotic, but holy hell, my lady bits are tingling. "What can I get you?"

It takes me a second to process he's asking about drinks. "Umm, surprise me."

He brings me a Moscow Mule. "You got one when you first got here," he says, and I'm surprised he noticed me back then.

"Good memory," I say and take a sip.

"You're not the kind of woman I could forget."

It's all I can do not to laugh, because I don't agree.

"You don't believe me?" he asks, moving close again.

"Me? I'm nothing special. I'm just...just me."

He takes my hand again, sliding his fingers to my wrist.

"I don't know you very well—yet—but from what I've seen, *just you* seems pretty damn special."

I laugh again and take a drink. "Thanks."

He looks down for a moment, considers his words, and then looks back at me. I know by the lust in his eyes, he's thinking about leaving and bringing me with. I want to go with him. It's been so long since I had sex. Russell and I stopped sleeping together months before the divorce. I've enjoyed talking to Luke, and I'm sure I'll enjoy him even more if we hook up.

It's just one night. I can handle it, right? Fuck. I don't know. Maybe I can't.

His eyes meet mine and that grin is back. I swallow my pounding heart.

"Do you want to get out of here?" he asks.

chapter
five

LUKE

*S*he hesitates, and my heart stops beating. I'm no stranger to a one-night stand—though it's been a while—but something about this woman has my stomach in knots over her hesitation. If she says no, then I'll be faced with going home alone, even if someone else comes with me.

Sharing my bed with someone, even just for the night, does little to fill the void. Physically, I might not be alone for those short hours, but I'm still just as lonely as I was before, though it pains me to admit that. I've had my fun chasing women. I've broken hearts and had mine broken a time or two, though it was never anything I couldn't recover from. I got a reality check a few months ago, and *that* I haven't recovered from. I don't know if I ever will. I do my damnedest not to think about it, but I can't keep the darkness out forever. When it creeps in uninvited, it evokes feelings inside me I want to torch and bury deep inside my soul.

It evokes feelings that make me long for *something more.*

Lexi pushes her hair back and her mouth opens. Her

eyes meet mine and it's like I can feel her heart beating right up against mine.

Fast.

Hard.

Exhilarated.

She wets her lips and inhales, moving closer without meaning to. "Yes," she whispers, her own words sending a shiver down her spine. Long lashes come together as she blinks. "Yes, I do want to get out of here."

Her eyes are wide, and she's clutching her purse tightly in one hand. The other rests on the bar, fingers just a hair from mine. Maybe she's never done this before, which explains the color on her cheeks. If it's an experience she's looking for, I know I can deliver.

"Great," I say. "Give me a minute to wrap up." She nods and goes to use the ladies' room while I close down the bar. Minutes later, we're headed out into the brisk night air.

"Where are we going?" she asks scanning the street, and I can't be entirely sure she knew I was asking her back to my place to hook up.

"I don't live far from here."

She comes to a halt. "I don't know you."

"You can get to know me," I say slowly, watching her face. As much as I want to get her naked, I don't want her to wake up and regret this in the morning.

She raises an eyebrow. "What if you want to take me home and kill me?"

"I want to do a lot of things to you, but killing isn't one of them. Well, not in the literal sense at least."

"How would you do it?"

"Do what?" I ask.

"Kill me. I need to know. Is it going to be slow and painful? Or fast and quick? I'd think if you're wooing me then taking me home, you'd have some sort of *Silence of the Lambs* thing going on, right? Why else would you take the time to talk to me and liquor me up?"

I laugh. "You liquored yourself up. And you're right. But it would be more *Dexter* style and I'd never get caught."

"That's what I thought," she says with a nod, and turns her head up to the sky. "It's kinda sad the stars are so hard to see."

I follow her gaze above us. The night is hazy, which, mixed with the light pollution, makes the stars impossible to see. I've seen them a few times on clear nights.

"It makes it easy to forget they're even there," she says, still looking at the dark sky. "Maybe if we saw them more often, we'd remember what's important. Sometimes remembering how small you are in the grand scheme of things helps you not be such an asshole."

"You're very philosophical," I say and take her hand and start down the street. She laces her slender fingers through mine and warmth goes through me.

"I've been told. I'm no Yoda, but I do have some pretty good theories on why the world sucks."

"Yoda? You like Star Wars?"

"I love it," she says right away. "I saw the new movie four times last December. I even took my six yea—uh, niece. Six-year-old niece. She liked it too."

"Gotta start 'em off young. And I saw it three times. You have me beat there."

She turns to me and smiles. "My friends told me not to talk about Star Wars. Or Harry Potter. So sorry you think I'm lame."

I can't help but laugh. "I don't think you're lame for liking either of those. I've never seen Harry Potter."

"Have you read the books?" We cross at a corner and start down the block.

"Nope."

"But you do read, right?"

"I like to," I confess. "I have more downtime right now than I usually do."

"What do you like to read?" she asks, and then shakes her head. "Books are another thing I shouldn't talk about. Unless you want to talk about it all night."

I look down at her, catching a glimpse of her dark purple bra beneath her black shirt. Talking about books is the last thing I want to do with her all night.

Isn't it?

Because talking to her right now is nice. Really fucking nice.

"Mostly thrillers. What about you?"

"The occasional thriller is good, but I prefer romance. Mostly erotic romance, or at least romance with some steam. I need some good action and descriptive sex in my books."

I blink. I wasn't expecting that. She goes on to tell me about the last book she read, and is talking so fast she's hard to keep up with. It doesn't take long to get to my house. I dig my keys out of my jacket pocket and unlock the front door. The alarm starts beeping, warning me that I have a mere thirty seconds to disarm the thing. Ignoring it, I step back, opening the door for Lexi. She tentatively steps in, and I follow behind her, shutting off the alarm and turning on the foyer light.

"Wow," she says quietly, looking around as she takes off her shoes. The house is big—very big—and a century old. It's been carefully restored over the years by my grandparents, and professionally cleaned once a week. I grew up spending holidays and part of the summers here. Yet it still feels like a museum, big, cold, and unwelcoming.

Though, the latter has nothing to do with the house itself.

"This place is beautiful," Lexi says and unbuttons her coat.

"It's all right," I reply with a half smile.

She's still looking around as she pulls her arms from her coat, and one of the thin black straps on her top falls off her shoulder. Lust hits me so hard I can't stop myself. I jump on her, pinning her between my body and the wall. The sudden move catches her off guard for a split second, and then her arms wrap around me and she brings her lips to mine.

I believe you can tell a lot about a person by the way they kiss. And the first kiss is particularly important in knowing how the night will go.

Lexi parts her lips slowly as her fingers curl into fists, balling the material of my shirt. I taste the strawberry lip-gloss she put on before we left the bar. She tips her head and opens her mouth, wanting more. I slide one hand up from her waist and cup her cheek, deepening the kiss. Her grip on me tightens when my tongue pushes past her lips, and her hips press into mine. I start to pull away, but Lexi isn't having it. She moves her hand to my face, bringing my lips back to hers. She takes charge, kissing me like her very existence depends on it.

Tonight's going to be a good night.

I move my lips to her neck, kissing and sucking her skin. Her head falls back against the wall, and her hands drop back to my waist. A moan escapes her lips, and it's sexy as fuck. I sweep my fingers across her delicate collarbone and find the strap that's already hanging off her shoulder. I walk my fingers up her arm and hook them under her bra strap, bringing it down as well. I run my finger along the fabric, then plunge my hand in her shirt, cupping her breast.

Lexi moans again, and I move my mouth back to hers. I kiss her softly, teasing, and circle my thumb over her nipple. She inhales deeply, and her breasts rise and press into my palm. A shiver runs through her, and she pushes her tongue back into my mouth as the same time she slips her hands under my shirt. Her touch is gentle and warm, yet full of lust. It feels so fucking good to have her hands on me, inching closer and closer to my cock.

I keep kissing her, feeling her nipple harden against my palm, and then move my hands down. I take her hands in mine and raise them above her head, pinning them against the wall. She pushes against my grasp, testing me, which is such a fucking turn on.

I'm kissing her again, hard, fast, and this time, feeling like my existence depends on it. She kisses me back with the same lust-driven desperation, arching her back so her hips press into mine. She widens her legs and I step closer, and I know it's driving her insane not to be able to touch me.

I smile as I kiss her, and tighten my hold on her wrists. I move my mouth to her neck again, kissing, sucking, making her moan. She twists her arm, breaking free from my hold, and brings it to the button on my jeans. With one hand, she pops it open and slips her fingers inside, finding my semi-hard cock and wrapping her fingers around it. She takes my lip between her teeth, and now I'm the one that's moaning. It's been so long since I've felt this much. The numbness inside me has grown into my new normal. I forgot what it's like to *feel*.

Fuck. I need her. Now.

I pick Lexi up and carry her through the dark hall and into the kitchen. The light from the microwave is on, casting a soft, golden glow over the room. I set Lexi down on the island counter, arms wrapped tightly around her slim waist. She pulls me to her, and we go back, laying on the counter and knocking over a bowl of fruit. Apples go rolling to the floor, but neither of us care.

Right now, all that matters is Lexi, and I'm living and breathing her kisses. Greed takes over and I want more. Need more. I grab the hem of her shirt and pull it over her head, dropping it behind us. I lean back just enough to look her over, to run my eyes over her body and appreciate her beauty.

I blink and look at her face, surprised that she looks nervous, casting a glance down at her middle.

"Don't be shy," I say. "You're fucking beautiful."

She takes in an audible breath, lips parting. "You really think so?"

It's like a switch was flipped, and she went from being Ms. In Control to insecure. For some reason it's making me want her more. Because it makes her real.

"God, yes."

She bites her lip and smiles. "Good."

"Take off your bra."

She blinks, unsure, but looks me right in the eye and nods. Another smile plays on her face, and she sweeps her hands up along her stomach, then slowly over her breasts. My cock presses against my jeans, begging to be touched again.

I lick my lips, watching with greed as she unhooks her bra. Her breasts come together and my cock aches as she undoes the clasp. She moves slow, purposely teasing me.

"You like this?" she asks coyly. "You want me to take it off, don't you? Then what are you going to do?"

God, this woman. One minute she's shy and insecure,

then the next she's talking dirty. I dive back down, lips crashing into hers. She takes the hem of my shirt in her hands and pulls it off, throwing it across the room. We collide again, and her large breasts crush against my chest. I put myself between her legs, scooting her to the edge of the counter. She runs her hands along the waistband of my pants, fingertips brushing the wet tip of my cock. Then she moves them back, dragging her nails along my back.

I'm so into her I don't notice her fingers brush over the large patch of scar tissue on my back until she touches it. But she doesn't stop, doesn't push me away, or ask for an explanation. She just moves her hand down and keeps kissing me.

I drop down, trailing kisses from her lips to her chest, and down her stomach. She drops back on her elbows, hands in my hair, as I unbutton her jeans. She lifts her ass up off the counter and I take her pants off, letting them fall to the floor. Mine come off next, dropping down to my ankles. I step out of them, putting my hands on the counter and gently pushing Lexi back. I part her legs and drop down, perching on the edge of a bar stool.

Starting at her ankles, I run deft fingers up her legs. She shudders when my fingers sweep across her center, still covered with her black and purple panties. I take one of her legs and put it over my shoulder. Slowly, I turn my head and kiss the tender skin inside her thigh. Her heat matches mine, and it pains me just as much to take my time. All I want is to come right now.

Her pulse pounds, beating against my lips. I move my mouth closer to her pussy, using every ounce of self-control I have not to jump onto her and fuck her senseless. I'll do that later. I'm going to make her come first.

I kiss, suck, nip at her skin, feeling her heat intensify.

Her muscles twitch and her breath quickens like she's on the verge of an orgasm. And I haven't taken her panties off yet. I lean back, taking my mouth off Lexi. I feel her eyes on me and look up, greeted with a "don't you dare fucking stop" glare. I flash her a grin, lick my lips, and put my head between her legs again, rolling her panties down her legs with more patience than I thought possible, until they're hanging from just one ankle.

I don't hesitate this time, and she cries out the second my tongue lashes against her wetness. She reaches down, taking a tangle of my hair as I go to town, bringing her to an orgasm in just minutes. Her legs tighten around my neck and she moans. I'm not done yet. I slip a finger inside, and feeling her pulse against me is so fucking hot.

She's writhing with pleasure, mouth open, eyes squeezed shut. Her hands are still in my hair, holding my head between her legs. It doesn't take long before she comes again, moaning loudly as the orgasm rolls through.

Her head falls to the side as she pants, and the red flush is back on her cheeks. She brings her hand to her chest, feeling her heartbeat.

"Luke," she groans unable to open her eyes just yet. She feebly reaches for me, and her hand lands on my shoulder, right on the patch of burned flesh. It's like it's not there, like my skin is normal and it doesn't bother her. She tugs at me, trying to bring me on top of her. The bar stool scrapes on the tiled floor as I stand and climb onto the counter, lowering myself onto Lexi. Her legs are shaking, and her embrace is weak. I put my lips to hers and she kisses me. Knowing she's tasting herself drives me wild.

"That was...was...intense," she pants, lips brushing against mine as she speaks.

"I'm just getting started," I groan, putting my mouth

back on hers. I take a handful of her hair and ball my fist. I move my mouth to her neck, teeth grazing her flesh. She inhales sharply, followed by another groan. Then she's reaching down, slipping her hand inside my boxers.

I melt into her the moment her fingers wrap around my cock, pumping up and down before need takes a hold of us both and we scramble together to get my boxers off. She bends her knees, welcoming me between her legs. I kiss her as I slide in, and holy fuck, she feels amazing. Lexi grabs my ass, nails biting into my skin as I fuck her.

She rocks her hips along with me, holding me close against her. She scratches her nails along my back, and the pain amplifies the pleasure. Knowing that kissing her neck does her in, I move my mouth there again, and moments later, she's coming again. Feeling her inner walls contract around my dick pushes me over the edge, and a minute later, I'm coming. Hard. Harder than I have in a long fucking time.

We're both panting, hearts racing. I lower myself onto her, chest rising and falling just as fast as hers. She drops one arm down onto the counter, and rests the other on my back for a second before she runs her fingers through my hair. I turn my face up to her, and put my lips on hers again.

The second we kiss, I'm hit with something else.

Regret.

And I know Lexi is all wrong for me. I'm not regretting something I *didn't do*. I'm regretting taking her home like this. Because as much as I'm trying not to admit it to myself, I know one night with Lexi is not going to be enough.

chapter six

LEXI

"*T*his is amazing," I say, sticking my fork into the cheese-covered pasta. I look across the kitchen at Luke. He's wearing boxers and nothing else, and is standing by the stove, sautéing mushrooms to top off the pasta. "Where did you learn to cook like this?"

He looks over his shoulder at me, and my heart flutters. I squash that feeling down, not wanting to feel anything but sex-driven lust for him. This is a one-night stand. In order to have no-strings sex, I need to have no feelings for Luke.

"My grandfather was a chef," he says. "He taught me everything I know, and after my parents split, I tried to pick up the slack and cook so my mom didn't have to. She worked crazy hours as a nurse."

Fuck. Me. I shove a forkful of pasta in my mouth to keep from talking. I like pasta. I love cheese. I'm still recovering from the epic fucking we just had and watching Luke—all tattoos and muscles—stand at the stove cooking for me is about to do me in.

I grab the stem-less glass of red wine in front of me and drink. *Way to pick them...* Not only is Luke the most aesthetically pleasing man I've laid eyes on, but he fucks like a sex god, can cook, and has this amazing house. I should get out of here. Because there has to be a catch. It's only a matter of time before he locks me in the basement or shows me his doll collection, right?

"Do you like to cook?" I ask, unable to control myself. I need to put down the wine. No more booze for me. But it's like my fingers are glued to that damn glass. Well, except when they let go to pick up my fork. Because cheese-covered pasta.

"I do," he says, giving me a half smile. "I hate washing dishes after, and I don't cook like this very often. But cooking reminds me of my childhood a bit. Call me lame or nostalgic, what have you," he adds with a chuckle.

The rest of my wine is gone. I squeeze my eyes closed and inhale, then open them and look around the kitchen. It's clean. Like spotless clean. There aren't any watermarks on the fridge dripping down from the filtered water dispenser, and there are no fingerprints on the dishwasher.

He's either gay, has a wife, or a housekeeper.

He's too good at sex to be gay—cover or not—and I see no evidence of a woman anywhere in the house. Do bartenders make enough to hire housekeepers? Or even live in this ostentatious house?

The alternative is just as hard to believe: that Luke is a unicorn. Rare and mythical, they just don't exist. Granted, I don't know him well, but from what I've seen, he's a nice guy who is easy on the eyes and can cook and fuck like a god.

Yep. I'm going to end up flayed in the basement. *Sorry, girls.*

"Want more wine?" Luke asks, coming over and spooning mushrooms in my bowl.

"No, I'm good, thanks."

He gets himself food and then sits across from me. We're both busy eating, and silence fills the room. It should be awkward, but it's not. Nothing about this is, and on some level, it weirds me out.

It's my high blood alcohol level, right? If I hadn't had anything to drink, this would be weird as fuck. Because sitting here in my undies and bra isn't something I do. I'm not a confident woman. I have stretch marks around my nipples from nursing two babies, and the muscles on my stomach never fully recovered from pregnancy. I have gray hairs that luckily are hard to see against my blonde locks, but they're there, reminding me of how much I struggle to get myself put together on a daily basis. I shaved my legs for the first time in days just for tonight, and my matching bra and panties were a rare Target splurge.

I feel like a hot fucking mess, and yet Luke is treating me like a queen. I'm scared if I blink this will all disappear.

"Do you want dessert?" Luke asks a few minutes later, standing and taking my empty bowl. I scan his body, admiring his abs and colorful tattoos. He has a patch of rough flesh on his shoulder going down his back. The lighting in here is dim but I think it's a burn. The colorful lines of his tattoos meld into a painful mess of melted flesh and scar tissue. Some may look at it and think it's ugly, but I find it sort of beautiful. Scars tell our stories, though most aren't visible.

"Um," I say and reach for the glass of water Luke set on the table between us. I take a long drink and let my eyes trail over his body. He looks as good as he felt, a mixture of muscles and ink, and a trail of hair that leads my eyes right to that thick cock. I grow wet thinking about him. "Yes, please."

His eyes narrow and he gives me that cocky smirk again,

one that promises he's going to fuck me so hard I won't be able to walk in the morning. He holds out his hand and helps me to my feet. I follow him up the grand staircase, which takes us to a large landing that looks over the foyer below. Light from the city shines through the windows, reflecting on the polished hardwood floors. There are several doors around us, and all but two are closed.

Luke's room is the farthest from us. His arms are around me the moment we crash through the doorway, falling backwards onto his bed, which is neatly made and smells like the sheets just came from the dryer. Seriously. Who is this guy? Is another mind blowing orgasm worth my untimely death?

Yes. I think it is. Because I know I won't have just one when it comes to Luke.

He wastes no time getting down and dirty. He lowers himself to me and I wrap my arms around his shoulders. Our eyes meet again, and I see something that I didn't notice before. Behind the cocky glimmer, past the confidence and the bad-boy smirk.

Desperation.

One that I know well. Desperation to belong. Desperation to be happy. Desperation to be loved.

To *feel*.

I can't kiss him hard enough. I run my hands down his back, pushing him onto me. The wet tip of his dick sticks out from the elastic of his boxers. I haven't had the chance to take a minute and admire it yet, but I know from feeling it inside me, he has a big, thick cock.

I arch my back, pressing my tender core against him. He removes my bra, and then puts his mouth to my neck, knowing that having his lips against me there is almost enough to make me come on its own. He doesn't take his mouth off me as he pulls my panties down, dropping them off the side of the bed. Every nerve in my body is awake and alive, feeling everything. Luke moves down, spreading my legs and plunging his head in between.

"I fucking love the way you taste," he mumbles, mouth against me. The stubble on his chin is rough against the flesh on my thighs contrasting against his warm, soft tongue. I lift my head and watch him work, feeling my muscles tighten as the pleasure winds tight inside. My head falls back on the bed, and I twist the blankets in one hand, and take a handful of Luke's hair in the other. My breath quickens as I climax. It comes on strong, sending pulses of pleasure through me, from my center all the way down to my feet, curling my toes. It runs up to my head, making my ears ring. I'm not aware that I'm pulling Luke's hair, twisting it in my grasp as I writhe beneath him. He doesn't stop, doesn't let up.

He slips a finger inside me, pressing against my inner walls, and finds that sweet spot that sends another jolt of pleasure to take over. He works his fingers in rhythm with his tongue. My legs are shaking from the force of the second orgasm that rolls over me.

An impeccable man with an impeccable house who gives impeccable oral? I am so getting skinned alive after this.

Luke moves on top of me, and presses his lips to mine. I'm in a temporary sex-induced coma, still feeling the orgasm pulse through me, ears still ringing, and stars in my vision. I couldn't get up and walk right now if the house was on fire.

Trying to catch my breath, I bring my arms up and push his boxers down. He moves his mouth to my neck and nips at my skin and he enters me, thrusting deep and slow. The feeling comes back to my legs and I grab Luke's hips, moving him off. I bite my lip and smile, then push him down onto the mattress. I climb on top, enjoying every minute of it.

"You are so fucking hot," he moans, taking my breasts in his hands. I let out a moan, relishing in how incredible this all feels. Not just the sex—which is abso-fucking-lutely amazing—but how free I feel. Sitting naked on top of Luke, enjoying the hell out of having sex with a man I just met. Finally owning my own sexuality is so damn empowering.

We come at nearly the same time, and then collapse onto the bed, out of breath. Luke pulls down the blankets and covers us up, pulling me close to him.

"I came inside you twice," he says, voice all breathy. "Sorry?"

His words hit me, and I realize he's only the second man I've ever allowed to enter me without a condom. I wasn't a virgin when I met Russell, but I'd been rather strict with my boyfriends before, terrified of an unplanned baby. "I have an IUD to prevent pregnancy. You don't have any diseases?"

"Not that I know of," he says. "You?"

"No, I'm clean."

"Good." I rest my head on his chest and pass out.

BRIGHT SUNLIGHT FILLS THE ROOM, shining through a large window that overlooks the street below. Luke's arm is draped around me, and his naked body is pressed against mine. I'm thirsty and need to pee, but I don't dare move yet.

I close my eyes and snuggle a little closer to Luke for another few minutes. All the alcohol is out of my system, and I'm thinking clearly for the first time since I met Luke.

He's basically a stranger—an attractive stranger who just might be a sex god—but it feels so damn good to have another warm body next to mine. I forgot how much I missed this.

I stretch out, and Luke tightens his hold on me. Part of my heart, the part that's been blackened and cold for so long, yearns for this to last more than just once, and I squash out the hope before it has a chance to take hold and set me up for disappointment.

Guys like Luke don't date women like me.

Divorced.

With kids.

And barely able to keep my head above the surface.

"Morning," he says softly, lifting his head off the pillow. His hair is a mess and he looks adorable.

"Morning," I whisper back, and he kisses my forehead. "I'm gonna use the bathroom."

He nods and flops back down, rolling over onto his other side. The sheets come with him, exposing his ass. And what a fine ass that is.

I put my undies back on and look around for my shirt. I can't find it, so I grab Luke's and pull it over my head as I walk, stopping when I open his bedroom door. We're on the second level, and I'm not sure where the bathroom is up here. I slowly pad down the wide hall, and can't help but feel like I'm on the set of *Gossip Girl*. I look over a balcony that's above the foyer. Seriously, how the hell can anyone afford a place like this?

I find the bathroom, pee, and spend a few minutes cleaning up my makeup and rinsing my mouth with water. I'm on my way back to Luke's room when I hear something downstairs. I freeze, hand on the balcony railing. A door opens and closes, followed by footsteps. My heart skips a beat and I rush back to Luke.

"Someone's in your house," I say, closing the door behind me. Shit. My phone is downstairs by the front door... which I don't think we locked last night.

"My brother," Luke mumbles into his pillow.

"What?" I crawl back onto the bed, hands shaking.

"My brother," he says, turning over. "He lives here too."

"Oh." I let out my breath, feeling a little silly for panicking. Living alone has turned me a bit paranoid. Russell was a good-for-nothing asshole, but at least would have provided enough of a distraction to a burglar to give me time to get the girls and lock ourselves in the bedroom.

"Come back to bed," Luke says and reaches for me. I'm about to lie down next to him again when I see the clock. It's after nine, and the girls might be up. I need to get my phone and make sure I didn't have a missed call from them.

"I will. In a minute."

Luke mumbles a response, still half asleep, and I slip out of the room and hurry down the stairs. Luke's brother is in the kitchen, but if I'm fast he might not see me, though I suppose it doesn't matter. He had to have heard us last night and won't be surprised to see me. I grab my purse and turn to dash up the stairs when I see him sitting at the island counter drinking coffee and eating toast.

Cole Winchester. My boss.

chapter
seven

LEXI

I can't help but stare. Standing here frozen like a deer in headlights is the last thing I should do, since I'm dressed in only last night's undies and Luke's black t-shirt. I need to move. Need to run up the stairs, barricade myself in Luke's room and never come out. Yet my damn feet won't move.

Cole picks up his toast, takes a bite, then sets it down. On the counter. The same counter my bare ass was on last night, getting fucked by—oh my God—*Cole's brother.* I inhale sharply as it hits me.

I had a naughty, dirty, one-night stand with my boss's brother. The blood leaves my face and I think I might pass out. I blink a thousand times, making sure this was really happening. Then Cole looks up and I dash out of sight, crashing into the wall. My face takes the brunt of the impact.

"Hello?" Cole calls from the kitchen. I hear the barstool scoot as he stands, and my legs have never moved faster in my whole entire life—and I was on the track team in college.

My heart is racing by the time I get to Luke's room. I close the door behind me and use every ounce of self-control I have not to jump into bed and hide under the covers. Luke is sprawled out on the bed, white sheets twisted over his legs, hiding his junk but leaving enough exposed to make me lust. Sunlight filters through, lighting up the bed.

He looks like something that belongs on a book cover. An erotic book, that is.

His eyes flutter open when he hears the door click, and he slowly sits up. Our eyes meet and my heart slows. There's something about him that's comforting, which doesn't make sense.

I don't really know him.

His body—that, I know. But what goes on inside that head of his, what his life is like...I'm clueless. Well, other than the fact that he's Cole Winchester's brother.

"I was a little worried you left," he confesses.

Hearing his voice takes away some of the panic. He sits up and reaches his hands over his head. Seeing his muscles flex as he stretches doesn't hurt either.

"I thought about it, but I can't find my clothes," I say coyly. My pants are still in the kitchen. With Cole. Maybe? I don't know. "And I can't go out like this."

He swiftly moves to the edge of his bed and grabs me by the waist, pulling me onto him. We fall back onto the bed and he slips warm hands under my shirt.

"Well, if that's the case I'm never giving them back." His lips meet my neck and I'm hit with mad desire for him all over again.

"Then I'll just have to steal yours."

"Fine by me as long as that means I can have you again." He runs his fingers down my spine, inside my panties, and grabs my ass.

"That can be arranged," I say. I'm looking into his eyes, moving in for a kiss when my phone rings. *The girls.* I jerk away so fast it leaves Luke looking hurt, and scramble to get my phone from my purse. My heart speeds up and I'm feeling guilty now for not checking it the moment I grabbed my bag.

It's not Russell's number. I let out a breath and silence Jillian's call. She's wanting details about last night, and probably wondering why I ignored the six texts she sent me. I have no other missed calls or texts. The girls are probably still sleeping. Seeing their smiling faces on my phone background reminds me that I'm so far from the woman Luke thought he was with last night.

He's a sexy-as-sin single guy, living it up with no regrets. I'm a divorced mom of two who questions her judgment every single day. He'd run away screaming if he knew the truth.

"Do you want breakfast?" he asks and gets up, going to the window. Holy hell...that ass. You could bounce a quarter off that thing.

"Uh, sure." Is breakfast standard after a one-night stand? This is my first go at this. I don't know the rules. Wait.

Breakfast.

The kitchen.

Cole.

I can't go down there. Cole can't know I'm here. He can't know it was my screams he inevitably heard last night. We'll never be able to look at each other the same if he sees me as that girl, the one who goes home from the bar with some random dude.

And Luke...Luke was fun. Saying he's easy on the eyes is an understatement, but he can't be anything more. Fun was nice, but I'm not looking for fun. I want a long-haul type of guy, and Mr. Tattoos and Muscles over here is the opposite of that, isn't he?

"Actually," I start, not sure how to word anything without sounding harsh. Though did Luke expect anything more? He offered to take me home after a short while of conversing. It's not like he expected this to turn into anything serious, right? "I should get going."

"Right. I'm sure you have shit to do."

"Yeah." I run my hand through my hair. "I do. My pants, though. Where are they?"

He strides over to his dresser and pulls a pair of pajama pants from the top drawer. "Downstairs, I think. I'll get them for you."

"That'd be great. Thanks."

He nods, and I'm not sure if that's disappointment I see in his eyes. He opens his door and lets out a huff, shaking his head. I follow his gaze and see Cole walking up the stairs.

"Luke. The kitchen is a fucking disaster. You left dishes everywhere," he says and I can tell right away he's pissed off. Panic floods my veins. He can't see me. Not like this. I do the first thing that comes to mind and grab Luke, twisting him around. I take a step back and sink down on the bed.

Luke flashes a grin and comes down with me. We kiss, and the sensation sends shivers through my spine and for a split second, I forget that my boss is in the hall. Then Cole grumbles and slams the bedroom door shut.

Crisis averted.

And yet I have no desire to stop kissing Luke. I widen my legs and welcome him between. His skin is still warm from being under the covers and feels wonderful against me. His tongue slips past my lips and he moves his hand down, pushing under the thin material of my panties.

Cole is no longer on my mind.

"You can't turn down breakfast now," Luke says, pulling on pants.

I sit up, holding the sheet over my breasts. "I am hungry."

He turns to me, flashing that cocky grin. "Coming that many times had to work up an appetite. Remind me, how many times did you come? I'm going to have to wash the sheets."

My cheeks—which are already flushed—redden even more. "Should I be apologizing for that?"

"Hell no. It's fucking hot to see you come." He zips his jeans and pulls on a long sleeved t-shirt. "Where do you want to go for breakfast?"

"Uh," I start. "Go out for breakfast? Not eat here?" I heard him, but I need the reassurance. And now I probably sound weird. Dammit. Wait...why do I care? I'm not seeing Luke again after this. I *can't* see him again after this.

"Yeah, I'm not the best cook."

I raise an eyebrow. "Seriously?"

"Fine. I know I'm a good cook," he sighs. "Not to bore you with family drama, I can't fucking stand my brother."

My heart stops beating in my chest. "Why?" I blurt, then kick myself. He doesn't know I know his brother, and it needs to stay that way. I didn't see Cole. Didn't recognize his voice. I reach over the bed for my underwear.

"Long story short, he's an asshole. Always has been, always will be."

I bite my lip and stick my legs in my undies, trying to gauge what's normal talk and what's prying because I'm pretty damn curious about my boss...who I've had a secret crush on for the last six months. "I'm sorry," I say. "I have an older sister. We hated each other growing up but now that we both have ki—that we both are busy with, uh, adult stuff we get along well."

"Lucky." He grabs shoes and socks and sits on the bed to put them on. "I'll get your clothes from downstairs." He kisses my forehead and dashes out of the room. I put my head in my hands and take a deep breath. What the hell kind of mess did I get myself into?

I seriously entertained the thought of having a relationship with Cole. Even if he wanted me, wanted to settle down and add another kid or two to our little family, I'd be the girl who slept with his brother.

Three times. And I don't regret it, not at all.

"Oh my God," I groan. My hopes for landing Cole might have been far-fetched, but hopes for continuing to work at Black Ink Press aren't. I can't lose my job. I'm barely getting by as it is. My phone buzzes again, and I clamor over the messy bed to get it. It's Jillian again, asking me what the hell is going on since she hasn't heard from me yet. I start typing a reply and stop, delete my words, and start again.

Luke comes back into the room, carrying my clothes, shoes, and jacket. His blue eyes are as clear as the cloudless sky above us. I look into them, feeling that odd comfort again. Now that I'm specifically looking, I can see similarities between him and Cole. They're both tall and broad-shouldered. They have the same defined cheekbones and chiseled jaw. Luke's hair is a bit darker and he has a certain ruggedness about him, making me think that he most definitely has a motorcycle and more notches in his headboard than should be legally allowed. Cole is refined, collected, and put together. God, those two are dangerously sexy in their own ways.

They're like the fucking Hemsworth brothers.

Luke tosses me my clothes and strides to the window again. His face darkens momentarily when he looks out at the city, and sadness pulls down his blue eyes. He takes a breath and that cocky grin is back. I divert my eyes as he turns, knowing he didn't mean for me to see that moment of truth behind the arrogance he carries around.

I wish I didn't see it. I wish all there was to Luke was tattoos and sex appeal. I wish he'd forget about me and I could get back to my hectic hot mess of a life. But that millisecond where his walls came down changed everything.

Because now I want more.

chapter eight

LUKE

*L*exi brings the mug of coffee to her lips and takes a drink. She visibly relaxes as the liquid goes down. I watch the muscles in her face go slack, and she even closes her eyes for a second or two. She raked her hair to the side in a messy braid, and is wearing one of my sweatshirts. Despite the bright sun, the air kept the nighttime chill, and the thin material of Lexi's top wasn't enough. She puts her mug down, looks at me, and smiles. I can't help but think I could get used to this.

Which is totally ridiculous, I know.

We started the night with a classic one-night stand: girl meets guy in bar, guy takes girl home. It can't be anything more...or can it? It might be ass-backwards, but maybe she'll see me after this, let me take her on a real date before we jump each other's bones again.

Or maybe not.

But if life has taught me anything in the last few months, it's that this life of bachelorhood isn't all it's cracked up to be. Having someone there, someone who knows me and my goddamn flaws and accepts me for it, helps when shit gets dark.

And it can't get much darker than this.

Lexi takes another drink of coffee, happily sighing. I smirk.

"Want me to leave you alone with that?"

"Huh?" she asks, putting the coffee down. "Oh, the coffee. Yeah. You might, or you'll get jealous by how easily I get off from just a little bit of caffeine."

I laugh. "From what I recall last night...and then this morning...the coffee has nothing on me."

She flushes a bit, looking innocent.

"How many times did you come last night? I lost count."

"Luke!" she whisper-yells. "You can't talk like that in public!"

"I can't? It seems like I am." Fuck. Pushing her buttons and making her flustered shouldn't turn me on. It's sexy as hell, and putting me at risk for getting a hard-on right now in the middle of the crowded cafe. "If anyone heard, *they'd* just be jealous."

"They take one look at you and they'd be jealous," she mumbles, trying not to laugh.

"Same to you."

She wrinkles her nose and laughs again, like the thought of someone wanting her is funny. Then she realizes what's she's doing and stops, looking embarrassed. Fuck. Seeing her like this—so raw, coming unhitched—is not helping the don't-pop-a-boner situation I have going on.

"That's not the first time you've acted surprised to hear you're desirable."

"I know," she admits, and her honesty takes me aback. "But it's in the past. I'm good. You're good. *We* were good." She buries herself in her coffee again.

"Last night you said you don't know me," I start. "Do you feel like you do now?"

She puts her mug down, lips curving upward. "Parts of you. And kind of. Though I do have some questions."

"Shoot."

"How old are you?"

"Twenty-nine. You?"

"Twenty-seven. What's your favorite color?"

"Blue," I answer.

"I like yellow. Now, these next few questions can make or break you as a person. Are you ready?"

I inhale, acting nervous. "I don't know. I'll give it a shot."

"Cubs or Sox?"

"Cubs," I answer.

"Do you like Nickelback?"

"Nope."

"Have you seen Game of Thrones?"

"Yes, every episode at least once," I tell her.

"Do you like horror movies?"

"They're okay. Nothing is a good as the slasher movies from when I was a kid."

"What do you do when one of those ASPCA commercials with the sad music comes on?"

"Change the channel as fast as I can."

She nods like she's mentally keeping score. "Well, Luke, you should be happy to know you are not a horrible person."

"I passed your test?"

"Yes," she says seriously. "You did."

We both laugh. "See?" I say. "You can know someone after one night."

"You know," she starts, grabbing an empty packet of sugar to fiddle with. "I've never done that before."

"Done what?"

She flicks her eyes to me, then looks back at the sugar packet, ripping it in two as she talks. "Had a one-night stand."

"Who says it has to be one night?" The words slip out before I have a chance to think about it. My heart thumps at the silence that follows. Shit. What the hell was I thinking?

"You want to do this again?" Her full lips pull into a smile.

"I wouldn't turn it down."

"Well, neither would I." Her eyes meet mine and she smiles. My chest loosens, making me realize how much I want to see this woman again.

~

"Luke."

A heavy hand falls on my foot and pushes it off the couch. I startle awake, fighting remnants of a bad dream for clarity. I blink, eyes adjusting to the bright afternoon sunlight coming through the living room windows. I fell asleep on the couch watching TV, and my mind, that traitor, took me back to the hell I left Chicago to escape.

Cole is standing next to me, eyebrows pushed together with concern. "You were having a nightmare," he says. "I assumed it was about...well, you know."

"It was," I confess and sit up, running my hand over my face. Cole is still standing there, still looking worried. It's odd and out of character, and about fucking time he played the role of big brother. Considering what happened, he's months overdue.

"Thanks," I mumble and look at the clock. "Fuck, I was asleep for hours. I meant to go to the gym. Have you gone yet?" I'm not exactly suggesting we go together, but I'll lay the offer out for him to take. We both work out. Why not share a cab?

"You wouldn't have fallen asleep and missed your gym time if you hadn't stayed up so late last night."

Just like that, my brother is an asshole. Maybe it *would* actually kill him to be nice for more than a minute.

"Yeah, well, it was worth it," I say and stretch, trying to mentally will my body to stop reacting to pain and fire. My heart is beating a million miles an hour. I flash a grin to cover up how panicked I feel inside.

"Maybe for you, but I don't appreciate being woken up in the middle of the night to whatever the hell you were doing."

"Oh, you know damn well what I was doing." Just the thought of Lexi naked on top of me, next to me, curled up in my arms, is enough to slow my racing heart.

"I heard enough. Spare me the details." Cole shakes his head.

"Don't be jealous. You could go out and meet someone too."

"That's not the way I want to meet someone. I outgrew the bar scene ten years ago." He shoots me a judgmental look. "The type of women who go home with you from the bar aren't the type of women I want to be dating."

A surge of protectiveness comes over me, and I have to defend Lexi. "That's bullshit."

"No, it's not. You're not going to meet a worthwhile mate from a one-night stand."

"Referring to a woman as a 'worthwhile mate' certainly doesn't make you one."

He shakes his head. "You know what I mean. Worthwhile in a sense that you'd take her home to see

Mom, or you think the two of you have a shot at a real relationship."

"You're still wrong. Because the woman I met and brought home with me last night is more than worthwhile. She's smart and funny and Mom would like her."

"She still slept with you on the first date. Wait, no, it wasn't even a date. That says a lot about her."

"Yeah, it says she likes to fuck, and there's nothing wrong with that. Besides, I'd rather know right away if things are good in the sex-department before I commit to a lady. Nothing ruins a relationship faster than bad sex."

Cole has always been on the conservative side when it comes to talking about sex and relationships. So of course, I make him as uncomfortable as possible. He gives me his trademark scowl and headshake, and goes into the kitchen. Needing to eat before I hit the gym, I follow him and open the fridge.

"You know, if you pulled that stick out of your ass you might be able to meet someone too. Or at the very least get laid so you stop being such a dick." I look over my shoulder at Cole, who has ingredients out for a sandwich.

"You're insinuating that you have further plans with your booty call," he says and puts two pieces of bread on a plate.

I grab the Tupperware of leftover pasta from last night and stick it in the microwave. "I do," I lie. "I told you, she's not like that. She's...she's different. She's nice and easy to talk to. The sex was great—really fucking great—but there's more to her than that. And not even you can deny women like that are few and far between."

Cole just rolls his eyes and looks away, concentrating on making his sandwich. Now it's my turn for sympathy, though I won't ever let Cole know it. Not all that long ago,

Cole proposed to his girlfriend, Heather. She was my partner in a school project way back in high school, and met Cole when she came over to work on it. They'd been on-and-off again ever since. She said yes only to say no a few months later, putting a halt on all wedding plans.

He shocked everyone by asking her in the first place since the two broke up and got back together more times than Ross and Rachel, and I think he only asked her to marry him because he had turned thirty that year and felt he *had* to. Still...being shot down like that'll fuck with anyone's mind, but when you're borderline psychotic and uptight like my brother, it turns you into even more of an asshole. And nobody wants to date an asshole. He's been single ever since, and has standards so ridiculous, no one can meet them. It's a defense mechanism to keep him from getting hurt again, but I'm not his shrink. I won't even attempt to get into that with him.

"You're going to call this mysterious wonderful woman?" he grumbles.

"It would be a loss not to," I say it to further our argument, but it couldn't be more true. Because Lexi really is different. There really was something more than no-strings sex between us. "And I'm dying to get her in bed again."

"You're crude."

"Just honest." I watch the timer count down on the microwave, stomach grumbling. "You know what'd be nice? It'd be really fucking weird, and I'm talking X-Files level weird here, but nice."

"What?" Cole asks flatly.

"If you showed just the tiniest bit of happiness when I say I met an amazing woman."

Cole huffs and raises his eyes to meet mine. "You need to disinfect the couch."

"The couch? Why?" I ask with fake innocence.

"You fucking know why."

I shake my head. "Nope."

"Because you two...you know...on it."

"We didn't have sex on the couch."

"I heard you down here," he grumbles.

"Oh, right. We *did* have sex down here. Just not on the couch. But where you're sitting...and eating...*that's* where we had sex."

chapter nine

LEXI

I get into the shower, head spinning. I do my best not to think about Luke. Or Cole. Or the naughty things I could do with both of them. At the same time.

The water starts to run cold by the time I'm ready to get out and face the world. I take my time toweling off and putting on lotion. Anything to buy myself time. Anything to keep my mind from going back to him.

To *them*.

I get dressed and grab my phone. A missed call and four missed texts stare ominously at me, and I scramble to make sure none are from Russell regarding the girls. They're not. The missed call is from my mother, and the texts are from Jillian and my sister Kara, who wants to know if I can do a playdate with the girls after school next week. I tell her most likely yes, and hope we can go. It's so hard committing to anything that's not five minutes from now.

I've always had a decent relationship with my mother, but we've become especially close after the divorce. The girls and I stayed with my parents for a few months until all the legal stuff was taken care of. As much as I hated living at home again, it made me appreciate all my parents did for me as a child. And even more so as an adult.

I call my mom back, welcoming a distraction. She asks how we've been and hints more than once she'd like to set me up with her friend's son, who is a doctor. Which she reminded me of at least three times in our ten-minute conversation. After we hang up, I reply to Jillian, asking her to come over. She answers right away that she's headed over. She knows it's serious to ask her to come from the city.

I grab a coffee mug, then switch to a wine glass at the last minute. Even though I drank enough to kill a whale last night, I need liquid sanity to get me through this. I down a glass of pink Moscato and lean against the counter. It'll be a while before Jillian gets here, not only because she's coming from Manhattan, but because she can't go anywhere without a full face of makeup. She's gorgeous without it, and has skin as soft and flawless as my toddler.

Needing to kill time, I log onto my computer and start reading that paranormal book. The writing is brilliant and I get sucked in right away...until I meet a demon hunter named Luke. Is that fate or what? I'm tempted to do a mass replace of the name to something different. I read another page. And another. Damn, this book is good. Good, but a little creepy. I get scared easily, so this will be a daytime-only read. Yeah, I know it's just a book and I can close it at any time. But it's so much more than that. It's so hard to explain to people who haven't experienced it though.

Once I flip open that first page, I get sucked in. Everything else fades away and only the words painted in front of me exist. My mind shapes the characters and places, putting personal touches on every single one of them.

That's the thing about books. Reading is an intimate process, as people and places take on those you're familiar with. And half the time I don't even realize it, and it just happens.

And it happened right then and there, because I jump when the doorbell rings over an hour later. I close the computer and fly to answer it.

"What the hell, Lexi?" Jillian says, bustling in. She's put together in an effortless way.

"You look like Han Solo," I say, eyeballing her vest and boots.

"Who is—never mind. Spill."

"How do you not know who Han Solo is?" I ask incredulously and close the door behind her.

"It's a Star Trek thing, I know," she says seriously, giving me a dead stare. "Kidding. I know it's Star Wars. You know I like messing with you. So please don't launch into the difference between the two again."

I just shake my head and wave her into the kitchen. I grab another wine glass, realize that it came out of the dishwasher dirty—and put away dirty apparently—and quickly stick it in the sink before she sees. I get another and do a nonchalant check for dishwasher residue.

"So, last night," I start. "I went home with that bartender."

"Ohh I know. What the hell happened? Was he horrible in bed? Have a small dick? Did you freak? Did he cry after he came? I heard some guys do that."

"What? No, he didn't cry." I go to the fridge and grab the wine, filling up both our glasses.

"You did freak, didn't you? It's okay if you did. It's understandable after all you've been through."

I turn back around and hand her the wine. I take a drink. "I didn't freak. The sex was amazing. I'm talking romance novel quality sex."

"Wow. So...what's the big deal?"

I close my eyes, remembering Luke's naked body tangled up in the sheets. He looked so damn good, and fucked me even better. And then I went downstairs and it all went to hell.

"His brother was home."

Jillian winces. "He walked in on you, didn't he?"

"No, thank God." I take another drink, thinking about what that would have been like. Suddenly, I'm laughing so hard I'm choking on the wine. I bring my hand to my face, certain wine is going to come out of my nose at any second, and start coughing.

"What the fuck is wrong with you?" Jillian sips her wine, eyebrows arched.

It takes me a few more seconds to control myself. "The bartender, Luke," I start, wiping my mouth. "He was great. Everything involving him was really great."

"Then what? Oh my God? Did you fuck his brother too?"

"What? No, oh my God no! That would have been really awkward because...because Luke is Cole's brother."

"Cole?"

"Cole Winchester. Our boss."

Jillian's mouth falls open a bit and she stares at me, blinking. "Mr. Hot Bartender is Cole's brother?"

"Yeah."

"And you had sex with him."

"Yes," I say, internally wincing. "Three times."

Jillian leans back. "Three times?"

"Yeah, twice at night and once in the morning. Jill, this is awful! I had sex with Cole's brother. Cole, who has made it abundantly clear he doesn't mix business with pleasure. And Luke told me they pretty much hate each other." I set the wine down and cover my face with my hands. "Oh my

God. We did it on the kitchen counter, and the next morning I went down to get my purse and there's Cole, sitting in the same spot where things got dirty, eating breakfast. Jillian, he didn't use a plate. He put his food where my ass had been! My ass and other...fluids."

Jillian's eyes meet mine and we both burst into wild laughter. She's shaking her head at me, trying to regain her composure.

"Did he see you?"

"I don't think so. I ran into a wall trying to get away. Literally. I hit it pretty hard."

She's laughing again, so hard she has to wipe away tears. "Lex, calm your tits. I don't know what you're freaking out over anyway. You slept with Luke, who happens to be Cole's brother. That's not against company policy or anything."

"But if he found out..."

"So what? I really don't think he's going to come up to you at work and say 'hey, remember that time you had a one-night stand with my brother?' or anything like that. He just won't mention it."

"I know but..." The confession dies in my throat. Jillian knows I have a crush on Cole, but doesn't know the depth of it, and certainly doesn't know how I've fantasized about him, both sexually and as a partner. Who the hell sleeps with the brother of the guy they've been crushing on for months? Oh right, me. "Of all the people, I go home with my boss's brother."

Jillian puts her elbows on the counter. "What's his house like? What was Cole wearing? And why does he live with his brother if they hate each other?"

"The house is amazing. It's one of those big historical homes that people shouldn't be able to afford. He had on a t-shirt and probably pajama pants. And I'm not sure. Luke didn't say, and I didn't ask. He dislikes him enough to take me out for breakfast instead of eating at the house just to avoid him, though."

"Wait. Back up. You and Luke went out for breakfast?"

"Yeah," I admit.

"One-night stands don't usually include breakfast the next day."

"He paid too," I blurt. "He asked for my number. And I gave it to him."

"Lexi! Shit. Okay, now we can freak out."

"Why? I doubt he'll call. And even if he does, this won't turn into anything. Luke is a well-written bad boy. And they don't go for single moms."

Jillian doesn't say anything as she looks at me. "Do you want him to call?"

I look away and shrug. "Nah. I mean, he was phenomenal in bed and we talked for hours like old friends, but he's nothing special."

She crosses her arms. "Really?"

"Really. It was one night...and then one morning. I knew going into this it wouldn't turn into anything more. Luke means nothing to me. We don't know each other. It's not like I can miss him or anything. Come tomorrow, I'll face Cole, get over my embarrassment, and move on. I'll be back to my old, single-mom self in no time. I won't even remember Luke, let alone think about him. Give me a few days and I'll be saying Luke? Luke who? I don't know anyone named Luke."

"Mh-hm."

She doesn't believe me. And to be honest, I don't believe me either.

~

"GOOD MORNING, ALEXIS."

"Cole. Good...good morning," I stammer, staring down at my coffee so hard the thing might burst into flames. My heart starts racing and my cheeks are red. I shift my eyes to Jillian, who's totally entertained by this. We're in the break room, filling up on coffee and carbs before work.

"How was your weekend? Did you do anything fun?" Cole grabs a paper cup and the pot of coffee.

Shit. He knows. He's testing me, right? He knows what I did this weekend because he came down for a midnight snack and saw me spread eagle on his kitchen counter with his brother's head between my legs.

"Yeah." I still can't look up. I can feel Cole's eyes on me, and I know he's wondering what the hell is wrong with me. I always talk to him or at the very least look at him. "You?"

"It was rather uneventful. I stayed home and caught up on work."

Home. I was in that home. Getting the shit fucked out of me *by your brother.*

"Me too," Jillian says, a smile on her lips. "I read this interesting submission about family, and it got me thinking about how much my brother has impacted my life. Do you have any brothers or sisters?"

Is she for real right now? I stare daggers at her.

"I do," Cole says simply and puts the coffee pot back.

"Interesting. And are you close with them."

"I wish I could say I was," he tells us and puts a lid on his coffee. "Gotta get to work. See you both at the morning meeting." He forces a smile and hurries out.

"What the hell was that?" I whisper-yell.

"Trying to get you info," she whispers back.

"I don't need info. I need to pretend this weekend never happened."

Jillian rolls her eyes and refills her coffee cup. "Answer when he calls."

"He's not going to call." I add creamer to my coffee.

"We'll see about that," she quips as we walk to our offices. I sit at my messy desk and push papers out of the way to make room for my coffee. I don't want Luke to call as much as I do, which is just as confusing as it sounds.

When I read more of that paranormal romance last night, the sexy demon hunter took on the form of Luke in my mind. I was halfway through a marathon sex scene before I even realized it, and once I did, I couldn't stop. Not that I wanted to of course. It didn't matter. Luke was a one-and-done fun time. And that's all he can be.

I spend my morning answering emails, checking social media, and dealing with a graphic artist who isn't grasping the concept of "subtle erotic romance". Then it's off to the Monday meeting, and back to my office until I stop for lunch. I'm printing out the first chapter of the book I just accepted that morning when Cole walks in.

"Paranormal romance?" he asks with a playful smile. Little wrinkles form around his lips, and his brown eyes sparkle. "Has hell frozen over?"

"Funny," I reply, still unable to look him in the eye. I should tell him that it's more romance than paranormal, and the heroine is one of the most likable I've read lately. She's honest and real without being whiny. She doesn't take shit but isn't a bitch. And she's brave, so incredibly brave, doing anything for the one she loves. I want to be more like her.

I should tell him all that, but I don't.

I clam up again, knowing that even though he didn't *see* me having sex with his brother, he definitely *heard* me. That house is big, but not big enough to drown out the porn star screams that came from my lips.

"Are you all right, Alexis?" he asks. I used to love hearing him say my full name. No one calls me it. I'm Lexi to everyone, even my mother calls me by my nickname. Now, hearing Cole speak all three syllables makes me feel like a kid in the principal's office.

"Yeah," I say and force myself to raise my eyes and look at his face. "I'm tired. I stayed up late reading and then had to get up early with the kids."

"Ah, gotcha. I'm looking forward to—" he cuts off when my phone rings. It's sitting face up on my desk and I don't think anything of it at first. Authors, agents, and other people from Black Ink are calling me all the time. But when an unknown number with a Chicago area code pops up, my blood runs cold.

Luke is from Chicago.

I'm not good at remembering numbers, but those digits look familiar. And if I slightly recognize them, then Cole certainly will. I desperately reach for it, and end up knocking my phone off my desk. In a mad dash, I dive to the floor, hitting my wrist on my desk. I internalize the pain, decline the call, and stand up. I squeeze my eyes shut, knowing there is no way around being totally busted. Maybe if I stay like this, standing still with my eyes closed, Cole will leave and I won't have to face him ever again.

Hah.

"Alexis?" Cole's voice is tight, and when I finally force myself to turn around, he looks caught off guard. "Everything okay?"

"Yeah, it is. I think that was my ex," I dumbly spit, cursing my ability to *not* lie on the spot.

"You think?"

"Yeah, yeah. I, uh, don't recognize the number or anything." Right, Lexi. Talk yourself into a hole. Just grab the gun and pull the trigger while you're at it.

Cole looks past me, staring intently out the window. He's too far away to see anything below, and the view isn't to die for or anything up here. He blinks, then moves his gaze to me, and suddenly, it's like he's looking at me for the first time.

The printer spits out the last page and a newfound silence fills my little office. Cole sharply inhales, takes a step toward the door, and nods.

"Let me know how the paranormal book is. And feel free to send anything my way it if gets too dark," he adds playfully.

"You remember that I don't like creepy stuff?"

"You sound shocked," he says with a laugh.

"Well, it's not something I talk about. Ya know, it's kind of embarrassing."

His brown eyes drill into mine, and I can't help but notice the similarities he shares with his brother. The differences stand out even more, and suddenly I feel a longing to look into Luke's cool blue eyes. "Consider it our little secret then." He gives me a wink before turning to leave. He shuts the door behind him, and I sink back into my chair and let out a sigh.

The voicemail from Luke haunts me, and I want to listen to it as much as I don't. I stare at the screen of my phone, feeling so conflicted I could scream. Then my office door opens, and I practically jump out of my skin.

"Get in here!" I hiss, waving my hand in the air like a lunatic. "Hurry! Close the door!"

Jillian dashes in, eyes widening with excitement. "What's going on?"

"Luke called," I say as soon as the door closed.

"Ahh, yes! I knew he would. I told you your breakfast date wasn't part of a typical one-nighter. What did he say?"

"I don't know. I didn't answer. Cole was in here."

Jillian laughs. "Did he see the call coming in?"

"I don't think so." I stand, phone in hand, and go to the window. Only a few seconds went by between the call and the voicemail. The message isn't long. "He left me a message."

"Luke?"

"Keep your voice down!" I whisper-yell.

Jillian rolls her eyes. "You haven't listened to the message yet?"

"No. I'm scared to."

"Why are you scared to listen to a message?"

"What if I don't like what he has to say? What if he wants to see me again, and then he doesn't like me? Guys like Luke don't date single moms, trust me. He's got that sexy tortured bad boy vibe down so well he gives Angel a run for his money. Maybe he found out I work for Cole and is going to yell at me. Or say we have to tell him! What if he already doesn't like me and is calling to tell me that."

"Lex!" Jillian stares at me, wide eyed, and holds up two fingers, an inch apart. "I'm this close to slapping some sense into you, though I don't think it'll work. Take a breath and calm down."

I inhale slowly and nod. "Okay."

"First, you gotta stop with the Buffy the Vampire Slayer references. No one gets them anymore. Second, Luke isn't going to call you just to tell you he doesn't like you or to yell at you. The fact that he called at all means you left an impression on him. Maybe he wants to fuck you again or maybe he wants more, I don't know. Listen to that message, and then call him back. And you know what? *You* should ask him out. I know you like him."

"I don't."

Jillian puts one hand on her hip and arcs an eyebrow. "Really?"

"Really."

"Right. Because you're freaking the fuck out over a guy you don't like. Not even a little."

I put my head in my hands. "I'll listen to the message. And maybe call him back. But I'm not asking him out."

"Oh, come on. The worst he can say is no."

"That literally is the worst. I don't know what alternate reality you live in, but here in the real world, getting turned down when you ask someone out is generally considered a bad thing."

She raises her hand, palm flat. "Don't make me slap sense into you."

"Please. I'll hit you back twice as hard."

"Bitch."

"Jerk."

"Lexi!" she cries. "Listen to the voicemail. He's calling you already, and that means he likes you in some sense at least. Hear him out. And if he's just after sex, you can be the one to tell him no...or take him up on it. There's no harm in having a fuck-buddy."

"Fine. Okay." I unlock my phone and pull up the voicemail, putting it on speaker. "Hey, Lexi. It's Luke. I was wondering if you want to get together again sometime, maybe repeat Saturday night but have dinner first. Call me."

I repeat the message, just to be sure I heard everything correctly.

"Oh, wow," Jillian says dryly. "He really laid the hammer down. You're right. He totally hates you. How dare he want to take you to dinner then have sex with you again. What an asshole."

"Shut up. He sounded a little nervous, don't you think?"

"Yeah, a little. Which is cute. Call him back now!"

I'm trying hard not to smile. Why did I think dating was so hard again? "I'll call him back. But not until we're out of the office."

Jillian hooks her arm through mine. "Good thing it's time for lunch."

"Should I tell him I have kids?"

Jillian shakes her head. "I honestly have no idea. If you think there's something going on between you that's more than sex, then probably."

"Right. Let him know before we get involved. Well, *if* he wants to get involved with me."

"Stop being so hard on yourself. He totally wants you. All of you. But I do agree, you should let him know before either of you get invested. Not everyone wants kids, and there's nothing wrong with that. It just means you're not compatible."

I nod and grab my coat and purse, my mind going to Luke. I am looking forward to seeing him again, even if it's nothing more than getting naked and sweaty together. I've never had a fuck buddy before, but maybe I'm finally old enough to give it a try. I'm not naive enough to go into it hoping things will work out and Luke will realize he can't live without me. Life isn't a romance novel after all, no matter how badly I want it to be. I'll put limits on it, and call it quits after a month so there's no risk of either of us getting attached.

A little harmless fun never hurt anyone, right?

I open my office door, finding myself a little hot and

bothered by thinking about a secret sex-only friend, and run right into Cole.

Two worlds collide.

"Heading out for lunch?" he asks us.

"Uh," I sputter, feeling like I got caught in the act. Again. "Yeah."

"Me too," Cole says. "Care if I join you?"

Now Jillian is sputtering. Never in a million years has Cole joined anyone for lunch. Jillian slowly turns to me, mouth open. She's speechless. Jillian is actually speechless. I've never encountered a time where Jillian can't form a sentence. My head might implode.

"Juice diet," Jillian blurts. "We're doing a juice diet and not eating real food."

Cole laughs. "When did this come about? I swear I saw the both of you eat donuts this morning."

"I had a bagel," Jillian quips. "I fell off the wagon this morning. Gotta get back on."

I know she's trying to help me, but we can't blow Cole off like this. For years, we've been inviting him to join us for lunch. And no one in this building will believe for a second I'm doing a fad diet. Let alone one that doesn't let me eat tacos.

"Might as well stay off," I say with a smile. "You know I'm not going to stick with it."

"Well then," Cole says, still smiling. "I have a table waiting at Mickey's. Do you want something? My treat."

Mickey's is a little pizza parlor tucked in an alleyway several blocks from here. They have the best cheese pizza and breadsticks and make their own sangria, which is borderline orgasmic. Jillian and I started going there for lunch back when they were a little hole-in-the-wall diner, but they've been discovered and are always insanely busy.

Getting a table requires name recognition or a hefty cash "holding fee".

Cole has a bit of both.

"Sure," I say because turning that down would be a huge red flag. And I'm pretty sure I've entered the Twilight Zone. "We haven't gone there in a while."

"Great," Cole says. "I'll meet you in the lobby."

He continues walking into his office to get his coat and wallet. Jillian grabs my arm and leans in.

"What the fuck is that about? Cole never goes to lunch with anyone."

"I don't know. I'm kind of freaked out."

"Me too. Like, call my mom, let her know where I'm going in case I disappear kind of freaked out. And how are you going to call—fuck, he's coming."

"I'll text."

Jillian rolls her eyes. "And just like that, you get out of calling him."

"Funny how things work out," I say, and a weird feeling forms in my stomach as Cole comes toward us. I'm not sure whose favor this is working out for.

chapter
ten

LUKE

*G*od, she's beautiful when she comes. All day, her face scrunched up in pleasure, eyes shut tight and mouth slowly falling open, has been stuck in my head. I'd say I don't know why this woman has affected me, but that would be a lie.

I want to see her again. I crave her unabashed honesty, the unfiltered way she talks, the way she sees the world. I can tell she's been hurt before, and she wears the past as armor. I want to know what happened to her, and I want to take away the pain.

I shouldn't.

I shouldn't care. I shouldn't think about her. Shouldn't long to be inside her again. And I sure as hell shouldn't have her number pulled up on my phone, finger hovering over the little green "call" button. It's only been a day. Hardly even twenty-four hours since I last saw her. I shouldn't want to call her.

I shouldn't. But I do.

Before giving myself time to back out, I call her. I lean back against the couch, feet up on the coffee table, and wait.

Her phone rings. Once. Twice. Three times. Then goes to voicemail. Three rings. Did she hang up on me? Do I even bother with a message? Fuck. Stop acting like a teenager. I want to see Lexi again. Everything I said about her being different is true. There's no reason to deny the intent was to hook up and move on, but something happened along the way, something unexpected. And usually, the unexpected is the most real. If there's a chance I can see this woman again, I have to take it. Have to try.

We regret what we don't do, after all.

"Hey Lexi," I start. "It's Luke."

My mind blanks and I feel like that teenager all over again, calling a girl for the first time. I've always been smooth with the ladies. What is it about this woman that has me clamming up?

"I was wondering if you want to get together again sometime, maybe repeat Saturday night but have dinner first. Call me."

I hang up and roll my eyes at myself. She's not going to call back after that disaster of a message. Shaking my head, I toss the phone on the cushion next to me and grab my food. I'm halfway through my Chinese takeout when my phone vibrates with a text. Holy shit, it's Lexi.

Lexi: *Hey, sorry. I'm at work and at lunch with my boss. I can't call. But I got your message. Is it okay if I call you later?*

Work. Right. She said she works downtown, with daytime office hours and lots of work from home. I'm curious about what she does.

Me: *I'll let it slide this time. How's your day going?*

Lexi: *Busy, but that's normal. What about you?*

Me: *Just getting started. I'm not much of a morning person.*

Lexi: *Me neither. I like being up late and sleeping in. If only, right? Stupid daytime work hours.*

Me: *I guess I'm lucky now in that aspect. I'm not good at getting up on time.*

Lexi: *Me neither. I like the night. There's something calm yet mysterious about it. The world is still and quiet, yet the darkness holds secrets. I stay up late reading a lot.*

Me: *Are you a big reader?*

She doesn't respond, and it throws me a little how much I want her to. But she's at work, and I got shit to do. I finish my food and carry my dishes into the kitchen to load them into the dishwasher. It's weird having free time like this. Weird, and probably the last thing I need right now given everything that happened. Maybe moving here was a mistake. I told myself it was a fresh start.

But really, I was running away.

My phone rings, and I'm totally not rushing through the hall to get it in case it's Lexi. And I'm not toying with the idea of getting her to talk dirty to me at work. Just imagining her cheeks flush and her eyes widen at my question turns me on. Watching her push her own limits is so fucking hot.

It's not Lexi, and I almost decline the call from my mother. She and my stepfather retired to Florida last year, and she calls a lot to check on things, specifically me. We talk for a few minutes and I assure her I'm fine at least three times before hanging up. I change into workout clothes, and am walking out the door when Lexi calls.

"Hey," she says and the sound of her voice warms me. "I got a minute away from the boss man. How are you?"

"Good. You?"

"I'm doing well, thanks. And yes, I'm a huge reader."

Oh right, the last thing I texted her was about books.

"Are you much of a reader?" Her question comes out rushed, like it all depends on how I answer.

"Yes," I say honestly. "I've had more spare time since

moving here and just finished that thriller that became a movie, *The Fake Wife*. It was great."

She doesn't respond, and now I'm wondering if she thinks there's something wrong with liking psychological thrillers. "Have you read it?" I meekly ask.

"More than once," she says slowly. "It really is a good book. The editing was great, don't you think?"

"Uh, sure. What are you doing this weekend?" I ask before I have a chance to ruin things. I don't know why, but it feels like I'm teetering on the edge with her, and I don't want to fall off and lose my chance.

"Nothing really."

"Can I take you out?"

"I'd like that."

"What about Saturday night?" I ask.

"Oh. I, uh, can't. Not on Saturday. Or Friday," she adds. "But I'm free Wednesday, which isn't a normal date-night, I know. And it'll have to be early. Sorry."

"Don't be sorry," I tell her, though the date and time are a little weird. I'll take what I can get. "Wednesday is fine. It means I can fuck you sooner."

"Oh my," she says, and I imagine her smile, which makes me think of her mouth, and my cock jumps at the thought.

"When and where would you like to go?"

"You're putting the pressure on me?" She laughs.

"Damn, you figured me out. I'm not too familiar with the city yet, or know what you like."

"There's a place not too far from your house that has the best tacos, if you like tacos."

"I do."

"Great, because I'd have to call this whole thing off if you didn't. I'll text you the address. Meet there at four-thirty?"

"It's a date."

chapter
eleven

LEXI

I put my head in my hands and close my eyes, letting out a heavy sigh. *Stay calm. Don't lose your shit.*

"Paige," I repeat. "You need to stop this right now. You get your teeth brushed every night before bed."

It's an hour past her bedtime, and by the way Paige is rolling around on the floor in tears, you'd think I'm trying to hook her up for electric shock therapy, not brush her teeth with bubblegum flavored toothpaste. I sink down to my knees, toothbrush in one hand, and reach for my three-year-old. Paige screams and covers her face with her hands.

"You are such a baby!" Grace yells, appearing in the doorway.

Paige lifts her head to glare at her sister. "Go away!" she screams back.

"Baby! Baby! Baby!"

"Stop it, Grace," I scold. "Go back to your room."

Grace stomps her foot and crosses her arms. "Why am I getting in trouble? I'm not the one acting like a little baby!"

"I'm not a baby!" Paige cries. She's certainly acting like

one. "You're mean! Go away!" She swats her hand in the air at her sister, but ends up hitting me in the face and knocking the toothpaste-covered toothbrush out of my hands. It clatters to the floor, getting pink toothpaste on the white carpet.

I close my eyes, anxiety and frustration rising.

"Grace!" I snap. "Please just go to your room!"

"I want a bedtime story," she replies as I reach for the toothbrush.

Paige leans forward. "No, *I* want a bedtime story!"

"Babies don't get stories," Grace taunts. "You're a baby! You're a baby!"

"No, *you're* a baby!" Paige bursts into tears again, and Grace continues to yell at her. I spent the thirty minutes I allotted for vacuuming the downstairs dealing with Paige's tantrum. I still have to clean up the spilled can of Pepsi on the kitchen counter, take out the overflowing trash before the dog gets into it, make lunches for the girls, empty the dishwasher, and do at least one load of laundry if I want clean underwear for tomorrow. And I promised Quinn I'd call her.

I'm at my limit.

Tears bite the corners of my eyes, and my heart speeds up.

"That's enough!" I shriek. Both girls stop mid-argument to look at me with wide eyes, and even Pluto hunkers down. I'm not a yeller. I hate raising my voice. Russell yelled at me nonstop during arguments, and it made me feel like crap. I make a point to *not* scream when I'm angry. It doesn't help anything.

The tears I'm trying to hold back come out in a fury. Paige's bottom lip quivers and she starts crying again, but this time because she feels bad. I set the toothbrush on the nightstand and hug my toddler. Grace runs into the room and throws her arms around me.

"I won't be bad ever again," Paige sobs. I don't remind her she promised the same thing two days ago.

"I'm sorry, Mommy," Grace says, sniffling. She presses her tear-soaked face against my cheek. I sit on the floor and pull both girls into my lap.

"It's okay, babies," I whisper, holding back a sob. "I'm not mad. I'm just tired. Very tired."

"We'll go to bed with no stories," Grace offers.

"I like reading you bedtime stories," I say. "Come on, let's get into bed."

I have Grace pick out books while Paige sits somewhat still while I brush her teeth—with minimal whining.

～

IT'S two AM by the time I go to bed, and I'm officially behind schedule. I convince myself that I'll catch up tomorrow. All I have to do is stay up pretty much the whole night, but one night of no sleep won't kill me.

I'm lying through my teeth, but if I don't think about it, I'll believe it enough to sleep and not lie there panicked about everything I have to do. To keep my mind from going there, I switch over to Luke. He brings on a different wave of anxiety, and it's not all bad. I'm looking forward to our date Wednesday, but won't allow myself to get too hyped up about it.

The guy is probably just after sex, after all.

I make a mental list of all the pros and cons to having a fuck buddy and check the time on my phone. Crap. I need to fall asleep *right now* if I want to have more than four hours of sleep before my alarm goes off.

Just as I start to drift off, I worry about what to wear. I'm coming from work, but can change before I leave the office. Or maybe put a sweater over a sexy black dress to make it office appropriate or something. Only I don't have a sexy black dress that can double as work and date clothes. I *do* have some extra cash saved up, but wanted to surprise the girls with the new American Girl bedroom set that just came out. I'm sure I can find something in my closet that will work. Finally, I fall asleep only to get up a few short hours later and start the hectic morning routine all over again.

I run into traffic on the way into the city, and there is a delay on the subway. I'm half an hour late for work, but no one even seems to notice when I slip in. No one, besides Cole.

"Hey Alexis. Everything all right?" he asks, coming out of his office and falling in step next to me as I make my way to the coffee.

"Yeah, just traffic. I texted Jillian. Did she not tell you?"

"No, she did. You look stressed."

"Thanks," I say with a strangled laugh.

"Ah, sorry," Cole says quickly. "I didn't mean it in a you-look-bad way. Because you don't look bad. You look the opposite, really. And a little...uh...stressed. I know how hard you work and want to make sure you know you're appreciated around here."

I turn and look up at him. Cole is a good foot taller than me. His brown eyes are kind, and he offers me a sympathetic half smile. "Thanks. Really. It means a lot."

"If you need anything," he starts, meeting my eyes, "don't hesitate to ask."

"Thanks, Cole."

He smiles and goes back into his office. I fill my to-go

cup with coffee and go into my office. Jillian is on the phone already, and I feel a little guilty that I'm happy about it. I'm not in the mood to talk to anyone right now, which sucks because I have a million phone calls to return.

Grumbling, I sip my coffee and get started. The first phone call I have to make is to Erin, which isn't a bad way to start the day.

"Hey, lady," she answers the phone. "How are you?"

"Tired," I sigh. "Bedtime took two hours."

"I remember those days," she says. "I don't envy you. Though I'd rather deal with that than having to leave a girl's night out to talk to my teenager about safe sex."

The thought makes me shudder. "I'm not ready for that at all."

"How was the rest of the night?" she asks. "Did you ever talk to that bartender?"

My heart skips a beat. "Uh, I did more than talk to him."

"No way! You got his number?"

"That and then some. We're going out Wednesday," I blurt. "I'll give you full details another time. I can't talk about it here."

"Ohhh, this sounds juicy!"

"Super juicy." I shake my head, thinking about the precarious situation. Erin and I get down to business, which is the asshole author she's representing. We scheme and plan a way to get an editor to want to work with her, then I'm onto the next project.

Wash.

Rinse.

Repeat.

I eat lunch at my desk, trying to make up for lost time. I'm so exhausted today I don't want to stay up late tonight, and I'm feeling guilty for not having good quality playtime with the girls. After dinner, I want them to have my undivided attention until bedtime.

I spend my last hour actually editing, and scramble to send an approved chapter to the proofreader before I pack up and head out. I get an email from Cole right before I shut down the computer. It's a form email, sent to all the editors here at Black Ink, reminding us that he's going to be out of town Wednesday through Friday at a book convention. I've never been to one, but from what I hear, any sort of large gathering involving people in the book world can get crazy. In good *and* bad ways.

Someday, I'd love to go to one. Especially since Black Ink pays for the airfare, hotel, and all meals. Someday, when the kids are older and leaving them doesn't cause anxiety. Though, I have a feeling I'll always have anxiety, even when they're married with their own children.

I pack up, rush to the subway, and then pick the girls up, surprising them with ice cream and a trip to the park to enjoy the warm spring air. I chase the girls around, playing tag, helping Paige climb on the playground to keep up with Grace. We're all laughing and having a blast, and my heart is full. I love my girls more than life itself, and one look at them is all I need to keep me from getting bitter.

Russell might be a miserable bastard, but he gave me Grace and Paige. He gave me my heart as much as he broke it.

"Mama!" Paige slows to catch her breath. "Can I swing?"

"Of course, baby," I tell her and scoop her up in my arms. She giggles as I kiss her cheeks. "Do you want to try the big girl swing?"

"Yes! Yes!" she cries. "I'm a big girl."

"You are getting so big!" I tell her, feeling a tug on my heart. Time goes by so fast. Both girls end up on the swings, laughing as I push them "so high they touch the sky". We leave the park to go home for dinner, take Pluto for a walk around the block, then rush around for baths and bedtime.

I'm exhausted when I sit down at my computer a little after nine PM. A new message from Katie James, the author of the paranormal book, greets me when I log onto my email. She's ecstatic to have her book published, and her enthusiasm makes me smile. I love when the authors I work with are excited about their books. I've seen nerves get the best of a lot of authors and take the fun out of publishing—not that I can blame them. I'd be a basket case weeks leading up to the release, and there might not be enough wine in all of New York to get me through the day.

I reply to her, set up a time during the day tomorrow for a phone call, and take a stab at the rest of my inbox. I get half a dozen emails answered, three requests sent to the marketing department at Black Ink, and read through a handful of submissions from agents. Then an email comes through from Quinn.

I expect it to be about her newest book, and am shocked and totally flattered when she asks me if I'm open to any freelance jobs. One of her friends has a book set to release in just a few weeks and the editor she had booked fell through at the last minute. She recommended me to her friend because I've been "the best editor she's ever worked with". She goes on to include a sample chapter and says her friend—who is an incredibly successful indie author—is willing to pay a rush fee.

Even without the extra fee, there's no way I could turn down that money right now. In fact, my mind flashes to working as a freelance editor for indie authors. I'd be just as busy, but I could work from home and not waste precious hours away from my daughters commuting into the city.

I push that thought far out of my head. I can't quit my job because I got asked to do *one* editing job. I reply to Quinn, who says she's going to forward everything to her friend. The extra work makes me anxious, but now I can buy the girls that doll bedroom set as well as take them shopping for new clothes this weekend.

It's nothing huge, but it's enough to send a surge of happiness through me, energizing me enough to tackle another chapter of edits before crashing for the night. I haven't been able to take the girls shopping without a ball of dread forming in the pit of my stomach as the total tallies up at the register. One of the best things that came from having my life fall apart is a newfound appreciation for the little things.

chapter twelve

LUKE

I'll admit, leaving the house just minutes after four doesn't make this date feel much like a date. The sun is still out, and the streets are busy with people leaving work. The dark of the night is sexy, and makes going home together after dinner more natural.

I throw my clothes in the wash and make my bed before I head downstairs to leave. Cole is out of town for work, thank fucking God. Why the hell did I think living together was a good idea? The best thing that ever happened between us was him going to college my junior year of high school. We went our separate ways from there, only seeing each other at the occasional family get-togethers, and when the house was bustling with cousins, aunts, uncles, and grandparents, it was easy enough to stay out of each other's way.

Now that it's just the two of us...no house is big enough.

It takes a tremendous amount of energy not to resort back to childlike tendencies when it comes to him. Like the other day, when I was finishing my coffee and saw a manuscript sitting on the counter. It had to be over a hundred pages printed out. Unnumbered. Knocking it off, watching the pages scatter across the tiled floor would be so satisfying. I didn't shove the pages to the ground, but only because I don't want to deal with him after the fact. He's been at my throat since the day I was born, and I still think people who say they get along with their siblings are lying.

I grab my coat, punch in the alarm code, and leave the house. I walk to the restaurant and get there early enough to get a table and order drinks. I take a guess and get Lexi a strawberry margarita.

At four-thirty, she texts me saying she's running late. Ten minutes later, I wonder if she's blowing me off. I finish my beer and prepare to leave. Then I look up and see her rushing through the doors. Her long blonde hair is pulled over her shoulder in a messy braid. The black leather bag on her shoulder must weigh a ton, and pulls her off balance. She's wearing boots over dark jeans, and an ivory-colored top that flows loosely around her thin frame. Her face is tight with stress, but the moment our eyes meet, it all melts away.

I stand, and it feels like ages pass as she navigates around servers and tables. She stops inches in front of me, brushing her hair out of her face.

"I'm so sorry," she says and sets her bag down. "There was a problem with a printer and..." She lets out a breath and looks back into my eyes. "I feel like an asshole for being late to our first official date." She pulls her lip in her mouth, nervously biting it between her teeth. Thinking about her mouth leads to thinking about *my* mouth, and where I'd like to put it.

Buried deep between her legs, of course.

I want to feel her come, pressed against my face, legs wrapped tightly around my neck. I want to look up just in time to see her come, to see the euphoria twist her face, eyes shut and mouth gaping open.

"Don't feel like an asshole," I say and pull her into a hug. "You're here now." Her arms go around me, soft breasts crushing against my chest. A soft, floral scent clings to her skin, and her hair smells like lavender. It's intoxicating.

I run my hands down to the small of her back, pushing her waist into mine. She's holding onto my shoulders, and neither of us care the older couple by the window is staring.

"It's nice seeing you again," she says, looking right into my eyes. God, she's gorgeous. The happenstance of finding a connection with someone I least expected is making lust build inside me at a dangerous rate. I want to knock the chips and salsa off the table, lay Lexi down, and fuck her senseless. Instead, I take a step back and pull out the chair for her.

"I take it your day was hectic?" I start.

She slides the margarita over and takes a sip. "To say the least. We ran into a crisis with a printer. You'd think the sky opened and the trumpets sounded by the way people were freaking out." She rolls her eyes and smiles. "But enough about work. I don't want to bore you with details. My days are boring enough even I get bored with it, so you definitely would get bored hearing about it. And I just said 'bored' like fifty times." Color rushes to her cheeks when she's embarrassed. Not a lot, but enough to give her an I-just-had-sex glow. It's fucking sexy.

"What about you?" she asks, changing the subject. "How was your day?"

"Uneventful, which is weird, but nice."

"Why is it weird?" She goes for the chips, and I'm glad she's a woman who's not afraid to eat what she wants on a date.

"I'm not used to this much downtime."

"Ah, right. You're new in town. What did you do before?"

"I was a firefighter."

Her eyes widen, and her hand hovers in the air above the chips. "You're kidding, right?"

It's a reaction I'm used to, a reaction I'm able to take advantage of more times than not. "Not kidding."

"So why you'd leave that and come here?"

Now *that* isn't something I'm used to. It's something I don't want to think about. Not now. Not ever. "I got hurt at work and...and...it's a long story," I say, eyes dropping from her face to the table. My mind flashes to the fire, smoke fills the room. The patch of burned skin on my side starts to ache like it always does when I think about getting burned. "A long boring one, and we're avoiding boring, right?"

Lexi gives me a tiny nod, and then smiles. Her shoulders relax and she reaches across the table, slipping her fingers under mine. She knows that was a bullshit line, but isn't calling me out on it. "How do you like New York?"

"It's different, that's for sure. But after this weekend, I find myself liking it much more."

Lexi tries not to smile. Tries, and fails. How is it possible for her to be so fucking adorable *and* sinfully sexy? "Well," she says, wrapping her long fingers around the stem of her margarita glass. "I'm happy to help."

"So," I say after we order our food. "Besides work and rocking open mic night, what else do you like to do?"

She bites her lip again, and I realize it's a nervous habit. Between the color rushing to her cheeks when she's flustered, and the lip biting, I really want to push her. If I'm lucky, she'll push back.

"Not much, to be honest. I like to read, binge watch shows if I have time. I'm finally caught up on *Once Upon a Time*. And be outside. I take my dog for walks daily when the weather is nice."

"You have a dog?" The three-letter word tugs at my heart and I think of Sadie.

"Yeah. Pluto. He's a scrappy little thing, but we—I—love him."

"Nice. What kind of dog?"

"We—I—think he's a Basenji mix, but I have no idea. I went to a dog rescue years ago to look at puppies, but when I saw a line—a literal line of people waiting to see them, I knew they'd get adopted fast. So, I asked to see the dog who'd been there the longest. I fell in love the second we met. Proves love at first sight exists, right?"

I laugh along with her, but I feel something inside me, something I haven't allowed myself to feel in a long time.

Hope.

"That's really kind of you. I bet the volunteers at the group were thrilled."

"They were, which makes it so much sadder to know that people don't want the poor old dog who's been there for months. And to this day, I have no idea why no one wanted him. He's kind of goofy looking, I'll admit, and he had some hair loss from mange at the time, but he's a sweet little guy who's good with kids and other dogs." She reaches for a chip and dips it in the salsa. "I'm not perfect, so why would I expect my dog to be?"

I lean back in my chair, that weird, warm feeling in my chest spreading. Lexi is so refreshing. So raw. So real.

"You don't have any pets, right?" she asks and brings the chip to her mouth.

"I had a black lab named Sadie that passed last year."

Sadness fills her eyes, and it's genuine. "I'm so sorry."

I look away and nod, the subject still painful. It was what set off the domino effect of the shittiest year of my life, and I need to repress and move on. That's the healthy thing to do, right?

"Well," she says. "If you ever need a dog fix, I'm sure Pluto will gladly play with you at the dog park. He likes going."

"If he brings his owner, I think I'd like that," I say and make her smile again, green eyes sparkling. "What do you mean by goofy looking?"

She laughs and digs into her purse for her phone. "I'll show you. He looks like a big Chihuahua."

"Are you one of those people who has a million pictures of your dog on your phone?"

"I am. It's so bad. I barely have any room left on my phone because of all the dog and ki—dog and cat photos."

"You have a cat too?"

"Uh, no. But there are strays. Lots of strays around the house," she says quickly and concentrates on her phone. She's swiping through a lot of photos as if she's looking for one of the dog, which doesn't make sense with what she just said about taking tons of pictures of him. "Here he is." She holds up the phone, but doesn't give it to me. Maybe I'm reading into this too much, but it's like she doesn't want me to take it and accidentally see another photo.

"He's a good looking pup," I say, looking at the photo of the golden brown dog. "Is he wearing a Ghostbuster collar?"

"Yeah, he is. I'm a bit of a fan."

"The original or newer one?"

"Original of course, but the new movie was actually really good. I'm a fan of remakes with a female cast."

We talk about movies and then music until our food arrives. The conversation never stops as we eat, and we continue talking and laughing after our food is gone and the plates have been cleared.

"Do you want to come back to my place?" I ask. It's forward, and I'm sure she knows I'm inviting her back to fuck. I just hope she knows I want more than what's between her legs.

I want *her*.

She checks the time on her phone. Right. She said she couldn't be out late.

"Yeah, I do," she says, eyes meeting mine. She pulls her arms in and bites her bottom lip again.

She's nervous.

Excited.

Pushing at the walls of her comfort zone.

And it's so fucking hot.

We leave the restaurant, and I take her hand as we walk down the busy sidewalk. Lexi goes back and forth between talking, hand loosely in mine, fingers intertwined, and going silent and tense. I can't figure her out, and it makes her all the more intriguing. When we get to my street, she gets her phone out of her purse and calls her neighbor, asking if she can let the dog out.

"She lets him out during the day for me," she explains, putting her phone back in her purse. "I don't live in the city, so I can't go home during the work day or anything."

"It's nice he gets out."

"Yeah. I feel bad for him being home like that. I didn't work the same hours I do now when I got him."

I nod. "I felt guilty leaving Sadie when I'd work overnight."

"Yes, guilty is exactly how I feel."

"Hey, he seems like he has a great home and has someone to let him out, so don't feel bad."

"Thanks. And Poppy likes having a job, so it's a win-win I guess."

"Poppy?"

"Oh, my neighbor. She's kind of crazy, but is great with animals," Lexi explains. "She thinks the government is out to get her, so holding a job hasn't worked out for her very well. She walks a few dogs in the neighborhood, and it makes her feel like she has a purpose. She's been taking Pluto out for us for over a year now, and it's worked out great."

"Nice," I say, noticing that she said "us". That's not the first time she referred to herself as more than one person. We walk up the stone steps to my front door. "My brother isn't home," I say as I unlock the door.

"Oh, right," she says like she's remembering information. "I mean, that's good. I think. Right? You mentioned you didn't really like him."

She's getting all flustered again, and the discomfort coming off of her is tangible. I punch in the code to shut off the alarm, and welcome Lexi inside. We go into the living room.

"Want anything to drink?" I ask.

"Just water," she says and I bring her a glass. "Thanks."

I sit next to her on the couch, hand falling on her thigh. She inhales quickly, breasts rising. I lean in, and place one hand on her face, cupping her cheek. Her eyes fall closed and she parts her lips, anticipating the kiss.

I put my mouth to hers, tongue slipping past her lips.

Her arms go around me, and passion doesn't spark. It explodes. We fall back on the couch, kissing with desperation, tugging on each other's clothing.

"Luke." She puts both hands on my chest and pushes me away. "Wait."

"Is everything okay?"

She takes another deep breath. "No. I really like you."

I laugh. "Thanks? Or sorry?"

"I'm not who you think I am."

We sit up. "What are you talking about, Lexi?"

"Me. Look...I think we both know that what happened the other night was supposed to be a one time thing, right?"

"Yeah," I say, relieved she brought it up.

"But this isn't one night."

"No, it's not. Fucking you once isn't enough," I say. "And being with you, just talking and hanging out...well, I like that too."

Lexi smiles, nose wrinkling. She's so fucking cute. "Really?"

"Yeah. That's why I asked you to dinner and didn't text you at three AM asking to come over."

"You are so logical," she says.

I take her hands in mine and gently pull her onto me. "You were saying something about not being who I thought you were."

"Right. Confession time."

I raise an eyebrow. "You're a serial killer, aren't you?"

She nods. "But I don't actually do the murdering. I have a crazed group of followers who do my evil bidding for me."

"I knew it. Well, I suppose I can overlook that. Just don't get me involved. I hate lying to the police."

"Deal. I'll hide the bodies before you come over."

"Glad we got that out of the way," I say and kiss her

again. Lexi is tense for half a second, then relaxes, melting against me. Whatever she had to say can wait.

I HATE BUYING PRESENTS, and it's not that I don't like giving. Because I do. It's because there's too much fucking pressure when it comes to gift giving. What you give someone carries too much weight, and it's fucking stupid. Give the wrong gift and you seem like you don't care. Didn't spend enough? Then you don't care either. Over give and you're just trying too hard.

I should just send Mom a gift card for her birthday. Going shopping on a Saturday was dumb on my part. The crowded streets are even more crowded than usual with weekend shoppers and tourists. I walk down Fifth Avenue, looking in the windows at the busy stores. The biggest difference between New York City and Chicago are the people. They say Midwesterners are more friendly, and it's true. Though it's not like I'm going out of my way to smile and wave at the people on the streets.

Deciding to just go into the next store I come across, I go into Saks and end up leaving with a silk scarf, then remember Mom moved to Florida and won't need a scarf anymore.

Dammit.

I'd rather eat the loss than deal with standing in line to return the thing. Sighing, I keep walking with a plan to go into the *next* store I see and buy something. Anything. Though I know no matter what I get, it won't be what she wants. She's made it abundantly clear she has all she needs and only longs for one thing.

Grandchildren.

With Cole being, well, Cole, and me dealing with my current situation, I don't think that will happen anytime soon. I ball the shopping bag in my hand and stop at the corner of Forty-Ninth and Fifth, waiting for traffic to let up so I can cross.

I'm not sure how I see her through the waves of pedestrians and cars, but I do. Lexi exits a building with red awnings, holding several large bags in one hand, and a little kid in the other. She hikes the toddler up on her hip and looks down at another child, instructing her to loop her arm around the shopping bags as they wait to cross the street.

Lexi looks up, and our eyes meet. A smile instantly spreads across her face, then it fades and her cheeks redden. Cars stop and people begin crossing, but Lexi doesn't move. She doesn't take her eyes off me either, and she brings her arm back to keep the older of the two girls from walking forward.

"Stalking me?" I say playfully when I get closer to her. Lexi doesn't laugh, doesn't shoot back with witty sarcasm. She just stares at me like a deer in headlights. Then she inhales sharply and takes a step back, getting out of the way.

"Hey, Luke. How are you?" she finally says, her grip on the children tightening. They look at me curiously. The toddler waves.

I wave back, and she smiles, then hides her face in Lexi's hair. "I'm good," I tell her. "You?"

"Good." Her eyes are wide and her shoulders are tense.

"Who are you?" the older girl asks.

"I'm Luke," I say.

"You look like Flynn," she says.

"Uh, thanks?" I nod, smiling at the girl who can't be much older than five or six. Her hair is darker than Lexi's, and she has the same eyes.

"Flynn Rider," Lexi stammers. "He's from a Disney movie. And you kind of do. I never noticed before."

"I hope that's a good thing."

"It is," Lexi says and smiles. The gesture seems forced, and she looks down at the girl, who's still staring at me. "This is Grace," Lexi says, introducing the older girl. "And this is Paige. They're my daughters."

chapter thirteen

LEXI

*L*uke looks from Grace to Paige, and then to me. He blinks once, twice, and then smiles.

"Nice to meet you. Looks like your mom took you shopping," he says to the girls, smiling warmly.

"I got American Girl stuff," Paige starts, and wiggles out of my arms. I set her down, and she launches into conversation with Luke, telling him all about her American Girl named Alyssa and the new bedroom set we just bought. Luke crouches down to her level and follows along the best he can.

"Is he your friend?" Grace asks, still curiously watching Luke.

"Yes," I say, aware that Luke can hear our conversation. "He is."

"How come I haven't met him?"

"We haven't known each other very long," I say, feeling embarrassment at the awkwardness rise.

"Can he come to lunch with us?"

"Uh, I'm, uh, not sure he wants to," I mumble, watching Luke mirror Paige's excitement about her new doll accessories. I haven't seen him since Wednesday, when I had all the intentions of telling him that I was a single mom. But I spent all the time I had doing non-verbal activities with him, and had to leave in a rush to make sure I was home in time for the girls. We've texted a few times since then, and he tried to get me to come to the bar again last night since he was working.

Obviously, I couldn't, and now he knows why.

"How do you know if you don't ask?" she quips, twisting my "how do you know you don't like it if you don't try it?" psychology around on me. Out of the mouth of babes, right?

Luke flicks his gaze up, having heard everything said. Turning and running away is so tempting right now. Only running while carrying Paige and all the bags and dragging Grace behind me isn't exactly the fast getaway I have in mind.

"We're going to get pizza," Grace says.

"Do the pizza dance!" Paige squeals.

Luke laughs. "What's the pizza dance?"

Paige lights up, thrilled someone asked her to show off her silly dance. She puts her arms up and starts wiggling her butt, then shakes her arms over her head and spins around, all the while shouting, "Pizza! Pizza! Macaroni pizza!"

I can't help but laugh. She's so stinking cute. And it's amazing how different she is than her sister, who was painfully shy until just recently.

"Macaroni pizza?" Luke repeats with a laugh.

"She calls pepperoni macaroni," Grace explains. "She's just a little girl."

Luke's smile widens. "I'm digging this pizza dance. You know, I do a similar one when I eat pizza. Or tacos." He looks up at me, still smiling. My heart—which is racing with fear over this going terribly wrong—skips a beat for an entirely different reason.

"How does New York pizza compare to Chicago pizza?" I ask.

"Doesn't hold a candle," Luke answers. "But, with the right company, it's pretty damn good."

"Do you want to join us?" I ask, feeling my heart lurch once again. "You don't have to. I mean, you're probably busy and all, right? Don't worry if you—"

"Lexi," he says, stopping my rambling. "Yes. I'd like to join you."

Now I'm smiling as wildly as Paige. "Good. And New York pizza is the best."

He stands and takes a step closer. "It's not even close." He looks down at the bags. "Let me take those."

"It's fine, I, uh, okay. Thanks." He takes the bags from me, and I shake my arm. I'm used to being a Bag Lady at the same time I carry Paige around, but this is nice. I pick Paige back up, sitting her on my hip, and take Grace's hand, ignoring her eye roll. She's six. I'll be damned before I let six be "too old" to hold her mother's hand. Besides...the streets of New York City skeeves me out a bit. Having Luke walk next to me helps, as much as I don't want to admit it. But I can't deny the dangers of being a woman in a big city.

"What are you up to today?" I ask as we walk.

"I'm trying to find a birthday present for my mother," Luke says. "Trying, and failing."

"Moms are always hard to shop for." I turn my head, and steal a glance at his handsome face. He hasn't shaved in at least a day, and the stubble looks good on him. Really good.

"I got my mom a scarf. She lives in Florida."

I can't help but laugh. A few seconds later, he's laughing too. We continue making small talk as we navigate the busy streets to the restaurant. Once we're seated and the girls are busy coloring on paper placemats, I turn to Luke.

"So...I have kids," I start. "Are you mad?"

He raises an eyebrow. "That's a weird thing to be mad about."

"But I didn't tell you."

"I wouldn't have guessed it," he admits. "Would you be mad if I told you that I had a son?"

I shake my head. "Do you?"

"No. No daughters either."

I reach for my water, catching a bead of condensation as it rolls down the glass. In some part of my brain, I know I should just stop talking. Stop prodding, Luke said he's not bothered by the fact I have kids. I need to leave well enough alone.

But, that's not my style.

"If you don't want to see me again after this, you don't have to. Not that you said you wanted to even before this, because you're totally not obligated to, so don't feel like you have to and my feelings won't—"

"Lexi," Luke says and puts his hand on mine. He's in the booth next to me, and leans in a little closer. "I'd kiss you to make you stop talking, but I'm not sure if that's okay to do in front of your kids." He looks across the table at the girls, who are still busy coloring. "I said I wouldn't have guessed you had kids, but that doesn't mean I suddenly don't like you."

I nod, and feel stupidly emotional. "Thanks."

He laughs. "You're welcome. And I'm guessing this is the reason you couldn't go out this weekend, right?"

"Right."

"I thought you were seeing someone else. Though now I

know you're seeing two people, and I don't think I can compete with them."

I squeeze Luke's hand, smiling. "No one can."

Paige looks up and wrinkles her nose. "Did you draw on your arm?" she asks Luke.

He extends his arm so she can look at his tattoos. "Someone else did."

Both girls are fascinated with the ink on Luke's skin. I lean back against the booth and watch, trying to stop my heart from fluttering. I don't want to think too much into this, to start hoping that Luke will be a part of my life. I don't want to get hurt again, and I need to be practical for the girls' sake. If I was to introduce Luke as more than my friend, that's opening them up for hurt as well. And I have to find someone who's good for me as well as for them.

As much as that stupid hope inside me tries to blossom, I need to remind myself any potential step farther needs to be reliable and responsible, and holds the same values I do. And I'm not sure what to make of Luke working part-time as a bartender and eager to have a one-night stand.

I know, I know. Pot, meet kettle. It's not the fact he had one-nighters. To each their own, and I'm so damn sick of hearing anyone—male or female—get slut shamed for doing something they *want* to do. What worries me is if Luke likes mixing it up, having that wild, crazy sex every time.

Because real life isn't that way. The sex isn't always wild and crazy. Sometimes it's boring, and sometimes it doesn't happen at all. Some nights I'll be too tired, or might just not feel like it since I pigged out on junk food right before bed.

No one could blame Luke if that's not what he wants. He's entitled to seek what satisfies him, just like I am. I just can't believe what he wants could ever be me.

I'VE LOST count of the number of lies I've told myself. I glare at the clock, hoping maybe if I stare long enough, time will somehow jump back two or three hours and I can collapse into bed. I swore I wouldn't work on the weekend, as well as stay up until three AM. I rub my eyes and trudge to bed, not bothering to close my computer or put anything away.

After lunch, we went for a stroll through Central Park—and Luke came with. He walked us to the subway, carrying our shopping bags the whole time. Not wanting the girls to see him as anything other than a platonic friend, we didn't kiss goodbye. Before he left, Luke said he wanted to see me again. We set a date for Friday, and thinking about it now, Friday seems so far away.

I strip out of my clothes and fall into bed, phone in hand. I open my text messages and send one to Luke, who should be getting home from work right about now.

Me: *Thanks again for today. We all had fun.*

Luke: *I did too. Why are you still up?*

Me: *Working, even though I promised myself I wouldn't take any home from the office.*

Luke: *Workaholic.*

Me: *I know. I'm the worst. Also, Friday is far away.*

Luke: *Too far away. Can I take you out sooner?*

His last text comes through, followed by one immediately after.

Luke: *You and your girls, I mean.*

I bite my lip to try to keep from smiling. I want to say yes, and start to type, then stop. How does this whole dating post-divorce thing work when kids are involved? When is it okay for them to know I'm dating again? Russell has a girlfriend. A girlfriend who sleeps over when the girls are there, a girlfriend he kisses goodbye in front of the girls. They know Mommy and Daddy aren't together.

Heartache suddenly hits me, and tears pool in my eyes. Paige doesn't know what it's like to have her parents together. She was just a baby when Russell and I split. Grace remembers, and has asked in the past if we're going to get back together. When Russ got together with his last girlfriend, it was hard on Grace to see her father with another woman. Is seeing me with Luke going to do the same to her?

I exit out of my texts and pull up a Google search. I enter "dating after divorce with kids" and click on the first article I find. Well, I've already screwed up, according to this. I shouldn't have let the kids meet Luke yet. Of fucking course. Leave it to me to mess something this big up.

I scan another article as fast as possible, knowing I need to reply to Luke soon or he's going to think I'm blowing him off. Guilt that the girls already met him comes in waves the further I get into this article. My only saving grace is that the meeting wasn't arranged, and we just happened to run into each other. Was I wrong to invite him to lunch?

As of right now, the girls know Luke as my friend and nothing more. I have male friends that I've hung out with before, and the girls have met them. I never thought anything of it since I had no plans of having a relationship.

I exhale, knowing I'm getting into dangerous overthinking territory. It was incredibly thoughtful for Luke to include the girls. He knows I can't go out during the week solo. Though I could. Mom will come over in a heartbeat if I asked her to, and I know she'll be happy to know I have a date. It's been a while since Russell and I legally split, and even longer since we separated. Mom's been hinting for a while now that I need to get back out there.

I go back to my text messages, erase what I started typing and send a new message.

Me: *Yes, I'd love that. Wednesday again?*

A minute passes before Luke replies.

Luke: *I work that night. Tuesday?*

Me: *That should work :-) Work out details in the morning?*

Luke: *Sounds good. I'll call you. Night.*

Me: *Goodnight, Luke <3*

I send the message, put my phone down, then worry the heart emoji was too much. I shake my head at myself, and lay down, falling asleep quickly.

chapter fourteen

LUKE

*B*eing with Lexi and not being able to touch her, to pull her close and press my lips to her is painful. Running into her on Saturday felt like fate. Out of all the people in the city, I see her.

There was a time in my life when I'd dismiss that as bullshit. I didn't believe in love or think there could be one person you're meant to be with. I've had girlfriends before, but always preferred to be unattached. Free to do whatever I wanted and all that shit. It was fine before. But now, after nearly losing it all, my priorities have changed. They say your life flashes before your eyes before you die, and I can attest to that. In some way, at least.

And in the moment when I didn't think I'd live to take another breath, everything changed. I lived my life for myself, and when it was all said and done, I had nothing because I had no one.

No one to share it with. No one to love or take care of. No one to take care of or love me.

It took almost burning to death to make me admit to myself that I was lonely.

Muted dawn light streams through the window. I roll over, trying to get comfortable. It's way too fucking early to be up, but I can't fall back asleep. Not with Lexi on my mind.

Finding out she has kids threw me for a loop. Not that it's bad or anything, just unexpected. I was drawn to her the moment I saw her, and every minute we spend together solidifies my want for this woman. The fact that she has two girls doesn't change that. If anything, it makes me nervous, and I've never been nervous when pursuing a woman before.

But those little girls raise the bar. Not only is Lexi's heart on the line, but theirs are too. And that's a lot of fucking responsibility. I don't want to fuck this up.

A few of my friends back in Chicago have kids. I'm at that age, edging on thirty, when single becomes the minority among a group. My interactions with children are limited, but I babysat before so friends could go out for date night. As long as the kids aren't assholes, we seem to get along just fine. Kids are fun. I like fun. No problems there.

Finally, I fall back asleep, not waking again until noon. It's Sunday, which means Cole is going to be home all day. Normally, the thought would bother me. But today, I don't really care. I plan to eat, hit the gym, then play video games. Easy day, and it'll be easy to stay out of each other's way. I stand, letting the blankets fall off my body, and walk across the cold wooden floor to my dresser. I get dressed and head downstairs.

"It's alive," Cole says, not looking up from the papers he's reading. A red pen is next to the manuscript. Ah, he's in edit-mode. Which for some reason makes him even more of a dick. If he hates his job so fucking much, then he should just quit already.

"Yep," I say. "And it's a great day to be alive." I open the fridge and get out ingredients to make an omelet. I can feel Cole's eyes on me, waiting for me to say something else and egg him on. Like I usually do. But I don't. Pushing his buttons doesn't seem fun today.

"You've missed half the day," he goes on.

I shrug. "Depends on how you look at it. I sleep the same amount of hours you do, just at a different time." I crack an egg and start mixing. "Want one?"

Cole looks up from the stack of papers. "Sure. Thanks."

"No problem."

"You're in a good mood. Is there a girl upstairs?"

"Not today."

Cole leans back. "She left already?"

I shake my head, trying hard not to let him get to me. Why does he have to be such an ass? In general, he's not the most pleasant person, but I know he's not like this to anyone else. Perks of being the younger brother, right? "She left over a week ago."

"You're still seeing the same chick?"

"I am. We went out yesterday. And I'm seeing her again Tuesday."

"If she gives it up that easy, I can see why you keep going back."

I turn away from the oven and stare at Cole. My patience snaps right down the middle, and I tighten my grip on the spatula, grateful it's not a knife. I can't promise no bloodshed right now. "Would if fucking kill you to be happy for me? I get this isn't front page news, but I'm seeing a fucking amazing woman and yeah—I'm in a good mood because of it. What do you want, Cole? You've been like this since the day I was fucking born and it gets worse every year."

"I don't have time for this," Cole says and stands,

gathering the manuscript. I really want to shove him and watch him drop fucking everything. Anger surges through me and the next thing I know, I'm inches from Cole's face.

"Leave me the fuck alone," he growls.

"Or what?" I tip my head. "What are you going to do? Hit me? Go ahead. Try."

Cole narrows his eyes and turns to leave. My arms twitch as I resist bringing my fist up to meet his face. My phone rings, and I take my eyes off my brother for a second to see who's calling. Cole uses that to his advantage and ducks out of the kitchen like a fucking coward. Not that I want him to start a fight. I know I'll own his ass, and though I can't stand him, he's my brother and I don't want any more bad blood between us than there already is.

Lexi's calling me. I exhale before I answer, and the moment I hear her voice, all anger melts away.

"Hey," she says, voice as smooth as honey. "How are you?"

"Good. Just getting my day started. You?"

"Good too. Tired, if I'm being honest. The girls got up at seven."

I move back to the stove and flip the omelet. "That's brutal."

"Yeah, but it is what it is, right? And it's my own fault. I'll go to bed early tonight."

I laugh. "Why don't I believe that?"

"Because it's a big fat lie. Tuesday...when and where do you want to go? My mom can pick up the girls from school so I can meet you somewhere in the city."

"You don't have to come to Manhattan."

"But that's where the good restaurants are."

I'm laughing again. "And there's nothing good where you live, which is...?"

"Brooklyn. And there are nice places here. Lots of them. But that's a far drive for you and—"

"I'm not the one with kids who has to get up the next morning for work. I promise I don't mind coming to Brooklyn."

"Right. Sorry. I'm not used to, uh, consideration."

"Well, get used to it."

∽

I PUT the car in park and double-check the address on the mailbox with the one I entered into the GPS. Seeing it's correct, I get out, and send Lexi a text to let her know I'm here, like she requested. I start up the sidewalk, looking at the two-story brick house. A light turns on inside a room in the front of the house, and a few seconds later, a dog barks.

Lexi texts me back, saying she'll be right out. It was her idea to meet like this, wanting to spare her kids a meet-and-greet. She fumbled over her words as she explained it to me, getting more and more flustered as she kept speaking, worried she was offending me. But I get it. Don't risk getting attached if it's not going to work out.

A few minutes pass before she comes out of the house. Her hair hangs in loose waves around her face, framing it perfectly. She's wearing a form fitting dark purple dress that highlights her curves in the best way. My mind jumps to slowly inching that dress up her thighs until her ass is exposed.

"Luke," she calls, and hearing her say my name isn't helping me not mentally fuck her right now. I stride over, meeting her halfway. My heart leaps the second my arms go around her, and I pull her in for a tight embrace. "You smell good," she says, breath hot on my neck. Would it be tacky to suggest fucking in the car? Because I don't know how long I can hold out.

"You look good. Better than good. Fucking amazing." I slide my hands from her shoulders to her hips, and bring them against mine. She tips her head up to mine, even in heels she's shorter than me, and kisses me. Her kiss is deep. Desperate. Passionate. Fucking in the car seems like a brilliant idea right now.

I press her tighter against me, blood rushing to my dick. What is it about this woman that turns me on so fucking much? We stumble back, clumsily kissing and walking, until we get to the car. I can't help it. I pin her between the passenger door and myself. I move my lips to her neck, gently brushing her blonde hair out of the way.

Lexi shivers and hooks her ankle around mine. The dog barks again, making us both break apart. It's like I forgot we weren't the only ones in existence.

"Before we go," she starts, letting her hands fall from around my waist. "Are you sure you don't mind that I have kids?"

"I don't," I tell her and take her hand, bringing it to my cock. "This is what you're doing to me, if that helps."

Color rushes to her cheeks. "It does." Her hand is still over my dick, and she tips her head, eyes going to my junk. "But this probably isn't helping you."

I wrap my arms around her and put my lips to her ear. "You have no idea how much I want to fuck you."

"I have a pretty good idea," she whispers back, and rubs her hand against me. I enjoy it for a second then take a step back.

"Let's go. Before I lay you down in the backseat."

She nods. "At least drive down the street first."

For a split second, I think she's serious. Then we both

laugh and I open the door for her.

"Just so you're sure," I say as we drive to the restaurant, "my feelings for you haven't changed since I found out you have kids."

"Good," she sighs. "And I'm sorry I didn't tell you before. I wanted to, but the right time didn't come up. And that night when we thought it wouldn't happen again, I didn't see the point of involving them, ya know?"

"You don't have to explain yourself, Lexi." There's enough baggage in my own past, shit that needs to be known before anyone wants to get serious with me. But just like she said, the timing has to be right for that crap to air. I take one hand off the steering wheel and put it on her thigh. She curls her fingers under mine, and changes the subject.

We talk about everything and anything throughout dinner, and there's never a dull moment. It's so easy to talk to Lexi, and being with her just feels right, as lame as that sounds. We order dessert after dinner, eating as slow as possible so this date doesn't have to end.

I walk her to the front door, arm around her waist. Before she can get her keys, my mouth is on hers again. Her arms go around my shoulders and I dip her back, holding her tight.

"Wow," she whispers, coming up for air. "You're quite good at that."

"I know." I grin, anxious to get her inside. She opens her purse and pulls out keys.

"I'd invite you in, but my mother is still here."

I blink. Shit. "Oh, right. I guess I'm not getting any tonight."

She shakes her head. "Nope. Sorry about that. You'll have to wait until Friday."

"You're worth the wait."

LEXI

"That was quite the kiss goodnight," Mom says the second I come in the door.

"Mom!" I exclaim. "You were spying on me?"

"I was merely trying to keep Pluto from barking and waking up the girls."

I take off my shoes and glare at my mother. "Sure, Mom."

"Why didn't you invite him in? I would have loved to meet him. From what I saw, he looks yummy."

"Ew. Mom. Never say that again."

Mom waves her hand in the air and laughs. Our relationship changed for the better after the divorce. I'm open and honest with Mom like I would be with a friend. It was a little weird at first, but now it's great. "I'm glad you went out on a date, Lexi. With a good looking man, no less. You're such a hard worker and deserve to be happy."

I blink back tears. Thinking about dating and happiness brings on an ocean of emotion. An ocean I will drown in if I think about it too much. "Thanks, Mom. I just hope I can do it right this time."

"Honey, you didn't do anything wrong before. We all thought Russell was a great guy when you met him."

"Obviously, we were all wrong." I sigh. "I don't know how to not make the same mistake twice. What do I do?"

"I wish I knew the answer."

I sigh. "Me too."

"But enough dwelling on what was or what could be. Tell me about your date! Did he pay? How much did he tip? Tipping your servers is important, you know."

"We had a really nice time. He's great. Easy to talk to, he makes me laugh, and he's a nice guy. He paid, and he tipped more than twenty percent. I'm not good enough at math to figure out the percentage in my head though."

"But?"

"But what?"

She raises her eyebrows and waits. I get my green eyes from Mom, but that's where the similarities end. My older sister Kara is a carbon copy of our mother, while I favor our father more. "You're going to find something wrong with him, some reason to push him away. I know you, Alexis."

Well crap. Mother really does know best. "There's nothing wrong with him," I sigh. "Not really. Just...say we go on more dates. And things are still good. I still like him, he likes me, and we want things to be serious."

"How is that a problem?"

"He's a great guy, Mom. Really great. But I don't know if he's, well, mature enough in some aspects to be a stepdad."

"You're not talking about sex, are you?"

"No, he's fine there, but I'll spare you the details."

"You've had sex with this man already?"

I sit on the couch and roll my eyes. "I'm an adult, Mom. I have kids. You can't pretend I'm an innocent virgin anymore."

Mom purses her lips. "What's that saying about cows and milk?"

"Anyway," I continue, ignoring her comment. "I thought I'd end up with someone who has a professional career and has their shit together. Someone the opposite of me who can keep me in line and tell me that soaking the crockpot in soapy water every day for a week isn't going to dissolve the burned Velveeta cheese that's stuck to the sides. Not a part-time bartender who lives with his brother."

Mom takes a seat next to me and pats my hand. "You just described Russell," she says gently. "And in the end, he did more than tell you to wash dishes."

Mom's words hit me, and I don't know why it took me until this very moment to realize that I was looking for Russell 2.0.

"You're right," I say slowly.

"Being organized and having a well-paying job is nice," Mom continues. "But that shouldn't determine who you date."

This revelation leaves me feeling naked and cold. I stoke Pluto's ears, mind going a million miles a minute. "I guess I thought having someone responsible like that was best for the girls. They need stability and security."

"*You* give them that. Alexis," Mom says and gets teary eyed. "The last few years haven't been easy on you. But not once have you given those girls anything but a stable, loving home, and all the security they need."

And now my eyes are filled with tears and my bottom lip is trembling. I look down at Pluto, trying to find a distraction.

"If you get into another relationship, those girls need a role model. They need to see a man who treats their mother like the wonderful soul she is."

Tears roll down my cheeks, which sets off Mom. "Okay," I squeak out. I snuggle Pluto, who's still wagging his tail from the excitement of me coming home. "I have no idea what I'm doing," I confess.

"None of us do, honey. If you like this man and he's making you happy, then keep going on dates. Keep it casual until you know if you want to make a commitment to him, and I'm not talking about marriage. It might take you a few months, it might take a few years. There is no time limit. And if the right man comes along, he won't put a time limit on your relationship either."

I nod, agreeing with everything she says. But being the First Runner Up in the Over Thinking Pageant, I've already run this scenario in my head.

"But what if whoever I end up dating wants kids of their own. I'm not getting any younger here, and it's not fair to make them wait."

"You're twenty-seven. I had you when I was thirty-two, and you turned out just fine."

"That's debatable."

Mom laughs and puts her arm around me. "Your father and I are proud of you, Lexi. You've dealt with a lot, and you've done it with grace."

I keep my sarcastic comments to myself. There's no need to alarm my mother by telling her I'm barely keeping my shit together.

"Thanks, Mom."

"I love you, honey."

"I love you too, Mom."

She hugs me and stands. "Now, get your butt in bed. I know you've been staying up late editing again, haven't you?"

"Not that late. Just until two or three AM."

"You're going to make yourself sick."

I exhale heavily. "I don't have much choice."

"Tonight, you do. Or rather, I do. I'm telling you to go to bed."

"Okay, Mom. I will. Thanks for watching the girls. They were good?"

"Perfect angels. Grace read Paige two bedtime stories they went to sleep with no problems. I'll watch them anytime."

I walk Mom to the door, watch out the window to make sure she got into her car all right, then go into the living room. I turn on *Gilmore Girls* and sit on the couch. I'm rewarding myself with one episode. Just one. Then I have to tackle the rest of the emails I didn't get to during the day, and edit one chapter of the paranormal book.

Three episodes, and half a dozen Oreos later, I'm hating myself on a whole new level. It takes me an hour and a half to meticulously go through a chapter. I have some major rewrite suggestions to make the character arc stronger, but if the author approves, it means going back into chapter two and changing things for consistency. It's a lot of work, but the book will be much better in the end.

I move onto emails next, replying, bookmarking, and making notes of shit I have to do until I can hardly keep my eyes open anymore. Mom did the dishes after the girls went to bed, thank God. I let the dog out, wipe down the counters, then call Pluto back in. The second he walks through the door, I can smell shit on his paws.

Literally. I make a move for him and he darts away, thinking this is a game. He makes it halfway across the kitchen before I hook my fingers under his collar. I grumble, cover my nose with my sleeve, and check to see which paw is the poop culprit. I clean the floor and his paw with a Clorox wipe to kill the germs.

I throw the wipe away and panic that the chemicals are going to burn his skin or seep into his bloodstream and poison him. A quick Google search tells me that my lack of judgment won't kill my dog as long as I don't ever do that again. Feeling guilty, I cuddle on the couch with Pluto while feeding him treats. I'm starting to doze off when he jumps up and barks.

"Pluto," I mumble. "What is—"

I cut off when a thump comes from the porch. My blood runs cold and I can't move. Pluto barks again. My hands shake. I don't know what to do. The lights are on, and I haven't closed any blinds. Whoever is outside can see right in.

My heart is in my throat. Pluto stops barking and sits by the door, growling. I hold my breath and listen.

Nothing.

But that doesn't rid me of fear. Feeling like I might pass out, I get off the couch and double check the locks. Then I turn on the TV to make it look like someone is up, grab a knife and my cell and run up the stairs. I check on the girls —both are sound asleep—and sit in the hallway outside their doors.

My first thought is to call Luke. I'm sure he'd come over, but he's at least half an hour away. The murderer lurking outside will kill us all before Luke can get here. Should I call the police? All I heard was a thump. It could have been anything from the wind to those damn giant rats Grace says she doesn't feed. Will the police even come out for this?

I rub my eyes, too freaked to be tired. Pluto joins me on the floor. I set the knife down, sliding the blade under the linen closet door to keep from stabbing myself or the pup, and wrap an arm around him. There's no way I'm getting in the shower right now. I lean against the wall, trying my hardest not to think about all the ways I could violently die while protecting my children.

Somewhere around four AM, I doze off only to be woken by Paige. She's having a nightmare again, and says there is a man in her doorway watching her sleep. Since I was just sitting against the wall right outside the door, it creeps me out more than it should. She's three. Having nightmares like that is normal, right?

Excuse me while I never sleep again.

I get in bed with Paige, jumping at every little noise. My head throbs from exhaustion, my body begging for some shut eye. I don't relax enough to fall asleep until the sun starts to creep up. Coincidentally, my alarm goes off right about then as well.

~

"You look like shit."

"Thanks, Jillian," I say, words slightly slurred.

"Are you sick?"

I shake my head and reach for the coffee. "I didn't sleep last night. Like at all."

"Go sit. I'll get you coffee."

My feet shuffle across the break room and I fall into a chair, folding my arms on the table to rest my head on. I listen to people milling about, cursing them for the sleep they got last night. My phone buzzes from inside my purse. I pull it out, blinking a few times to get my eyes to focus so I can read the text.

Luke: *I had a great time last night, even though it didn't end up with you naked.*

Me: *Next time, promise ;-) and I had a great time too. I'm surprised you're up already.*

Luke: *A certain someone was on my mind and I couldn't sleep. How's work going?*

Me: *Just getting started, but it's going to be a long day. I didn't get much sleep last night, which is always fun.*

I send the text, then worry I'm coming off as too whiny. Though at this moment, I'm too exhausted to care. And I *do* get whiny when I'm tired.

Luke: *Is everything okay?*

Me: *Yeah. Just busy with work then Paige didn't sleep well. She's going through a nightmare phase and wakes up a lot at night and I can't get her back to sleep.*

Luke: *I'm heading out to the gym in a while. Want me to bring you coffee? I'll tell the barista we have a Freddie Kruger situation going on and ask for double shots of espresso.*

His words bring an instant smile to my face, and a familiar flutter passes through me. It's familiar, yet hasn't been felt in a long time. Before I can answer, Jillian comes over, handing me my coffee.

"Here ya go." She sits next to me, adding no-calorie sweetener into her own coffee. "Was this a result of your date last night?"

"I wish, but no." How the hell was I able to pull all-nighters in college? Since when did I get so old? "It was the result of poor time management, working all night, then what most likely was a demonic spirit in my house. It knocked on the door at three AM and then woke Paige up."

"Someone knocked on your door at three in the morning?"

"Maybe. I heard a noise, and Pluto barked. It freaked me out too much to sleep, so I sat in the hallway guarding the girls until I dozed off, then Paige woke up saying the man was watching her sleep again."

"I've been saying you need to get that place blessed," Jillian quips. "But for real...you look rough, Lex."

"I'm okay," I say and bring my coffee to my lips. "I'll go to bed right after the girls do tonight and then I'll be back to normal."

She nods, not convinced. "How was the date?"

"Really good. We get along really well, like more than I've gotten along with any guy before. Is that weird? Shouldn't the beginning of whatever this is be filled with awkward moments and uncomfortable silence?"

"Maybe you finally found the one."

I take another drink of coffee and grumble. "I know we're literally in business of fairy tale love and happily ever afters, but that doesn't exist. It's not real life. There isn't one person out there for everyone. Some people end up alone. Or worse: with the wrong person."

"You're grumpy when you're tired."

"Sorry. I know I am." I take another drink of coffee, waiting for the caffeine to take effect. My right eye has been twitching as a result of being forced open. All I want to do is close my eyes and curl up on the floor right now. "That's two times we've been out and not slept together."

"I knew he liked you. Taking you out for breakfast was a dead giveaway he didn't want a one-night stand." Jillian leaves the table and goes to the counter, filling a bowl with fruit. She's skipping her usual bagel and she put that fake sugar crap in her coffee. If I weren't so tired, I'd lecture her on how unhealthy it is to do another fad diet.

I rest my head on my hands, relishing in the forty seconds of silence where I can close my eyes. Visions of my bed flash before my eyes. I can smell the detergent on my sheets, feel the soft comforter wrap around my shoulders.

"Lex?"

I startle up, blinking. "Yeah?"

"Are you sure you're all right?"

I run my hand over my face. "Totally."

"I'm worried about you. Your hands are shaking."

I put them on the table. "I'm fine."

"Hun, you're not. You should go home and rest."

"Who should go home and rest?" Cole says, striding into the room holding a ceramic coffee mug. He stops short, taking in the sight of me. "Alexis? Are you okay?"

"I'm fine," I reiterate. "Just exhausted. Work, plus the kids kept me up all night."

Cole immediately looks concerned. "You don't have to work at night. You know that, right?"

"I know. I mean, I was working." I shake my head. "No. Hang on. Let me think on it a minute."

Cole comes over and takes a seat next to me, signaling to Jillian to give us some space. "Is everything all right?" he asks quietly. "Everything at home?"

"Yes. Really. We're all good and happy. It was a rough night. I stayed up a bit later than necessary answering emails. Then I thought I heard someone on my porch, and to be honest, it freaked me out. And my toddler has nightmares sometimes that wake her up, and it's hard getting her back to sleep after that."

"Someone was on your porch in the middle of the night? Trying to break in?"

"I heard a noise," I explain. "Nothing definitive. Just...a noise. So, really, I don't know. Being alone with the girls...it makes me feel vulnerable, as much as I hate admitting that."

Along with being emotional and whiny, I ramble when

I'm tired. It's a weird defense mechanism I developed in college. Keep talking so I don't fall asleep in class. My words might not make much sense, but at least I'm awake.

Cole's brown eyes fill with concern. "Why are you here?"

"I work here," I say slowly.

Cole laughs, and I see slight similarities to Luke. "I mean, why didn't you call in and take a sick day?"

"I'm not sick."

"You haven't taken a sick day all year. Go home and get some rest."

"You mean that?" I ask, feeling such relief I could cry.

"Yes. I need you sharp and focused. Forcing yourself awake isn't good for you, Alexis. Go home and go to bed. No emails. No editing. Take care of yourself."

Tears fill my eyes. "Thank you," I squeak out, hardly able to keep from crying at his kindness. Cole's such a good man. He hugs me, gently patting my back. He wears the same cologne as Luke. It's unsettling, and makes me want to push him away. That smell is my Luke-smell. It reminds me of Luke. Cole can't remind me of Luke. It's just not right.

"Don't worry about it. And I mean it," he says, offering me a hand to help me to my feet. "No work."

I nod, wipe my eyes, and pick up my purse. I thank him again, tell Jillian I'm going home, and get into the elevator. I pull up Luke's unanswered text and reply.

Me: *No need. I look like such a hot mess the boss is sending me home to sleep.*

A minute later, my phone rings. I get out of the elevator and emerge into the lobby.

"Hey," I answer.

"Come over," Luke says right away. "And crash here."

"That sounds tempting. But I should head home. Maybe

pick up Paige early and cuddle with her and Pluto on the couch."

"Lexi, if you're exhausted it's not safe to drive. Not to be a downer, but I've seen some nasty accidents caused by people falling asleep at the wheel."

Oh right, he was a firefighter and responded to accidents like that. I don't want to risk anyone, let alone my baby.

"You work downtown, right?" he asks. I told him I work in publishing, which is true, but vague enough to not raise questions. "I live downtown. Come here, nap for a few hours, then go home. It's safer for everyone. And I get to see you."

"You raise several good points. I'm not imposing if I come over?"

"Well, now that you mention it, you are. Which is why I invited you over in the first place."

"Hah. Very funny. I'll see you soon. Have coffee ready?"

"I'll put on a pot right now."

I get a cab, and arrive at Luke's in a few minutes. Excitement to see Luke sends a jolt through me, and I'm not at risk for falling asleep on my feet after I knock on the door. My heart swells the moment I lay eyes on him. His hair is messy from sleep, and he's wearing plaid pajama pants and a white t-shirt. He pulls me into an embrace, and I rest my head against his muscular chest. He kisses my forehead and takes my coat, hanging it on the coatrack in the foyer.

"Thanks for letting me come over to sleep."

"You don't have to thank me. Though I'd be lying if I said I wasn't hoping to get a quickie in before you pass out." He flashes his famous grin and I'm smiling back at him, shaking my head. "You should come upstairs and take those pants off. They don't look comfortable to nap in."

"Nice try."

He takes my hand and leads me upstairs. "Don't deny it."

The bed is unmade, and the clothes Luke wore last night are in a pile on the floor. Seeing his room look real, look lived in, feels comforting. Luke faces me, putting his hands on my waist.

"Let me help you get that shirt off. That won't be comfortable either. And your bra...I hear those are the worst."

I laugh and shake my head, looping my arms around his shoulders. "Then what will I wear?"

"Sleeping naked is natural, you know. Experts recommend it."

"Well in that case, be my guest."

Luke pulls my shirt over my head, and I unhook my bra. My pants come off next, and I'm left in a light pink cami and my underwear.

"Are you really that tired?" Luke asks, looking at me with lust in his eyes.

"Exhausted. But I think I can give you fifteen minutes."

"Thirty."

"Twenty."

He smiles and kisses me. "Deal."

We fall back into bed, and Luke spoons his body around mine. He holds me tight and kisses the back of my neck.

"This is nice," I whisper, eyes falling shut. Luke runs his fingers up and down my arm, relaxing me and lulling me into sleep. I'm in that hazy state between wake and sleep when he moves his hand down my front, over my stomach and into my panties.

I moan at his soft touch, little pulses of pleasure jolting through me. Keeping my eyes closed, I roll onto my back and push his hand between my legs. He sweeps his fingers over my clit, then slips a finger inside. I reach for him, hand landing on his hard cock. He groans and nuzzles his head against me. I tug his pants down and move onto my side again so he can enter from behind.

I'm so fucking comfortable in Luke's bed, wrapped in soft sheets and under warm blankets. The air is cool in the room, a perfect mix for snuggling and sex. My eyes are still closed and my mind feels almost drunk, hovering close to sleep yet even closer to coming. Luke thrusts deeper and faster, fingers still rubbing over my sweet spot.

I love the slow burn of lazy sex, the way we both get closer and closer together and come at almost the same time. Luke holds himself against me, moaning as he climaxes, and then relaxes against the bed, arms still around me. After a moment passes, he goes back to massaging my shoulders, and I'm asleep in minutes.

~

"What the hell is this?" a loud male voice booms from the doorway.

I startle awake, bumping into Luke, who's still tangled up next to me sleeping. I'm facing the window, blankets pulled up to my shoulders. I'm comfy and warm and don't want to move, don't want to get up and see if someone is actually yelling at us or if I dreamed it.

"Luke," the person in the doorway yells, and my heart stops beating. I know that voice.

Oh.

My.

God.

Heavy footfalls echo off the walls as he comes into the room. Tangible anger fills the air.

Cole.

chapter sixteen

LUKE

"*L*eave us alone," I grumble, pulling Lexi closer. Cole's expressed his distaste over me having a woman in the house but this is a whole new level of bullshit. I'm in my room. Asleep. During the work day, where he just pops in for lunch then heads back to the office half an hour later.

Cole stomps in, rage in his eyes. "What is this?"

I take my arm off Lexi, who tensed up the minute Cole came into the room, and sit up. "What the fuck are you doing? Get out of here."

His eyes aren't on me, but on Lexi. Is he trying to get a good look? Save an image of her for the spank-bank later? A surge of protectiveness rises inside me, and I jump out of bed ready to punch Cole in the fucking face.

"Alexis?" he asks and I stop short. Lexi is Alexis. She told me she doesn't like going by her full name, and even her parents caved and now call her Lexi. How the fuck does Cole know her? "Alexis," he demands.

"Leave her alone," I say and move around the bed, putting myself between Cole and Lexi. "I don't care what history you have with her. You're not barging in here like this." I straighten my shoulders and step closer to Cole. "Get out," I say through gritted teeth. "Now."

"It's okay, Luke," Lexi's voice shakes. I turn my head. She's sitting up, holding the blankets to her chin. Her eyes are wide, and her face pale. Her eyes are on me, but it's like she's trying hard to avoid looking at Cole.

She does know him.

They do have a history.

I've never been more jealous in my whole life.

With my head turned, Cole advances, raising his fist to hit me. I catch his wrist and twist his arm. Cole tries to punch me again, and I shove him back. I really don't want to hit him, knowing that I could beat his ass easily. Always could when we were younger.

"Stop!" Lexi yells. "Luke! Cole! Stop it!"

Cole jerks his head toward her, throwing a look so full of judgment I can't help it. My fingers curl on their own accord, and I pop him right in the face. Cole's hands fly to his nose, and Lexi lunges forward, grabbing my arm and pulling me back onto the bed. She stays behind me, and it takes me a second to realize she doesn't want Cole to see her half naked. I pull the blankets over her lap, giving her privacy.

Cole lowers his hands, looking for blood. He's not bleeding; I didn't hit him hard enough for that. Though if he says something again, he'll be on the floor. His eyes narrow and he shoots daggers at Lexi.

"I can't believe I let you go home for this! You lied about your kids keeping you up all night, didn't you? So you could leave for...for *him*. Un-fucking-believable." He shakes his head then storms out.

"Oh my God," Lexi stammers and scrambles off the bed.

She picks up her pants and falls over in her panicked attempt to put them on. "Oh my God."

I blink, too stunned for it to make sense right away. Then it hits me. "Cole's your boss."

"Yes, though he might not be much longer because I probably just lost my job," she says, so stressed she might cry. But her words bring a smile to my face. She and Cole haven't hooked up. He's not a jealous ex-lover.

Just her boss.

Oh fuck. And she's probably right. Cole's a bitter bastard and hates me. Anything associated with me is hated by default.

"Lexi," I start and she shakes her head.

"I have to talk to him," she blurts, still struggling to get her pants buttoned. Giving up, she leaves the room, only to come back to look for the rest of her clothes. Her eyes are filled with tears and I suddenly feel terrible about this.

"I'll talk to him," I offer. "Lay back down if you want to."

She shakes her head. "No. I can't. I...I should explain everything. If he thinks I lied just to get out of work, he could fire me. I can't lose my job. I could lose the girls. Russell would love that. He'd take them away in a heartbeat."

Russell must be her ex. She briefly told me she was married for five years and those five years were full of heartache.

"You're not going to lose your job. Cole can't fire you for this."

"Yes, he can." She nervously plays with her hair. "He'll come up with something else. Something little and work related but really, it will be because of this."

I put my hands on her shoulders, and she relaxes. "Stop.

He's not going to fire you. Cole's an asshole, but he's not going to risk a lawsuit over firing you for no reason."

She blinks away her tears. "You think so?"

"I know so." I kiss her, wanting to take away her fear.

"Why do you two hate each other so much?"

I shrug. "I honestly don't know. He's always been that way, and it's only gotten worse."

"Then why are you here?" she blurts. "Sorry, that was rude. You don't have to tell me. Actually, you shouldn't tell me right now because I really should talk to Cole."

"Put on your bra first. I can see your nipples through that shirt."

Her eyes fall shut and her cheeks redden. I know she's not embarrassed about me seeing them, but if I can, Cole could too. She gets dressed, checks her phone for missed calls from the girls' schools, and smooth's out her hair.

"Want me to come with you?" I ask, even though I am anyway.

"Yeah. I don't like being yelled at."

"I won't let him yell at you." I take her hand and together we go downstairs. Cole is in the kitchen, staring at his lunch.

"Cole?" Lexi asks meekly. "Can I talk to you?"

He looks up from his food and glares at me. "To you. Not to him."

I raise my hands and take a few steps back, going into the hall. I'm out of Cole's line of sight but still able to hear everything he says, just in case I have to jump in.

"I didn't lie to you," Lexi starts. "I really didn't sleep last night because I was working and up with Paige. I was going to head home and Luke suggested I come here since it's closer. The plan was for me to sleep a bit then drive home. It's at least forty-five minutes to commute from the office to my house, and that involves taking the subway, then driving from there to home."

A few seconds pass before Cole speaks. "You two are... are together?"

I inch forward. Lexi and I haven't discussed status in any way, and I'm suddenly nervous for what she's going to say. I'm never nervous. Never anything less than completely confident. Lexi is my kryptonite.

"Yeah," she says, but doesn't sound sure. "We are. You're not going to fire me, are you?"

"No. I'm not going to fire you, Alexis. A guy like Luke is the last person I thought you'd go out with, but who am I to judge?"

"Thanks."

"How long have you two been together?"

"Not long. We met not this past weekend, but the one before that. So like two weeks." Lexi's words die in her throat as the realization hits them. Cole knows we had sex on the counter. He heard us fucking three times over the course of just hours.

And now Lexi knows he heard her screaming my name as she came.

"Well, see you at the office tomorrow," Lexi says, voice tight.

"Yeah, uh, see ya."

She leaves the kitchen, face beet-red. "Work is going to be fun tomorrow," she grumbles. We move into the living room.

"You work with my brother."

She nods. "I have for years. Small world, right?"

"It's more shocking than finding out about your kids," I say it as a joke, but as soon as the words leave my mouth, I wish I could take them back. Lexi tenses, physically reacting to her discomfort.

"That came out wrong. Lexi, I like you, and I want to keep seeing you, if you'll have me."

She shrugs. "I suppose I'll keep you around. You're good arm candy, after all."

"That's all I'm good for."

"You're not too shabby at a few other things." She wiggles her eyebrows and I laugh. "You know, no one has ever gotten in a fight over me like that before. I guess it really wasn't over me, but you know what I mean. So, thanks for defending my honor. I think. Maybe? I really should stop talking." She takes a deep breath and leans against the couch.

"Are you still tired?" I ask.

"I'm not sure. I'm still running on adrenaline and good old-fashioned fear right now. But I slept for longer than I meant to, so I think I'm good. I should get going so I can surprise Paige. I'll take her out for a late lunch or something. Are you sure you still want to go out Friday after learning all this?"

"All this, meaning...?"

"Working at Black Ink Press with your brother and me having kids."

"Yes."

"Good." Her hand lands on my thigh. She gives me a tight smile, and I know she's still uncomfortable with everything that just happened. Fucking Cole. "I really should go."

"Right." I walk her to the door, give her more than just one kiss goodbye, and assure her that I'll call tomorrow instead of tonight since I work and it'll be late by the time I get off. Once she's gone, I go into the kitchen acting like I'm in here just to get myself lunch. Cole is eating his sandwich at turtle speed. He's willing to be late for work in order to have a go at me. Great.

"This whole time you've been talking about this amazing woman, you've been talking about Alexis," he says.

"Yes. *Lexi*, as she likes to be called, is amazing. Which you should know since she's worked with you for years."

"You know she's divorced and has kids, right?"

"Yeah. I had lunch with them over the weekend," I shoot back. "They're great kids."

"What the hell are you doing with her?"

"If you need me to answer that, you have more issues than I thought. Which wouldn't surprise me." I fill a glass with water and sit at the island counter. "Why do you care? You might be her boss during the workday, but once she leaves that office she's free to do what—or who—ever she wants."

"I've known Alexis for a long time," he tells me, and he's not just stating a fact. He's bragging. "And I know she deserves someone better than you."

I roll my eyes. "Like who? You?"

Cole's eyes meet mine. He smirks, and the look says it all. He's had no romantic interest in Lexi in the years he's known her. He never made a move once she became single again. But now that he knows I like her, now that he knows it's *her* who's made me so happy the last few days, he'll do anything to take that from me.

"Yes. Someone exactly like me."

LEXI

"Mom told me you went on a date last night," my sister Kara says.

Last night seems like so long ago. The power nap I took snuggled up next to Luke helped immensely, but I'm still dragging. Paige and I took Pluto to the dog park and then the pet store, and ran out of time to take him home, which is why he's in the car barking at us. Kara has cats, and Pluto gets along with them too well. In an I-want-to-play-with-you kind of way, that results with him chasing them throughout the house. We tried it once, and poor Pluto got his invitation inside rescinded permanently.

"I did."

My always enthusiastic sister beams. "Good, Lex. I don't want you to be a lonely spinster forever."

"Technically, I can't be, right? I have kids."

"Well, whatever. And Mom said this guy—Luke, right? —is very good looking. Tell me about him!"

"I don't know him very well yet. But he is incredibly handsome, is great in bed, and so far, has treated me well."

"Don't do that!"

"Do what? Sleep with him? Did Mom tell you to tell me that?"

"Huh? No. I suppose it's a little soon to be sleeping with him. I made Jeff wait until our wedding night, after all."

I roll my eyes. "Sure you did."

"I did!"

"And that's why Taylor was born eight months after your wedding."

"She was early."

"She weighed nine pounds."

"Anyway, what I mean is don't say 'for now' like you expect him to turn into You-Know-Who."

I sigh. "That's what the therapist said too." I went to therapy for six months after the divorce, which is all insurance allowed me. "I can't compare, and I can't project my disappointments in Russell onto the rest of the world. But..."

"But it's hard. I get it, and I'd do the same. Are you going out again?"

I nod. "Friday."

"Ohhh! He must think you're pretty good in bed too," she teases. "Have you said anything to the girls yet?"

"Not about us dating. We actually ran into him over the weekend, so they know who he is, but I told them he was just a friend. I won't introduce them to any new partner until we're serious."

Kara nods. "That's a good idea. Tell me more about Luke!"

I laugh. "Well, there's this one thing you'll find really funny. You know my boss, Cole?"

"The hot one you claimed to not have a crush on?"

I make a face. "Yeah, him. Well, Luke is his brother."

Kara's green eyes widen. "Really? Is that how you met him?"

And now I'm laughing again, telling my sister how Luke was supposed to be my first one-night stand. "So, say this does work out. What the hell will I tell the kids when they ask how we met?"

"You can say you met at a bar. You don't have to give *all* the details, Lexi."

"Oh, right. Stop being so logical."

"I'm the older sister. It's my job."

"Thanks." I stand from the kitchen table and go upstairs to find the girls. Kara's daughter Taylor is seven, and gets along well with Grace since they're so close in age. Paige likes to hang out with the "big girls", and doesn't get to see her cousin as much as Grace does. She wants to stay a while longer, and sometimes I'm such a sucker.

I can't leave Pluto in the car, so I walk him around the block while the girls play. The things you do for your kids, right?

"You never once thought about having them settle it in the bedroom?"

"No," I tell Jillian the next morning. "I might be making an assumption here, but I don't think Luke or Cole would be into that."

She presses the button on the elevator to take us up to the office.

"Hey, you never know until you ask."

"I don't think *I'm* into that."

"Threesomes can be great if the guys know what they're doing. Speaking from experience here."

An older lady going up with us turns around and I wince, expecting her to scold us for being openly crude.

"She's right," she whispers. "It's better if at least one of them has done it already before. And if they have you're in for a treat." The elevator stops. She winks and gets off.

My mouth hangs open a little.

"If that's not a sign from God, I don't know what is."

I elbow Jillian. "No. I'm not having a threesome with Luke and *him*."

"What, is Cole Voldemort now?"

"No, but he works in this building," I whisper as more people get on the elevator. "I'm already unsure if I'll be able to make it through the day without dying of embarrassment as it is. Please don't add to it."

She gives me an innocent look. "But this is fun. My life is boring. I'm living vicariously through you."

I shoot her an incredulous look. "Really?"

"Okay, no. But I like playing with fire. You know that. And it's even more fun when I'm not the one who's gonna get burned."

"You are such a narcissist. Why am I friends with you again?"

She laughs and loops her arm through mine. "Years of mind games to slowly build a co-dependence."

"Ah, right. How could I forget?"

"That was my goal all along."

"You are good."

She smiles. "The best. Learn from the master."

I laugh and leave the elevator, going on autopilot to the office. As soon as the big, bold letters that spell out BLACK INK PRESS are visible on the double doors, I freeze.

"I can't go in there."

Jillian stops short and turns around. "Yes, you can. And you will."

I shake my head, heat rising in my chest. "No."

"Lex, the weirder you act, the weirder it will be. Cole isn't going to say anything to you about this. He's professional. And we're all busy. Oh, and yesterday the gossip going around was something happened at the UK division which makes for all sorts of drama that you know will carry over here."

"I hate that hearing that gives me peace."

She pats my back. "Looks like I'm not the only narcissist." We get coffee and food, and then head into our separate offices. Cole is in his office, on the phone with the door closed. I watch him for a second through the large glass window. His back is turned, and I can tell he's stressed by his body language.

I hope I'm not adding to that stress.

My inbox is so full I get a warning that I'm running out of space. It takes the entire morning to sort through emails. An hour before lunch, I'm feeling sluggish and need more coffee. I went to bed before midnight last night, but of course, sleep was elusive and I laid in bed obsessing over the current situation.

The easiest thing to do would be to call things quits with Luke. I have so much going on right now, I don't have time for drama. We've only seen each other a few times, after all. It's not like he's my boyfriend or anything. There'd be no hard feelings, and we'd leave knowing that we just weren't compatible.

But that's a big fat lie and we'd both know it.

Because I've never felt more in tune with someone than I do with Luke. And, again, we've only seen each other a few times. He's the first man I've been with after my divorce.

Well, second, technically, if I count that disaster date Mom set me up on a few weeks after the divorce was final. She thought it would be a good distraction with no anticipation of a relationship. I knew right away it was a waste of time when my date ate his French fries one by one. With a fork.

Everything about Luke is wrong. From the way we met, to his lack of a full-time job, and him being the first guy to hook up with after the divorce.

Yet everything about him feels so damn right. And I have no idea what to do.

Someone knocks on my office door, making me jump. I look in the reflection on my computer screen and see Gavin, the assistant editor. I'm bad about delegating tasks because telling someone what to do is a bit awkward. Though at the same time I know Gavin likes having shit to do. I was an assistant once and would have killed to do actual work instead of bringing coffee and printing off manuscripts.

He leaves with a smile and I get a sense of relief to be able to take several things off my to-do list. Then I'm back at it until lunch, and I'm meeting an author downtown to go over a new book pitch. I use the camera on my computer as a mirror, trying my best to pull my hair into a stylish messy bun. I give up and put my blonde locks into a side braid instead.

My phone rings, and I grab it off my desk without looking, thinking it's an agent who promised he'd call this morning and hasn't. I flick my gaze down to my cell, and my heart lurches when I see Luke's number. If I'm going to stop seeing him, I shouldn't answer. I should let his call go to voicemail, see what he has to say, and then call him back tonight and explain that this just isn't going to work out.

If I don't believe it, will he?

"Hey," I say, answering his call.

"Hey, Lexi. How are you?"

"So far, so good."

"Really?" he asks. "Everything is as normal as it can be? I've been sitting here all morning feeling guilty about making your work day stressful."

That's not cute or anything. Nope. Not at all. "Really. I've been in my office all morning though, so I haven't had a chance to run into Cole yet."

"I feel like I should apologize."

That's not cute either. "You didn't do anything wrong. It's just a weird coincidence." I lean back in my chair, day already better just by talking to Luke. I close my eyes and let out a breath. I shouldn't feel this much for a man I hardly know either. It's because he's the first man in a seriously long time to show me affection, and it feels good. So fucking good.

"A very weird coincidence. Though, it makes moving from Chicago suddenly seem worth it."

Oh, Luke. It's like he knows I'm trying to cut ties and he's purposely making it harder.

"Lexi?" he says when I don't respond. "Are you still there?"

"Yeah," I say and my voice shakes. "Sorry, this is just…it's just a lot."

"For that, I am sorry."

"Thanks," I say, knowing he means it, and silently curse him for *not* being the asshole bad boy I thought he was when I first laid eyes on him. "How was work last night?" I ask, changing the subject. He tells me about work, and then we start talking about totally random subjects. He makes me laugh and lose track of the time, and I don't know how he does it. Just minutes ago, I was trying to psych myself up to pull the Luke-plug, and here I am, cuddling the phone against my ear wishing he was here with me.

Well, not *here*, but somewhere together. I imagine his piercing blue eyes and stubble-covered face. His face makes me think of his body, all inked and muscular. And now I want to feel his skin against mine, have the weight of his body pushing mine down onto the mattress.

Stop.

I'm getting turned on and I have to get up, walk through the crowded office and have lunch with June Lee in half an hour. Luke and I say goodbye, both looking forward to tomorrow night. Talking to Luke has eased my nerves enough that it's a bit of a shock when I walk out of the office and see Cole.

Right. He caught me in bed with his brother just twenty-four hours ago.

"Hey, Lexi," he says. "How are you?"

My mouth opens but no words come out. Cole has never called me by anything but my full name. "G-good. I'm good. You?" I fiddle with the strap on my purse, feeling like everyone in the office is watching, like everyone in the office knows Cole's brother has fucked me into oblivion more than once.

And I liked it.

"It's been one hell of a day, and it's only noon."

"Oh, the whole UK thing?"

"Yeah. One of the editors over there leaked an advanced copy of Emma Stark's Guardian books."

"Crap."

"Yeah...it's a shitstorm."

"I can only imagine." My fingers wrap tighter around the worn leather strap on my purse, fighting the urge to disengage eye contact and make a run for it.

"Headed out?"

I nod. "I'm meeting June Lee to go over a pitch."

"Ah yes, I remember that now. Mind if I join you? Not to lunch, just on the way out?"

Yes, I do mind because this is awkward as fuck. I smile. "Sure."

He waits until we're nearing the elevator to speak. "It doesn't have to be awkward," he starts. "And I hope you don't feel like our relationship has changed. You're still one of the best editors I have, and I respect the hell out of you. Which is why I feel compelled to say this: you can do a lot better than my brother."

My mouth opens only to close again. I have no idea what to say to that. He's complimenting me the same time he's insulting Luke, a man I'm starting to like very much. Which makes the whole thing insulting to me.

Cole touches my hand and looks me in the eye, smiling. "But I don't have to tell you that, right? You know how great you are. Tell June the whole editorial staff is excited for her new book."

He walks away, leaving me speechless. I can still feel the gentle swipe of his fingers on the back of my hand. I blink and shake myself. Bewilderment takes over, and I get into the elevator unaware of my surroundings. I'm not totally sure, but I think Cole finally did the one thing I'd been hoping he'd do for the last year.

I think he was hitting on me.

chapter eighteen

LUKE

*C*ole is up to something. I fucking know it. We were home at the same time for several hours before I left to go to Lexi's house, and he didn't say a single thing to me. He avoided me, and looked smug doing it.

Or maybe I'm going insane. Slowly losing my mind, bit by bit. Cole's childhood ambition of getting rid of me might finally happen. It's not like he'll come visit me in the looney bin.

My phone rings when I pull onto Lexi's street. Linked to the car, a Chicago number saved in my contacts as Caroline flashes on the dash. Panic rises inside of me and I'm choking on smoke, feeling soot build up inside my lungs. I decline the call and park in front of Lexi's house.

Caroline doesn't leave a voicemail, and it's not the first time she's called me since I packed up and left Chicago with only a few hours notice. I kill the ignition and close my eyes, leaning against the leather seat of my Chevy. *Don't think about it. Don't think about it. Don't think about it.*

Feeling in control again, I pocket my keys and walk to the front door. The dog barks before I even knock, watching me from a front window. Lexi is right: he does look like a big Chihuahua in a way. I knock, anxious to see Lexi. Because as much as I'm trying to deny that all thoughts of the past are dead and gone, the fire is burning hot and bright in my mind and I can't put out the flames.

But she can.

"Luke, hi." Lexi opens the door and holds her dog's collar. "Pluto, sit. Sit. *Sit.*"

I crouch down, letting the dog sniff me. He stops barking and starts wildly wagging his tail.

"He's friendly," she says. "He's a good watch dog, but a lousy guard dog."

"Hey buddy." I pet the dog and step in, closing the door behind me. Pluto jumps up for attention, ignoring Lexi's commands.

"He's so well trained, as you can tell."

"It's all right," I say with a laugh. "I don't really mind."

Lexi grabs a squeaky toy and throws it. The dog takes off and jumps onto the couch, chewing his toy. I straighten up and take a good look at Lexi. Her hair is swept to the side in a bun, with loose curls hanging around her face. The blue dress she has on is sexy yet casual, and low cut enough to give me a preview of her tits.

"God, you're beautiful." I pull Lexi to me by the waist. She loops her arms around my shoulders and stands on her toes to kiss me.

"You're not so bad yourself."

The second her lips touch mine, red hot lust explodes inside me. I step forward, pinning her against the wall, and kiss her hard.

"No one else is home, right?" I whisper between kisses.

"Just us," she pants, hands traveling down my chest to my belt. She wants this just as much. "Come in." Her lips press to mine and we clumsily walk through the foyer into the living room. The TV is on, but I pay no attention to what's playing. There's only one thing I want to see right now, and that's Lexi. Preferably naked.

Lexi sinks down on the couch. I make a move to kneel over her but she stops me, putting her hands on my hips and shaking her head. She's perching on the edge of the couch, eyes focused on the button of my jeans. She licks her lips and looks up at me, smiling coyly as she undoes the zipper.

Holy fuck, where has this woman been all my life?

Lexi inches my jeans down little by little. So slow it's fucking killing me. She moves closer, lips grazing my skin. I close my eyes when her tongue runs along the V line my muscles make, moving down toward my cock. She plunges her hand inside my boxers, grabbing my cock, pumping it a few times before she takes it in her mouth. She keeps this up, bringing me close to coming and then slowing down and taking me back, and it's driving me insane in the best fucking way possible.

I moan, and grab a fistful of her hair. Her hands work in rhythm with her mouth, sucking, licking, moving fast then slow, fast then slow. The buildup feels so fucking good. I open my eyes and look down. I didn't think it was possible to get more turned on, but seeing Lexi's lips around my dick sends me over the edge. A shudder runs through me as I come, and Lexi wraps one arm through my legs, holding me tight in her mouth. She swallows everything and wipes her mouth. I pull my pants back up, forgoing the belt.

"You are so fucking hot," I tell her and sit down, turning Lexi away from me. I kiss her neck, and Lexi shivers. Keeping my mouth against her skin, I pull down the zipper of her dress and trail kisses from the back of her neck to between her shoulders. Gently, I push her down and move over top of her.

I slip my hand under her dress and into her panties, rubbing her clit. Lexi's breath quickens and her nails press into my flesh. When she's close to coming, I stop and sit up, stripping her of her underwear. Lexi parts her legs, expecting me to pick up where I left off.

Instead, I lay down.

"Come here," I tell her. Lexi's green eyes meet mine in question, but she sits up and moves on top of me, straddling my lap. "Up here."

"Luke, what...?"

I grab her thighs and pull her onto my chest, pushing her dress up and out of the way. She tenses and looks down at me, face between her legs.

"Take your dress off."

She takes her lip between her teeth, nervous. Shy. Feeling exposed. My cock starts to get hard again. Slowly, she reaches down, gathering the hem of her dress in her hands, and lifts it over her head. She's not wearing a bra, and her hard nipples begged to be touched. I run my fingertips over her thighs, up her stomach, and to her wrists. I take them in mine and pull them behind her back.

That flush comes back to her face, spreading down her neck and over her breasts. She is so incredibly sexy right now. I pull her arms, making her arch her back, which pushes her sweet pussy against my face. I lift my head, open my mouth, and press my tongue against her.

Lexi moans, flexing toward me. I tighten my grip on her hands, not taking my mouth off her. I can feel the pleasure wind up inside her as she squirms on top of me, riding my face. She pulls against me, trying to break her arms free. Her thighs tighten and she cries out as she comes.

But I don't stop, don't let up. I let go of her arms and grab her hips, grinding her core against me. Lexi falls forward, body curling around my head, hands in my hair, as she comes again. She's panting when I let go, helping her move down and lay on my chest.

"We missed our dinner reservation," I state, not that it matters. There's plenty to eat here.

Lexi just moves her head up and down, unable to speak. She shivers, and goosebumps break out all over her flesh. I look around for a blanket, taking in my surroundings for the first time. We're in the living room on an L-shaped sectional couch. The TV is mounted on the wall across from us, and a pink dollhouse is in the corner. A dog bed filled with toys and treats is next to that, underneath a decorative table.

Pluto is laying on a pastel-colored blanket in the corner of the couch, and I feel bad making him move to get it. I cover Lexi up and drape an arm around her. The dog walks over, stepping on both of us, to lick my face.

"Enjoy the show, buddy?" I ask, and reach out to pet him. Lexi laughs and lifts her head up, eyes meeting mine.

"My hair is a mess, isn't it?"

"I prefer it that way."

"Good. Because I can't fix it like how it was. My sister came over and did my hair for me. I wanted to look good for you."

"You don't have to do anything special to look good. I think you always do." I push her hair back and kiss her forehead. "You're beautiful, Lexi."

She buries her head in my neck, and I can feel her smile. "I'm glad you think so."

"I don't think. I know." I put my hands under the blanket and squeeze her bare ass. "We really did miss our dinner reservation. Do you want me to cook for you?"

Lexi lifts her head and looks at me, blinking. "Are you real? I'm not imagining all this, right?"

My fingers find her core, still hot and wet. "Does this feel real?"

"Yes," she moans. "So real. And I'm in desperate need of groceries. I was going to go grocery shopping every day this week, yet it just didn't happen."

I laugh. "Well, you are busy."

"I am. Very busy. But I'm also not the best time manager. Like today at work, I wasted time reading an article about vaginal knitting. They put the yarn up there and pull it out. It's considered art."

"I, uh, I really don't know what to say to that. Other than they could probably sell it to the panty sniffers for a high price."

"That's what I said!"

"So that's what you do at work," I say, blocking Cole from my mind. People talk about work. It's a normal thing to do. We spend more time at work than we do anywhere else during the week. Work is a part of Lexi's life. And my asshole brother just happens to be in it.

"Well, my career is heavily based in erotica. Comes with the territory. I was researching weird fetishes for an author and came across the whole vagina-yarn thing."

"It's so off-putting when you say it like that."

"I know! Dick-yarn has a much better ring to it." She narrows her eyes. "Stupid men and their penises ruining everything for us women again."

We both laugh and I stretch my legs out underneath Lexi, carefully sliding them out from under the dog. "What do you want to do for dinner? I don't know about you, but coming always makes me hungry."

"There's a great little burger place not far from here. It's usually not too busy and it's cheap. You can get a cheeseburger, fries, and a drink for eight bucks."

"That sounds good to me. You're not going to get mad at me later for taking you to a burger place over the fancy place we planned?"

She shakes her head, messy hair falling into her face. "No. I've been craving a burger and fries for a while. And it means I can wear jeans and a t-shirt instead of this dress and heels."

Fuck. She is perfect.

◞

"Where were you?" Cole demands as soon as I step foot into the house Saturday afternoon. I stayed the night at Lexi's house Friday, and we spent half the day together today not doing anything in particular, besides enjoying each other's company.

And sex.

We did have sex more than once. More than twice. On Friday. We fucked again after breakfast this morning and then again before I left. I haven't had that much sex in that short amount of time since college. Having that strong of a sexual connection with one person should feel unnatural.

But it doesn't.

Not at all, and the more time I spend with Lexi, the stronger that connection becomes. Every time I see her makes me want to see her even more, and leaving gets harder and harder. Especially when I come home to this.

"Why do you care?" I hang up my leather jacket and take off my shoes. Cole is sitting at his desk in the study, which is right off the front foyer. The entire house is styled and furnished specifically for Cole. Logically, it makes sense.

The house doesn't belong to just him, but I was living in Chicago with no intentions on moving back to New York. I had friends, a life, and a career I was proud of.

Then it all went up in flames. Literally.

Cole moved in not long after our grandmother passed, which is also logical since we didn't want this place sitting empty for longer than necessary. He's lived here for years, and has spent a great deal of his inheritance on making this place his and his alone. It never bothered me before. I'm a laid-back guy. I've witnessed firsthand way too many times how short life can be, how everything can change in an instant. Don't sweat the small stuff takes on a bigger meaning when you never know if you'll make it out alive from one job to another.

But standing here looking at Cole sitting behind that pretentious oak desk is pissing me the fuck off.

"I didn't set the alarm last night because I thought you'd be home."

"You're such a fucking liar. You set the alarm when I'm at work and know I'm coming home. I don't owe you shit, but I'll tell you where I was. Though you already know or else you wouldn't care. I was with Lexi."

"What exactly are you doing with her?"

"Well, at 7:03, I knocked on the door. At 7:04 she answered."

"I could do without your attitude." He puts his pen down, making sure it's perfectly parallel to the pages he's reading.

"Good. Because you do not want to know what was transpiring at 7:07."

"Luke," he starts. "Listen...Lexi is my employee. I don't want things to get weird for her. If your plan is to have your fun then never see her again, stop."

"That's not my plan. I don't know why you refuse to remember me saying I like her."

"I know you. You're not the settling down type."

I shrug. "People change. Just look in the mirror. You went from being a bit Type A, to full-on asshole."

"You're hilarious," he says dryly.

"Yep. I'm a one-man show. I'm going up to crash. I'm exhausted from all the sex I had with *your employee*." I wave my hand and walk up the stairs, snickering at Cole's face. When it comes to pushing his buttons, I'll never grow up.

LEXI

"We need to go on a double date," Kara says. It's Monday afternoon and she dropped Grace off from school to save me a trip. We're sitting in the kitchen drinking iced tea while the girls play upstairs. "Because I'm starting to think Luke is a mythical creature. If Mom hadn't seen him when she was spying on you, I'd worry you lost your mind. Again."

"That's very possible, and it's even more likely I never got it back in the first place. My poor mind is just out there wandering around. Though it was nothing but mush years ago. It's probably just a crusty dried-up puddle now."

"You are so weird." My sister shakes her head. "Are you going out again this weekend? Let's all go!"

"I have the girls this weekend."

"Mom will watch them. All three girls can stay over. They'd love that."

I wrinkle my nose. "But if I miss this Friday night with them, I have to wait a week to have another."

"They haven't had a cousin sleepover at Mom and Dad's in a long time. They'll love it. Mom will love it. And you need to take time for yourself. Especially since things are going so well with Luke."

"They're going really well. So, shouldn't I back off?"

Kara raises an eyebrow. "Please explain."

I sigh. "Don't you think it's weird the first guy I date has this much potential?"

Kara shrugs. "Not really. I mean, you didn't get set up on a blind date. You decided to talk to Luke because you sensed there was something there."

"I thought he was hot, and I was drunk."

"That's all it was?" she questions. "You didn't talk to him before that or anything? You just said 'hey, you're hot. Let's go back to your house and have sex, stranger'?"

"Basically. I did slip him a note that side 'Want to fuck? Check yes or no' to make sure he was down, and to eliminate the exchange of verbal words."

"I'm being serious, Lexi! If we all go out together, I can give you an opinion on him. You know I'm really good at reading people."

I grumble but agree. She didn't like Russell at first, and it caused us to lose a year of sisterly friendship. I wanted her to be happy I was in love with a man who wanted to marry me, and she told me he gave off a negative energy that clashed with mine. I called her a stupid hippy and said she had no idea what she was talking about. I'm still eating my words years later.

"Maybe." I let out a sigh and lean back in the kitchen chair. "I wish we'd gone about this a different way, and I wish I'd gone out on some of those dates Mom tried to set up so I'd have some more experience under my belt. Wait, that came out wrong."

"I think I know what you mean, and you need to stop.

You don't have to date a certain number of duds before you find that one person made for you."

"I don't know if I believe anyone is made for each other anymore."

"You don't mean that."

"I do," I confess. "I don't want to. I want to believe I have a soulmate out there whose love is the kind of love I read about in romance novels. But...I thought I had it once, and I was wrong. Why do I deserve a second chance? Why would I meet the man of my dreams after I already had a wedding? Already had kids? Nothing we do will be the first for me, and that's not fair. Say Luke *is* that guy. He shouldn't get jipped on those experiences. He should be able to be excited for his wedding. He should be able to go through the pregnancy of his firstborn full of question and fear right along with the mother of his child. I'd be one of those annoying old ladies sitting on a rocking chair on a covered porch telling him how it was back in my day. It's just not fair to him. He deserves it, but I don't. I already had it once, and it all fell apart."

"Sometimes things have to fall apart to be put back together. Your pieces weren't in the right order and were all jumbled up inside. Now's your chance to not only put them where they need to be, but to shape them yourself. Make *you* who you want to be, and that includes dating super -exy men who like oral and cooking. Goodness, Lexi, you do realize how much of a catch he is, right?"

And now I'm smiling at the thought of Luke.

"That's what makes this so hard."

Kara gives me a cold, hard stare. "You really did lose your mind, sis."

Exasperated, I sigh and rub my eyes, not caring if I smear my eyeliner over my face. It wasn't neatly applied in the first place. I did it on the subway. Yes, I was *that* girl this morning. "The first guy I date isn't going to be *the one*. He just can't. Because that's too easy, and life isn't easy. Trust me, I know firsthand how shitty the world is."

"Lexi," Kara says softly and puts her hand on mine. "Life isn't a fairytale. Life isn't a book. Life isn't a movie. There is no formula you have to follow in order to find happiness. Your job revolves around romance books where things happen in a somewhat predictable order, right?"

"If the book is well done, it's not predictable," I counter.

She purses her lips. "You know what I mean. You and Luke didn't anticipate finding a spark. But you did. And personally, I think the more unexpected love is, the better it is."

"I don't love Luke."

She smiles. "Not yet. Give it a few months."

I roll my eyes, refusing to let myself get too hopeful. The last time I let my mind wander to the "maybe it'll work out" category, I slept with his brother.

"Just have fun, Lexi."

I smile and nod, not bothering to get into it further with Kara. It's easy to say what someone should do when you're not the one doing it. "Okay."

"Great. I'll text Mom about a cousin sleepover Friday night."

~

"CAN your double date be a triple date?" Jillian asks the next morning. She opens her notebook and takes a seat at the conference table. I plant my feet on the ground and push, sending the rolling chair across the room. There's something about sitting in a rolling office chair that makes me incredibly lazy. Why walk when I can roll?

"That would be fun. Luke won't care."

"Great." Jillian's red lips curve into a perfect smile. "Where are we going?"

"Some new place downtown. Kara already made reservations for six-thirty."

"No one does anything that early."

"I know," I sigh. "And it'll be a headache for me to go home, get the girls to my parents' and then get ready on time. I'm hoping I can get my shit done and leave after lunch on Friday."

"I'll help if I can."

"Thanks," I tell her, knowing she's just as swamped with work as I am.

Christine, one of the publicists for Black Ink Press looks at me from across the table. "You have a date, Lexi?"

"She does," Jillian answers before I can fumble over my words and spit out "no". Christine came here from another big publishing house around the same time I got hired. I love when she's assigned to work with my authors. Christine is a boss lady when it comes to marketing.

"Ohhh. Tell me about him."

"He's a really great guy," Jillian goes on. "Super sexy too. I saw him once."

I give Jillian my best side-eye and smile politely at Christine. "What she said. I met him a few weeks ago and we really hit it off." I can't lie when it comes to Luke, even though everything inside me screams to shut the hell up.

"I'm glad," Christine says and I know she means it. My divorce and lack of love life after has been the topic of office discussion multiple times. It's not surprising since those of us who work together primarily edit or market romance novels. Nosing around in each other's love lives comes naturally to half of us. "I thought you looked happier lately. You've been getting some, haven't you?"

I can't lie about that either. "Maybe."

Jillian leans forward, enjoying this way too much. "I've heard the details. The man is hung like a horse and likes to lick—" she cuts off when Cole walks into the conference room.

"I feel like I interrupted a secret meeting or something," he jokes and goes to the head of the table.

Christine laughs and if looks could kill, Jillian would be dead on the floor right now. "Lexi's seeing someone," Christine says. If I'd been seeing any other man, this wouldn't be a big deal. At all. Everyone would heckle me over it, then we'd drop it and move on. "About time, don't ya think?"

Cole returns her smile, not missing a beat. "Yeah. About time."

I turn my head down, thinking I need to call Luke just to put out the fire that's burning on my cheeks. This meeting needs to get started so it can end. Though, there's really no need for this meeting anyway. One email asking for updates would save us all time.

My phone buzzes, and I pick it up. Since we're constantly taking calls from people in the book world, we're allowed to have our phones at meetings, as long as they're face down and on silent. I flip mine to see who texted me. I mentally grumble when I see Russell's name, saved in my phone as "The Ex". I had him under a more colorful name than that but toned it down for the sake of moving on and letting go of anger.

I sigh, already knowing that he's going to come up with a million reasons why he can't take Grace to the dentist next week. I purposely scheduled her appointment so she'd go during her lunch break and would have time to grab food with her father before returning to school. It would be a fun little excursion for her, and Russ works just fifteen minutes from her school.

"You are such a fucking asshole," I mutter when I read his response of not having time to take her because he's "really busy".

"Russ?" Jillian asks, looking over her shoulder.

"The one and only."

I shake my head, doing my best not to get angry as I type a reply. This is exactly the type of thing that led to me finally going through with the divorce. Russ will do anything to make my life hell, even if it means disappointing the girls. Grace was looking forward to having lunch with her dad.

"Alexis," Cole snaps. I jerk my head up. "No personal phone time during meetings."

The energy in the room shifts, and it suddenly feels a million degrees in here. The meeting hasn't started, and no one has ever cared about phone use. And how does he know this is a personal convo? He can't hear anything I've said to Jillian. There's only one reason he'd care: he thinks I'm texting Luke.

I set my phone down and nod, trying to develop psychic powers that will make people stop staring at me. I'm as embarrassed as I am pissed. I got scolded like a child in front of a majority of the marketing and editorial staff. What the hell?

Forty-five minutes later, the meeting ends and I hightail it out of there and into my office, closing the door. Luke, who'd been at work last night, texts me to say good morning. I smile and text him back, telling him about the awkward meeting. He laughs, says I shouldn't worry about Cole, and promises to call me at lunch. I get to work, ignoring Russ's attempts to bait me into a text message fight. It's been two years and he still won't give up trying to piss me off.

I skip lunch today, grabbing a sandwich from the break room and eating at my desk. If I want to leave early Friday, I need to get a head start now. I go nonstop until the end of the day. Rain is falling outside the window, crashing down onto a sea of umbrellas below. I twist my hair into a messy bun, wishing I had bothered to check the weather before I let. I didn't bring a coat. Or an umbrella. Oh well. It is what it is.

I pack up my shit and head out, saying bye to Jillian on my way. Cole's leaving his office, and I speed up to avoid him, but the guy is tall and his long legs take big strides and now he's behind me, stepping into the same elevator.

Dammit.

"Hey Alexis," he says, buttoning his coat. "I thought the end of the day would never come."

So we're back to normal? He's not mad at me over the Luke incident? Well, the Luke texting incident that didn't really happen.

"Uh, yeah. It was a long one."

"How are your girls?"

"They're good."

"I bet they're getting big now." He smiles.

What is happening? I return the smile, nervously forcing my lips to curve up. I stare straight ahead, wishing the elevator will go all *Tower of Terror* on us and rapidly drop to the main level. Without crashing and killing us, of course. I just want out.

"I meant what I said about things not being awkward," Cole says as we stop at another floor. Two more people squeeze in.

"It's not."

He gives me a look. "Seriously. Don't feel like you have to sneak around."

My eyebrows push together. "I don't know what you're talking about."

"Last night," he whispers. "It's fine with me. Whatever you and Luke do is your business."

Another forced smile. "Right." I wasn't over last night. Luke was working. Did he bring someone else home?

LUKE

"Yes, Mom, I'm doing just fine." I exhale and sit on the couch. I've been on the phone with my mother for the last twenty minutes. Since she moved several years ago, I really don't mind talking to her on the phone. She usually fills me in on the happenings in the neighborhood, tells me how many alligators she's seen on the golf course, and gives me a weekly recap of her trips to Disney World.

Yes, *weekly*.

She and my stepfather live only twenty minutes away, after all. And no one likes Disney shit more than my mother.

"Are you still going to the doctor?" she asks.

"I don't need to."

"But isn't it recommended?"

"Depends on who you're talking to. I'm fine. Healed the best I can be, so now I just need to move on."

"How's that going? Have you made friends in New York? Are you looking for another job? Not at the fire station, I hope. What about going back to school? It's not too late to change professions, you know. You're young. Talented. Smart, too. Have you decided if you want to stay? There's lots of job opportunities in Florida, you know. Disney treats their employees like gold, I hear."

"Mom, one at a time, please."

"You know I worry about you. You are still my baby."

"Yeah, yeah. And really, I'm fine. I'm seeing someone," I blurt, bypassing the other questions. I haven't decided what to do yet. Being a firefighter was my calling. Saving people, going in when others run out...that's what I'm meant to do.

At least I thought so. But I've been wrong before.

"A girl?"

"No, Mom, a monkey I met at the Central Park Zoo. I have to sneak in after-hours so I don't get arrested. Bestiality is frowned upon in New York."

"Luke, stop it. Tell me about this girl!"

"Her name is Lexi." As soon as the words leave my lips, everything transcends. I've never told my mother about anyone I was with before. There was no point, even if I was exclusive with whomever I was hooking up with. I knew it wouldn't last, knew there was no point in taking them home and going through the motions of meeting my parents. They wouldn't be around long enough for the next holiday anyway.

"How did you meet her?"

"At work. My work. The bar. She was out with friends and we just got to talking."

"Oh, how lovely! How long have you been dating?"

"Just a few weeks. She's great, though."

"I'm sure. If memory serves me, this is the first time you've even mentioned a woman to me. So this young lady must have made quite the impression on you."

That and then some. "She did. She has kids. Two girls."

"Oh, so is she divorced?" Mom tries hard not to make assumptions about anyone. Years of being a trauma nurse has made that second nature for her.

"Yeah. She has been for a over a year."

"Do you know the details of it?

"Not really," I confess. "It hasn't come up."

"I'm sure it will if you keep seeing each other. Now are you getting along with your brother?"

I do my best not to burst out laughing. I tell Mom we're doing just fine, and end the call. It's getting late in the afternoon, and that means Cole gets home soon. I look around the living room at the minimalist decor and think it's a shame Cole didn't leave one thing as Gran had it. This house was her pride and joy. Yeah, it was in major need of updating, but keeping one or two of her hideous floral paintings or one of her many doilies, would hold the right amount of nostalgia, reminding us of our childhood.

I suppose I could change things. Go to the storage unit and dig through the mountains of crap and find some of Gran's decorations. The house is half mine, after all. If I decide to stay in New York, then what? Why should I have to leave the house that is partially mine? It pisses me off just thinking about it.

I leave the house before Cole gets home, and am reminded right away how different my life is here. The city is unfamiliar, filled with strangers. It makes me miss everyone I left behind in Chicago, but if they cared about me at all they'd know why I can never go back.

It's nearing seven by the time I make it home, bag of Chinese takeout in hand. Lexi said she'd call after work, and I haven't heard from her yet. The last few days she's called me when she left the subway and was on her way to pick up her girls from her sister's house. I'm sure she's busy with her kids, trying to do dinner and help with homework or whatever, and will call later.

Lexi has always kept her word before, calling when she says she will, though I've learned to give her a thirty-minute grace period before I suspect the worst. And the worst usually is some sort of horrific accident. I've seen the worst of the worst, from scraping flesh off the pavement after motorcycle accidents to spending more hours than I thought humanly possible looking for missing body parts alongside the road.

I sit at the island counter, scrolling through news articles to keep my mind busy as I eat. Cole comes into the kitchen, opens the fridge, and takes out one of his nasty green smoothies.

"Expecting a call?" he asks, eyeing the phone in front of me.

I shrug and break an eggroll in half dipping it into duck sauce. Cole is still standing there, watching me. He doesn't say anything else, but he doesn't have to. The eggroll crunches under my fingers.

"What did you do?"

He shakes his head. "I didn't do anything."

"Bullshit." I drop the food on my plate and stand. "You don't like that I'm involved with Lexi. What did you do?" I say each word slowly through gritted teeth.

Cole laughs. "Look at you all desperate for answers. It almost makes me think you really like Alexis."

"I do. And she likes me. So what the fuck did you do?"

"All I told her was that things don't have to be awkward. She doesn't have to sneak in and out of your bedroom anymore like she did last night."

"She hasn't—" I stop mid-sentence. "You made her think I brought someone home with me last night."

"You mean that wasn't Lexi I heard leaving in the middle of the night?"

I don't think. I act. And right now I'm flying around the counter. My hands land on Cole's shoulders and I shove him back.

"What the fuck is wrong with you?"

He stumbles back, green smoothie sloshing out of his glass and onto the floor.

"Why?" I demand. "Why do you hate me so much you'd hurt Lexi just to get to me?"

Cole stumbles back against the counter. "I didn't hurt Lexi," he rushes out. "If anything I helped her. She's too good for you and needed to get out before she wasted any more time."

"Oh, so now you care about her. Really fucking funny way of showing it." I ball my fists, wanting to hit him repeatedly. "You're such a fucking asshole." I whirl around, needing to get out of here before I do beat his ass. I grab my phone. "She's going to find out what a piece of shit you are."

Cole laughs. "Hardly. You think she'll believe you over me? I've known her for years. It's been what, less than a month since you've known her? And calling to tell her you didn't bring anyone else home sounds like you have a guilty conscious. Why bring it up if it didn't happen? And I bet she's going to need someone to comfort her when it's all said and done."

I shake my head. "You're un-fucking-believable." Phone in hand, I storm out of the house. Cole's a miserable bastard, but he's right about one thing: he has the upper hand when it comes to Lexi's trust. Their relationship might be strictly professional, but she's known him for years. The only way she'd take my word over his if she felt as strongly for me as I feel for her. Panic rises in my chest, and I don't know how to fix this. Calling her and telling her exactly what happened —the whole truth and nothing but the truth—sounds far-fetched, just like Cole planned. She might believe me, but it's a small ass chance. It doesn't matter how small of a chance it is. I have to take it.

Because I'm starting to fall for her.

chapter twenty-one

LEXI

I slowly pull my arm out from underneath Paige and army crawl to the foot of the bed. I hop over Grace, landing silently on the floor. Pluto takes my spot between both girls. I smile, standing there in the dark looking down at my babies for a minute before tucking them back in and yawning my way downstairs and into the kitchen.

The girls wanted to snuggle in my bed with me, and there was no way I was saying no to that. Especially tonight. Because as much as I try not to think about it, I do. And it shouldn't bother me, but it does.

Luke was with another woman last night.

We set no rules, no expectations. For all he knows I could be seeing other men. I roll my eyes at myself. Luke knows how busy I am and how much time I don't have set aside for dating. I wouldn't have time to see other men. But still...I shouldn't be mad at him, shouldn't feel such intense disappointment.

But I do.

I thought there was something more between us,

something that pushed others out of the picture because for that moment, we were enough. I was wrong, and it's better to find out now rather than later.

The stupid part of me that clings to hope says it's still possible to continue this with Luke. After all, we never said we'd be exclusive. Maybe after a talk we'd come out on the same side.

Or maybe not.

I fill a glass with wine and sit at the kitchen table, head in my hands. Editing a romance novel is the last thing I want to do right now, and the only reason I planned to work tonight was so I could get off work early and be ready for a date. A date with him.

A date that probably shouldn't happen.

I sip my wine and take a deep breath. Even if I don't go on a date Friday, I still want to get ahead on my work. I can take a half-day Friday and spend it with Paige. If I'm really good and on top of shit, I can take her into the office with me, let her entertain herself with books and my Kindle, then hit the town for a mommy-daughter day before Grace gets out of school. Letting Grace play hooky is tempting. Maybe all three of us will fake sick and spend the whole day just lounging around the house.

My phone buzzes with a text. It's from Luke. I bite my lip, holding my cell to my chest, and decide to see what he has to say.

Luke: *Long day?*

I stare at his words, not sure how to respond. Should I come out and ask him about last night? He told me he worked, then came home and crashed. Leaving out part of the truth is a lie, right?

Me: *Yes.*

I send my one word response and then feel like an ass.

Luke is free to see other women. And he'll probably want to after this. It's for the better. Luke is a free spirit. Expecting someone like him to settle down—with a single mom of two, no less—is a lot. I twist my ring around my finger, looking at the gemstones as they twirl. Four stones make up the band. A ruby for Grace's birthstone, citrine for Paige, emerald for me, and peridot for Pluto. There was a diamond in its place for Russell's birthstone, but I sold that sucker for grocery money and replaced it with the cheaper stone when I could afford it.

I think of Luke and realize that I don't know when his birthday is. There's a lot about him I've yet to learn and was looking forward to figuring out. Is it too late?

Yes. Yes it is. Because we're not compatible.

~

"So you're canceling the date?" Jillian asks me Wednesday morning. We're in her office, sipping our morning coffee. She's eating a donut, and I'm not hungry. Which is a red flag that this whole Luke seeing other women thing is really upsetting me.

"I think so. I just don't see the point. We clearly want different things out of this. I'm looking for something long-term with hopes of forever on the horizon. He just wants sex. A lot of sex apparently. And if what we're doing isn't coming close to being enough now, he's only going to be disappointed later."

"Maybe he's the kind of guy who has to fuck every day."

"Then we're really not made for each other."

She waves her hand at me and picks up her phone, going through her email as we talk. "What I mean is, if you become more official, then you'll see each other more. He'll get some on the regular."

"I have two kids."

"And there are people with three kids. And four kids. And more than that."

"What are you getting at?"

"They're still doing it and they have kids. You can't get three kids without fucking while you have just the two."

I sigh. "I know. It's totally possible to have a sex life post-children. My fear is it's not the kind of sex life Luke wants."

Jillian puts her phone down and gives me a hard stare. I know what she's about to say is going to be harsh. Harsh, but true.

"Why are you pushing him away?"

"I'm not. He's the one sleeping with someone else."

"Have you talked about *not* sleeping with other people?" she asks and I shake my head. "Then why don't you go out Friday and talk to him about it. I'll be there. Your sister will be there. You have backup."

"How about I go to the bathroom and you ask him if he's seeing anyone else?"

"Oh sure," Jillian quips. "Then you can call your mommies and ask if it's okay to have a sleepover."

"Funny."

"Sometimes I don't know what to do with you, Lex. But seriously, no matter who you date, this topic is going to come up. You both need to lay out what you want and what your expectations are."

"You make it sound easy."

"Saying it *is* the easy part," she sighs. "Getting them to follow through—hah—that's a different story. But don't let my lack of engagement ring scare you. I can tell you like this guy, and from what you said he seems to like you too."

"I do like him," I confess. "Figures, I meet a nice guy who's not just related to our boss but is his brother."

"No one said love was easy."

"*Life* ain't easy."

Jillian holds up her hand. "Preach." Her eyes go back to her phone. "Today marks seven days," she grumbles.

"Since you went crazy, killed your horses, and were pushed into the well?"

"Huh? No, and that's not how that movie goes. You'd know if you weren't too chicken shit to actually watch it. Seven days past the deadline I gave Ren Fairchild. He hasn't turned in anything. No book. No chapters. Not even a page. And he hasn't returned my emails. He's still posting on Facebook, so I know he's not dead in a ditch somewhere. I swear to God, I will call him over and over today until he answers and gives me the fucking book."

"Have fun with that," I empathize with her, knowing the stress a late project puts on you. I live on day-to-day organized chaos, and shifting one project around for another can cause the whole precariously placed mess to collapse.

Cole catches me the second I leave Jillian's office. He has a glimmer in his eye and he looks me up and down before he waves me over. I'm both angry and relieved in terms of Cole. Angry he had to open his mouth and say something, ruining the facade of happiness I'd built around me. And relieved that I know the truth about Luke. I knew I was going to get hurt in the end.

Because love is fucking stupid.

"Good morning, Alexis," Cole says. His eyes meet mine and he holds my gaze, smile growing. "Did you do something different to your hair? It looks different. It's a good different, of course."

"Um, I parted it on the other side." I swallow hard and force myself to take a steadying breath. Looking at Cole reminds me how much I like Luke. God, my heart is a moron.

"It looks nice. Anyway, I was hoping you were free for lunch."

"Lunch?" I dumbly stammer.

"Yes. That meal between breakfast and dinner. I made a few notes on that paranormal book I wanted to go over with you. Marketing is suggesting a title change. *Cursed* has been used many times."

I nod, thankful this is about work. "I agree. I've been trying to get Katie to come to that conclusion on her own. She's so excited about this she went out and ordered business cards and stuff that say she's the 'author of the Cursed Series' and I don't want to put a damper on her mood. It's helping her write the second book."

Cole smiles, stepping closer to his desk. He puts his hand on the shiny wooden surface and leans forward. "You're so considerate, so thoughtful."

"Thanks." I fidget on my feet. "So lunch...do you want me to meet you here or the conference room?"

Cole laughs, and I can't help but think it sounds forced. "No, nothing formal. Let me take you out and we'll go over details."

"Uhhh, okay." Cole is my boss. We have a work matter to talk about, and I agree the title of Katie's book needs to be changed. But talking about it over lunch like this? It's just... weird. And it's leaving a bad taste in my mouth, one that makes it hard to concentrate on work. Needing a distraction, I start going through submissions. It only takes about three thousand words of a book to know if it's something I can work with or not. The author's voice has to jive with me, and if not, we're just not a match. Those three thousand words don't have to be at the beginning of a novel either, and more times than not, I suggest rewrites to the beginning of the books I take on.

I forward my rejections to Gavin, who has to do the dirty work of telling the agents we're not interested. One book is actually really good, but is a historical fiction. I don't edit historical fiction, and being sent a book outside of my preferred genre annoys me. It's clearly listed what genres I accept, and historical fiction is not one of them.

I write the agent back, telling her that the book is good but would be better suited with another editor and have forwarded the submission to her. An hour and a half later, and I'm feeling better. Back to normal.

Books have a way of doing that.

Then I'm fighting with the marketing department over the change in plans for a book that I edited several months ago, a book I believe can do incredibly well if given the exposure it needs.

And now it's just half an hour until lunch. Fuck. How much I don't want to sit down with Cole resonates loud inside of me, and I pull out my phone, ready to text Luke. But as soon as I unlock the screen, he calls me. I answer on the second ring.

"Hey," he says, sounding surprised I answered.

"Luke, hi."

"How are you?" he asks, and my heart is not fluttering from the sound of his deep voice.

"All right. It's been a hectic morning. But things are calming down now. What about you?"

"I'm good too. Just got back from the gym. Are you mad at me, Lexi?" he asks, and his bluntness catches me off guard. I don't know what it's like to have the confidence to just say what's on my mind like that.

"Yes. No. Maybe. Wait. Let me start over. No, I'm not mad at you. You have every right to see other women and I should have told you sooner that—"

"Lexi," he interrupts. "I swear to you, I'm not seeing anybody else. I don't want to see anybody else. There's no way anyone in the whole fucking world would compare to you."

I take a breath and stare out the window, brain going a million miles an hour. His words are making me swoon, but I shouldn't believe him. Believing is going to lead to heartache.

"Cole said he heard someone in your room."

"He lied." Luke's words are harsh. Angry.

"Why would he lie?"

"He doesn't like me. I'm sorry, Lexi. You got dragged into a big fucking mess. He doesn't like me and will do anything to take me down. Including hurting others. Don't take it personally."

I lean back in my chair, heart hammering. Russell was the same way. Dead set on hurting me, he didn't care whom he stepped on in the process. "I know someone like that, and they're no picnic." A few seconds pass as I process everything. I'm not sure what to think, and I'm even more clueless to how I should feel.

I've known Cole for years. He's never been anything but nice and professional, making it hard to see him as the vindictive asshole who wants revenge on his younger brother for some reason. Even before I crushed on him, I considered Cole a friend. When I was married, I wished Russell would be more like him. Cole always seemed like such a nice guy.

I feel like I'm walking on eggshells, eggshells that are also ticking time bombs. If dating Luke means my boss will forever hate me, retirement will seem a *long* way off. And if things do work out with Luke? Cole will be my brother-in-law. How fucking awkward is that?

What am I doing?

Luke is right: this is a mess. A hot fucking mess.

"Lexi?"

I shake myself. "Yeah? Sorry. Still here. Just trying to wrap my head around everything."

"Let's meet for lunch. Give me a chance to explain face to face."

"Yeah, that'd be great. Wait, no. I have to work through lunch. Cole, actually, needs to talk to me about the newest book I took on."

"Of course he fucking does," Luke grumbles. "He's playing you, Lexi."

My heart speeds up again and nerves shoot through my body. This is making me so uncomfortable. I don't want to be put between brothers. Not this way.

"I don't know, Luke. There is an issue with the title."

"And that has to be worked out over lunch?"

I shake my head and then realize Luke can't see me. "We work over lunch a lot. Sometimes I like it because I can take an extra long lunch break yet still have it count as work."

"Stop defending Cole."

"I'm not. I...I...." I stammer. "I don't know why you're mad at me."

Luke lets out a breath. "I'm not. Not at all. Lexi I...fuck... I'm not mad," he repeats. "I don't want to upset you. I'm sorry."

I'm not used to men apologizing to me. "It's okay," I tell

him and see Cole leave his office. "I have to go. I'll call you later, okay?"

"Okay," he says and I hear hurt in his voice. "Goodbye, Lexi." His words come out slow and heavy, like it's the final goodbye. And maybe it is. It should be.

I put my phone away and let out a breath. My entire body is tingling, my heart is still beating rapidly, and my cheeks are hot. That was one of the most awkward conversations I've ever had.

Cole knocks on my door and I wave to him through the glass, letting him know I'll be out the door in a second. I grab my purse and sweater, and walk out of the office with Cole. It's a beautiful day, but Cole insists on having the Press's driver chauffeur us three blocks away to the restaurant where he has reservations.

The place is ultra modern, expensive...and packed. "I'm surprised you were able to get a table," I say as we're seated right away.

Cole laughs. "I have my ways."

I order a lemon water and look over the menu. There aren't prices listed with the entrees. Stupid pretentious restaurant. I decide on a salad with salmon, tell the waiter, and then get out my iPad so I can pull up the files and notes I have saved for Katie James' book.

"Worry about that later," Cole says when I bring it up.

"Uh, okay." I put the iPad aside. If the point of going out to lunch was to discuss the book, then why aren't we discussing the book?

"You know," he starts, "my mother was a single mom for many years, working and raising us."

I nod. "She was a nurse, right?"

"Yeah, how did you—oh. He told you."

"Uh, yeah." I fiddle with the cloth napkin in my lap, eyes

landing on the steak knife. I might need it to cut away the tension around us. "He told me."

Cole's brown eyes darken and his face twists into a scowl. Thank God the appetizers arrive. I waste no time digging in, welcoming a distraction.

"Anyway," Cole continues. "I never realized as a child how much she did for us. So I want to make sure you know that you're doing a great job."

"Oh, wow. Thanks." It's a great compliment. Being told I'm a good mom beats out any and everything else. My girls are my number one priority. Doing right by them is more important than anything else.

"I don't think I've ever asked you," he goes on. "Have you always lived in New York?"

I nod, mouth full. "My family is from Brooklyn," I say after I chew and swallow. "What about you? Did you always live here too or did you live in Chicago before?"

Cole raises an eyebrow. "We're from here. Apparently Luke didn't tell you why he moved to Chicago?"

"No, he, uh, hasn't. Not yet."

"He was going to the University of Chicago. Pre-med. And then got kicked out and never moved back home."

I lean back. Blink. Holy information overload. My stomach flip-flops. I take my time eating another piece of bread topped with artichoke dip, looking around the restaurant as if it's interesting.

"I had to confirm the final headcount for the annual Book Cruise this morning. You're not going?"

I shake my head. For the last several years, Black Ink Press has taken part in a book-themed cruise that brings authors, agents, editors, publishers, and even movie producers together. Every year I'd entertained the thought of going, and every year going never happened. "I'd love to go but can't leave my girls."

"It's just five days."

"That's a long time. The weekends are hard enough when they're with their dad."

Cole smiles, a move that used to make my heart go pitter-patter like a schoolgirl. "You deserve a break. And what's better than an all-expense paid cruise to the Bahamas?"

The trip isn't totally free. I'd get a free room on the ship, one of the cheapest and smallest available. Any upgrades that are pretty much required to have a good time are paid for right from my pocket.

"I'm slightly terrified of getting hit with one of those giant waves that flips cruise ships over."

Cole laughs. "That's incredibly unlikely."

I shrug. "I like to play it safe."

Cole tips his head and slowly parts his lips. "Is that really what you're afraid of?" His foot brushes against mine under the table.

What the hell? I shift my weight and cross my legs, moving my foot away from his. Maybe he was just stretching his legs and not insinuating whatever the hell he's insinuating. He can't be.

Because he's my boss.

And I'm falling for his brother.

Wait, what?

Falling? Luke? Me?

No.

Fuck. Yes. I was. *Was.* But I can't. Shouldn't. I need someone who's committed, someone who wants a steady relationship. Luke says he's not seeing anyone else, and I want to believe him. But...I just don't see why Cole would lie.

I clear my throat and go for more of the appetizer. "So, do you have any title suggestions for the book?"

"No. We can have marketing put together a list."

"Good idea." I force a smile and put the bread down, my appetite gone. Cole didn't take me to lunch to talk about the book. That was never his plan.

Luke was right.

And I've completely fucked up.

LUKE

My feet hit the pavement in a steady rhythm. *Alice in Chains* blasts in my ears and I'm focusing on nothing more than moving one foot in front of the other, navigating around the slow joggers on the Central Park Loop. I can't think about anything more or I'll explode from anger. And Cole has to come home at some point tonight. If he's smart, he'll stay away or else he'll be leaving in a body bag in the morning.

Lexi isn't going to call me. She's not going to answer if I call. Cole manipulated her, the sick fucker, and she bought it. I lost her, and the icing on the shit-cake? Cole is going to fucking gloat about this for the rest of his life.

What's even worse is thinking of the pain this caused Lexi. She's been through enough, already had one asshole fuck with her life. Indignation surges through me at the thought of anyone mistreating Lexi and her girls. I pick up the pace, running faster and faster.

And then it hits me.

I'm running away.

Again.

I used to be the one to run in when everyone else ran out. I left Chicago thinking I could never be that man again, that he had died in the fire and was long gone. Fuck that. I'm done running away.

My pulse is pounding but I don't stop, don't give up. I keep running, leaving Central Park and emerging onto the busy streets. Darting through walkers. Around cars.

Anything to get to her.

I have no plan as I get into the elevator. Lexi might not even be here. She could still be at lunch and then what? It doesn't matter. I'll cross that bridge when I come to it. I get off on the wrong floor and have to impatiently wait for the elevator to come back down. It works out in my favor, though, because as soon as the doors open up on the right floor, I see Lexi.

She's walking next to Cole, her back to me, and is tense. She's uncomfortable with whatever the fucker is saying to her. He says something and laughs at his own joke. Lexi forces a smile and turns her head to look up at him, being the polite person she is. I don't know what makes her turn around, but she does and her eyes meet mine.

"Luke," she whispers. Cole whips around, face paling. I stride forward, grab Lexi by the waist, and put my lips to hers. She's frozen in place, but the initial shock wears off after only a second. Lexi's arms fold around my shoulders, and I dip her back, tongue pushing into her mouth.

Someone inside the office cheers and another cat-calls. But we don't stop kissing. My heart is on my sleeve and I'm giving this my all. I stand Lexi upright and break away, keeping my face just inches from hers.

"You are the only one I want to kiss. The only one I want to fuck. The only one I want to be with. There is no one else."

"Luke," she whispers. "You were right about everything. I'm sorry." Tears pool in her eyes. She blinks them away and kisses me, hands landing on my cheeks so she can bring my mouth to hers.

"Don't apologize."

Lexi lets out a deep breath and visibly relaxes. She rests her head against my chest, and I protectively wrap my arms around her, moving my gaze to my brother. His eyes meet mine, full of rage. I shake my head, trying to let him know I don't want to cause a scene at Lexi's work. Which happens to be his as well. Cole narrows his eyes in a threat, letting me know we'll pick this up later, but goes into his office, shutting the door.

"What are you doing here?" Lexi asks.

"I wasn't going to let him take you away from me. I had to show you I mean it: I don't want anyone else but you."

A tear rolls down her cheek. I catch it with my finger and wipe it away.

"Sorry." She wipes her eyes. "No one has ever told me that before."

"Get used to hearing it."

I kiss her forehead, heart still racing. "You don't have any more time left for lunch do you?"

"No, why?"

"I might have been hoping for a quickie in a broom closet."

She raises her eyebrows. "What about a blow job in the bathroom?"

"Are you...really...you'd do that?"

Lexi laughs and shakes her head. "Not in the bathroom. I don't want to smell other people's shit while your dick is in my mouth."

"I'm not sure how far I can take this joke before it crosses a line."

"If you're referring to blumpkins, that's too far."

"It's a bit shocking you know what those are."

Lexi shrugs. "After I told you about vaginal knitting nothing should shock you anymore."

"I will never find another woman like you." I kiss her one more time, and then step back. "I don't want to cause trouble here for you. Well, any more trouble."

She nods and runs her hand over her hair. "I'm not going to have to come identify you or Cole at the morgue, am I?"

"Nah, our mother will do that."

"I'm serious, Luke. If Cole could kill you with psychic powers, you'd be dead on the floor. I saw the way he was looking at you. What are you going to do?"

"Avoid him? Lock my door when I sleep and don't leave my drinks unattended. And I promise not to kill him."

"That's so convincing." She looks up into my eyes. "So...we're good?"

"Yes. Let's pretend this never happened. I want you, and everything is perfect."

"And the date is still on for Friday?"

"I always intended on taking you to dinner and then making you come so hard you can't walk the next day."

Lexi's green eyes widen and she tries not to smile. Tries, and fails. "People might hear you!"

"I don't care."

She covers her face with her hand and shakes her head. "I'm looking forward to our date Friday."

I kiss her once more, lips lingering. "Me too."

LEXI

*M*e: *There's no way the date is happening tonight.*
Luke: *Is everything okay?*

Me: *Girls are still sick. I'm exhausted, crabby, and don't feel well myself now.*

Luke: *That's two days of you getting no sleep and not feeling well. I'm coming over. Don't try to convince me otherwise.*

I put the phone down and close my eyes for half a second. Then Paige sits up, reaching for the trashcan.

"Here you go, baby," I say and hold her hair back. There is nothing worse than seeing my babies sick. I got a call from Grace's school around ten yesterday morning saying she had thrown up. I called Russell asking if he could get her and let her hang out at his house until I could get there, but he didn't answer my call or return my message. Refusing to let my poor girl sit and be sick inside the nurse's office, I had Mom pick her up. And now Mom has the flu.

We made it through Thursday night only to wake up to sweet little Paige dealing with the nasty stomach bug. Grace is keeping food down but still has a fever, and Paige seems to be—hopefully—at the end. Taking care of sick kids is physically exhausting and emotionally taxing. And I'm not sure if that slight stomachache I have is the start of something more than feeling nauseous from lack of sleep.

I re-band Paige's ponytail, help her take a sip of water, and then get up to empty the trashcan and recheck Grace's temperature. I realize I forgot to feed Pluto dinner in all the chaos. I give him extra to make up for it, and text Luke back.

Me: *I won't.*

Luke: *I'm on my way.*

Relief floods through me, and I'm anxious to see Luke. I haven't been able to talk to him much since Vommageddon started, and I was only at work a few hours before leaving to get Grace. Cole was in a meeting with one of the owners of Black Ink, and I was able to avoid seeing him all together, which worked out perfectly since he avoided me like the plague the rest of Wednesday.

The kiss was the talk of the office the rest of that day, and I told people the guy I was seeing was out for a run and decided to surprise me. Which is the truth, just not the whole truth. And I also left out the part where Luke is Cole's brother. I didn't lie about that, not technically. Just left that out as well.

I help Grace get into the bathtub, dealing with a mini tantrum about the water temperature. She likes it hot, but has a fever and can't do that tonight. Then I pick up as much as I can around the house, and make sure Grace is washed and rinsed before she gets out and dressed.

Paige is next for a bath, and cries the whole time because she doesn't feel well. It breaks my heart that she doesn't understand a quick wash to clean the barf from her hair will make her feel better in the end, and *not* fighting me will make this whole process go a lot faster. I get her dressed and wrapped up in blankets on the couch, turning

Disney Junior on the TV. She's asleep before Luke gets here.

Pluto wags his tail and jumps with excitement. He's a medium sized dog, tall and leggy but doesn't weigh more than forty pounds. Still, it's annoying to have a dog jump all over you.

"Hey, babe," Luke steps inside and pulls me in for a hug.

"You shouldn't get too close. And no kisses."

"The flu is airborne," he says. "I'm already exposed just standing here. So I will kiss you if I want to."

"Fine," I say and lean up. Luke's kiss doesn't disappoint and even though I'm feeling fifty shades of shitty right now, it awakens little nerves throughout my body. "What's this?" I ask, taking a grocery bag from him.

"Ingredients to make you chicken noodle soup."

"You don't have to do that."

"I know I don't. I want to. I'm here to take care of you, Lexi." He kisses me again, and then takes off his shoes and follows me in. Paige is still sleeping on the couch, and Grace is curled up next to her watching TV. She sits up and watches Luke for a few seconds before turning to me, waving me to come over.

"Is that the same guy who had lunch with us after the American Girl Place?"

"He is. This is my friend, Luke." I turn back to Luke and motion for him to come over. "Do you remember him?"

"Yeah." Grace smiles, getting shy like kids do. "He's the Flynn Rider guy."

"Right. He's here to help me take care of you girls and is going to make us soup."

"Can I help?"

I push Grace's long hair back out of her face. "Maybe

another time, sweetheart. You're still sick and I want you to rest."

Grace makes a face, and the attitude actually makes me happy. She must be feeling better. "Fine." I kiss her forehead and remind her to take small sips of water every once in a while to keep from getting dehydrated.

Luke and I go into the kitchen, and I set the bag of food on the counter. "Sorry about the mess," I say. "Washing dishes wasn't a priority the last two days."

"I understand. I'll help."

"Being here is more than enough help on its own. Thank you."

"You don't have to thank me. Taking care of my girlfriend when she's sick shouldn't be out of the ordinary."

Towards the end of our marriage, Russell would get mad at me if I was sick. And if that sickness lasted longer than twenty-four hours, I was faking it for attention. And that included the morning sickness I had when I was pregnant with Paige. He claimed I made myself throw up for thirteen weeks straight to get out of heavy housework.

"Well, it's nice." I open the dishwasher and make a face at the smell. It really should have been run yesterday. I try loading it with lightning speed before Luke gets hit with the scent of several day-old milk cups. Pluto rushes over and starts licking the dishes. I shove as much as I can into the dishwasher, and start it up on a heavy cycle.

"I'll vacuum later," I say, brushing dog food crumbs into a pile, and grab a broom and dustpan from the hall closet. "I don't want to wake Paige up." I sweep up the crumbs and dump them in the garbage. Sometimes when I'm feeling really bad about my housekeeping—or lack thereof—I watch an episode of *Hoarders* and instantly feel better.

Works every time. The glass of wine I have while I'm watching doesn't hurt either.

"I'll take care of it," Luke tells me. "Go lay down or shower or something."

My head is throbbing and I want so desperately to lie down and close my eyes. Or shower. I know I have the faint smell of kid-puke clinging to my skin. And probably on these PJ pants.

"I can help you with the soup."

"No," he says defiantly.

"You don't mind making it by yourself?"

"That's why I came over. Go rest."

"I'm fine."

He raises an eyebrow. "Really? You're perfectly fine."

"I might be slightly achy."

"Slightly?"

"Everything hurts and I'm dying. Better?"

"Much. So go get some sleep."

"Okay, the girls—"

"I can handle it," he interrupts, looking through the doorway at Grace and Paige, who are still both on the couch. "Go. Don't make me carry you to bed. You need sleep, especially if you're fighting the same flu the girls have."

Tears well in my eyes, and I hurry up to my room before Luke has a chance to see. I'm thinking hard, and cannot come up with a time where Russ took care of me like this. Not even in college when we first met. Actually, the first time I was sick—really sick—he was a mixture of concerned and annoyed that we missed a party. In fact, he sat with me for a while as I hacked up a lung from pneumonia, huffing and puffing about being bored, and left with his rock solid rationalization that he shouldn't be around me so he wouldn't get sick.

He left me alone in the University urgent care to go to that party.

Why the fuck did I marry him? Just thinking about it embarrasses me. Causes me shame. The bad times shadowed the good even before I became Mrs. Winters. It's done and over. I can't change the past, can't take back what is done. I can only grow and learn from it.

I take a shower, and lay down in bed still wrapped in a towel for what will only be a "couple minutes" before I go downstairs and check on the girls and make sure Luke can find what he needs to make us soup.

Two hours later, I wake up. I sit up, a bit of panic going through me. Luke is watching my kids. I should check on them. Now. I rake my fingers through my hair, twist it into a bun and get dressed. I'm halfway down the stairs when I realize that this will be the first time Luke sees me with no makeup and super messy hair. My socks don't match, I'm not entirely sure my leggings aren't on backwards, and I'm wearing an oversized t-shirt that says "Harlow's Harlots". Explaining that it's the name of a fan group for Quinn Harlow will most likely slip my mind and he'll be left wondering, not that I care.

I could go back up the stairs, put on makeup and brush my hair. Or I could get this over with now. Break the ice and keep things real.

I go with the latter, and descend the rest of the steps. The stairs empty into the hall that runs behind the living room, and I can hear Luke's voice before I reach the last step. I slow, and look in. Grace is passed out now, but Paige is up and sitting close next to Luke as he reads to her.

Be still my heart.

I cover my mouth with my hand and smile. Pluto spots me and jumps off the couch, giving me away.

"That was a short nap," Luke says, turning around. His eyes meet mine and he doesn't recoil from the sight of me. Which is good, because this is how I look 90% of the time when I'm not at work. He smiles, and my heart melts. Having a man look at me like that—in all my sick glory— is something I've always wanted. I wanted it bad enough to try to make things work with Russell, to put up with the heartache in hopes things could work out. I've wanted it so fucking bad that now that I have it, I'm terrified of losing it.

"I didn't really mean to fall asleep."

"Mama," Paige coos and turns around. "We're reading Olivia Pig!"

"How are you feeling, baby?"

"Good. I want milk."

"She's been asking for it," Luke tells me. "I assume that's a no from you too, right? I told her we'd ask you."

I nod. "Let's give your tummy a little bit longer. You can have Jell-O and some soup."

"I already had soup," she pouts. "Bring me milk!"

"Paige," I say sternly. "We talked about demanding stuff."

"Please?" she adds.

"In a bit. You don't want to get sick again, right?"

She makes a face and leans back on the couch. I sit on Luke's other side, and he puts his hand on my thigh. It's a small gesture, and I don't think Paige will even notice. Luke and I are only seeing each other, but it's still too soon to bring the girls into this. For now, Luke is just my friend in front of them.

"Can we do popcorn and a movie?" Paige asks.

"We can watch a movie," I say. "But let's do Saltines instead of popcorn." Paige grumbles again being overdramatic about crackers, making Luke and me laugh. I get up to get crackers and water for Paige, and soup for myself.

"Hey," Luke says to her. "That guy...Fin Rider...what's he in?"

"Flynn," Paige corrects. "He's in *Tangled*. I have that movie. It's my favorite!"

"Let's watch it."

Paige jumps off the couch and flies to the entertainment cabinet to get the movie.

"Kids recover so fast," Luke says. "The flu knocks me out for a week. I feel old."

"It has nothing to do with your age," I tell him and pop the movie in. Paige runs back to the couch, and Pluto jumps up next to her, trying to steal her crackers. "It's because you're a man."

"That's low."

I laugh. "Right, it is. I mean, you do have a genetic predisposition to walk the line of life and death every time you get a cold. The flu is no laughing matter."

Paige rests her head on me, and I rest my head on Luke. He casually slips his arm around me, and things seem right in the world. Once the movie ends, I get both girls into bed, let Pluto out, and then sit on the couch with Luke once more, flipping through Netflix to find something to watch.

Halfway through the action movie Luke picked, I fall asleep. He gently shakes me awake when it's over, offering to carry me into my room.

"I can walk," I tell him, rubbing my eyes. "But thanks."

I stand and stretch, then wrap my arms around Luke's body. I can feel his muscles through his thin t-shirt, and he smells intoxicating, a mixture of cologne and the scent of leather that clings to his skin from his jacket. I step closer, hips against his.

"Feeling any better?" he asks.

"I am, thanks to you."

"Good." He pulls me closer, and I can feel the outline of his dick through his sweatpants. He's not even hard, yet feeling that thing against me is a turn on. "Should I sleep on the couch?"

"I'm not sure. Probably. Maybe? I don't know." I look into Luke's blue eyes. "Dating with kids is confusing. I'm not sure what's right or wrong, and I'm just going off of what I've been reading on the internet. The general consensus is to go with what feels right, and what we're doing right now does. I *want* you to come to bed with me, and the fact that you even offered to sleep on the couch makes me want you even more."

"Well then," he says and raises his eyebrows. "I think it's settled."

I take his hand. "Yes, it is."

We go upstairs to get ready for bed. I dig through the linen closet for an extra toothbrush for Luke, who goes into the bathroom once I'm out. I close my bedroom door and get into bed, debating on changing into a sexier nightie rather than my Harry Potter pajamas. But as soon as my head hits the pillow, I'm overcome with tiredness, and the only way these PJs are coming off is if someone else takes them off for me.

Which just might happen. And suddenly, I'm nervous. I'm not worried about us being heard or even having one of the kids walk in on us. I can be quiet and the door does have a lock. What scares me is how this is working out. Everything I thought impossible is happening.

I met a great guy who accepts me *and* my children. A guy who I look at and see potential for something more. Something lasting.

And I'm fucking terrified of losing this.

Luke comes out of the bathroom and strips down to his boxers. I admire the dark shadows casting over his body as he climbs into bed, immediately wrapping his arms around me. I hook my leg over his and put my lips to his. Luke moves a hand to my face, cupping my cheek before sliding his hand to the back of my head.

The man knows how to kiss.

The kiss leads to other things he knows how to do, and only minutes later I'm moaning into my pillow with his head between my legs. Twenty minutes after that, we're both panting, satisfied, and ready to sleep. Or at least I am. Though I'll gladly lose sleep for sex with Luke.

We get redressed, and I slip out of the room to check on the girls. Pluto is in bed with Grace, tucked under the covers right next to her, and Paige is sound asleep. I give each girl a kiss then get back in bed with Luke. He cuddles with me, wrapping his body around mine and softly stroking my hair until I fall asleep.

I could get used to this. I *want* to get used to this.

"Goodnight, Luke," I whisper.

He kisses the back of my neck. "Night, Lexi."

I close my eyes and fall asleep in just minutes, and sleep soundly for the next six hours. Someone knocking on the door wakes me up way too early. Pluto barks and runs downstairs and into the small foyer. He barks a few more times, then stops.

"Expecting someone?" Luke grumbles.

"No. Maybe it's telemarketers. Except not the ones that call but go door-to-door. They have a name, but I'm too tired to think of it."

Luke chuckles. "Want me to tell them to get the hell off your porch?"

"Nah, they'll leave in a minute." I reach for my phone to check the time, and remember I left it downstairs in the living room. Judging by the sunlight coming in the window, it's right around seven AM. I roll over and put my head on Luke's chest. He folds his arms around me and pulls the blanket up to my shoulders. I'm falling asleep when someone knocks again, causing Pluto to bark.

Luke sits up. "I'm going to tell them to fuck off."

"Okay."

I stretch out, watching Luke step into his sweatpants and walk out of the room. Sunlight hits the patch of scar tissue on his back. It starts at the base of his neck, goes over his right shoulder and extends to his midback. My knowledge on burns is zilch. But I do know whatever happened to Luke had to be incredibly painful. Is it still painful? I've run my hands up and down his back many times and he's never so much as flinched.

The sound of the deadbolt shooting back echoes up the stairs. The master bedroom is the first one off the stairs, and voices carry right up here. Pluto's tags jingle as Luke opens the door.

"Who the hell are you?" the person on the porch asks. I shoot up. You have got to be fucking kidding me. What is he doing here?

"Who the hell are *you* and what are you doing knocking on the door so fucking early?" Luke throws back.

"I'm here to see my kids."

chapter twenty-four

LUKE

I immediately size up the jerk who hurt Lexi. He's not as tall as me, and nowhere near as built. I can't fault him for being bad-looking, and he's well dressed and put together for being so early on a Saturday.

"Get the hell out of my way," Lexi's ex says, trying to push his way past me. I square my shoulders and don't move.

"Russell." Lexi comes down the stairs, anger spread across her pretty face. "What are you doing? You woke me up." Lexi's eyes meet mine and she gives me a tiny nod, signaling me to step aside and let the asshole in. The dog goes crazy to see him, and the guy just stands there ignoring the pup.

Russell eyes me up and down, staring at my tattoos a moment too long. "I can see that. Who is this?"

Trying to be decent, I give the guy the benefit of the doubt. His kids are in here, and a strange man answered the door. "I'm Luke," I say and extend my hand. "Lexi's boyfriend."

He doesn't shake my hand. Instead, his nostrils flare and he turns to Lexi. "How long as this been going on?"

"A month or two—it doesn't matter," Lexi says. "What are you doing here?"

"The better question is what are you doing here?"

"Oh, grow up," Lexi shoots back.

"You're the one not acting very grown up."

Lexi lets out an exasperated sigh. "What do you want?"

"I wanted to check on the girls and see if you needed anything. I figured you could use some help but I see you have that covered. Are they still sick?"

"They seem better, and they're still sleeping. Don't wake them up."

"I'm not going to wake them up," he snaps, still ignoring the dog who's doing everything he can to get his attention.

"Say hi to Pluto," Lexi tells him.

Russell rolls his eyes but pets the dog. It's weird knowing there was a time when the dog and the ex lived together in this house. Lexi sighs. "We're fine. I'll tell the girls you stopped by."

"I'm here to see my kids. You can't make me leave. Especially with him here. I'm not sure I want him around *my* girls."

"Luke has met the girls before and they like him."

Just then, one of the girls—I can't tell which one—calls for Lexi.

"Hang on, sweet pea," Lexi quietly replies. "I'll be right there."

"I got it," Russell says and goes through the living room to the stairs.

Lexi turns to me. "So, that's my ex. This is shaping up to be a great weekend."

"It's fine. I figured I'd meet your ex sooner or later. I didn't figure I'd be half naked when I met him though."

Lexi smiles and shakes her head. She still looks tired, and I want her to go back to bed, get some more sleep, and let me make her breakfast later. We go into the kitchen and Lexi heads straight for the coffee pot. She stops and looks at the oven for several seconds.

"Did you clean up or am I going completely crazy?"

"I did. When you were sleeping."

The smile is back on her face again. I'll do anything to make her smile. To hear her laugh. To make her happy.

She sits with me on the couch while the coffee brews, resting her head on my shoulder. A few minutes later, her ex comes down the stairs.

"Paige was thirsty. I let her have a bit of water and she's back asleep now," he says. "Do you want me to take them later so you can rest?"

Lexi shakes her head. "No, they should just stay home."

"My house is their home too."

"You know what I mean. They should stay put. The last thing they need is to be stuck in the car for half an hour when they could very well get sick again. You can stay and hang out with them here. I don't care."

Russell just nods and stares at me. He's judging, not that I give a fuck. "Lexi, can I talk to you privately?"

"I really don't want to get up," she grumbles. "Can it wait?"

"It's about the girls."

"Fine."

I put my hand on her thigh. "You stay. I'll go upstairs and get dressed."

"Thank you."

"Of course." I kiss her and hope it pisses off her ex. What

an idiot to let Lexi go. Though if things hadn't played out the way they did, Lexi and I wouldn't have met.

"What?" Lexi asks her ex. I slowly go up the stairs, still able to hear their conversation.

"You let a man sleep over?"

"Don't even start," she tells him. "You have a girlfriend. You've had a girlfriend—multiple girlfriends at that—since the day we split."

"But I don't have them stay the night when the girls are with me."

"If I could roll my eyes any harder, they'd get stuck in the back of my head. That one with the fake tits, Botox and lip injections lived with you for a few months."

"This is something we need to talk about, to agree on."

"You have got to be fucking kidding me," Lexi says. "You want me to get you to agree on whoever I date?"

"You can't just bring strange men into the house with my kids, Alexis. I do get a say on that."

"No, you don't. I don't say shit about the women you date, and you've dated some real winners."

"That's not the point!" Russell yells. "You let a man I don't know sleep in the same house as my girls. That's not okay with me!"

"You know why he stayed the night? He stayed so he could take care of me and help with the girls. You know being up for two days with sick kids isn't easy. Luke isn't the girls' father and yet he put in more than you did the last few days."

I smile at Lexi's words and go into the bathroom. Once I close the door, I can't hear anything else that's said. I get dressed, brush my teeth, and move to the top of the stairs. I need to hear the exchange of words to know if I should give Lexi space or tell her ex to shove off. All is quiet below, and when I go down, I find Lexi sitting on the couch with her eyes closed.

I grab a blanket and sit next to her, pulling her in my lap and covering her up. "Go back to sleep."

"I was kinda thinking I should work. I'm so behind."

"Work can wait. You look exhausted, Lex."

"I am. Just a bit."

I kiss her forehead and run my hands over her hair, having noticed that helps her relax. She rolls over, gets comfortable, and falls asleep in just minutes. Pluto jumps up and weasels his way under the blanket covering Lexi. I laugh and lean back on the couch, not wanting this to end.

Lexi is unlike anyone I've ever met before. She's making me want things I never knew I wanted. I want to keep seeing Lexi. I want to get to know her better, to have her fall for me like I am for her. I like this: the house, the dog, and even the kids. I want to keep going, keep seeing each other and growing closer and leave the past behind me.

For good.

Never talk about it. Never think about. Never go back. Never bring it up.

I want to let it burn. Though I of all people know it's dangerous to play with fire.

"Dammit," Cole mutters when I walk into the kitchen Sunday evening. I stayed with Lexi all weekend, playing with the girls so she could sleep and then catch up on her emails. I played princesses and dolls, and every other fingernail is painted hot pink, courtesy of Grace. "I was hoping you were gone for good."

"Yeah. Gone and left all my stuff."

"That didn't stop you before."

I freeze in the threshold of the doorway. Cole is sitting on the couch reading a book. He doesn't look up from the pages as he speaks.

"Picking up and leaving everyone and everything behind is kind of your thing, isn't it?"

My fingers curl into my palms, nails digging into my skin. "You know what happened." My heart hammers in my chest and my nostrils flare. "Seventeen days. That's how long I was in the hospital, and you never once came to see me. You don't fucking care about anyone other than yourself, do you?"

"The same can be said for you," Cole retorts, keeping his cool. His lack of emotion pisses me off even more, and I know he's doing it on purpose.

"Bullshit! I've never done anything to you."

Cole looks up from his book. "You really think so? You know exactly what you did."

"I have no idea what the hell you're talking about. I left. Went away to college and stayed away. It's impossible that I did something so horrible it caused you to hate me like this."

Cole stands, slamming the book shut. "It's what you didn't do, and you goddamn know it." He throws his book onto the floor. "Someday the same thing is going to happen to you, and hearing you deny everything makes me that much more excited for the day it does."

I shake my head, having no idea what the fuck Cole is talking about. "Whatever shit you're holding onto, let it go. Lexi and I are together, and nothing you try to do can stop it."

"Try?" Cole laughs. "I'm not trying at all. When I do try, you'll know. Trust me."

LEXI

"So when you say he made you soup, you mean he opened a can and microwaved it, right?" Erin asks. It's Monday morning, and we're having lunch together, along with Lori and Jillian. I brought them up to speed on everything that's happened between Luke and I...including that one person he's related to.

"No. I mean he chopped up carrots and celery and cooked the chicken himself."

Lori puts her hand to her chest. "That is so sweet. He's a keeper, that's for sure."

I reach for my water and nod. "So far things are going great. Well, besides the constant storm cloud of awkwardness that comes from dating your boss's brother."

"And you have no idea why they don't get along?" Erin asks.

I shake my head. "Luke told me they never really did as kids, and it just got worse as they got older. I think Luke eggs Cole on a little bit, but none of it makes sense to me."

"What if you and Luke get married?" Lori starts. "Then

Cole will be your brother-in-law. You'll see him at Christmas and birthdays."

"Dude, no. I don't even want to think about marriage," I say, even though I already entertained the thought for half a second. "And really, I don't know if I want to get married again. It didn't work out so well for me the first time."

"But what if Luke wants to get married? You shouldn't date him if you don't want to get married."

"She'll cross that bridge when she comes to it," Jillian says and flicks her gaze to me. I give her a look that says "thank you", and agree with her. I love Lori and know she means well, but she has a hard time accepting the fact that not every woman wants to get married, have babies, and live traditionally.

"Right. It hasn't been that long yet."

"Speaking of not long," Erin starts. "The Ink and Paper Gala is coming up fast."

"I already got my dress," Jillian says. "Like three weeks ago. Maybe four."

Black Ink Press has put on a literacy gala every year, honoring our authors and celebrating the behind-the-scenes workers who bring the books to life. It's a huge event, with celebrities and famous authors attending. I've gone before, enjoyed the ever-loving shit out of it, and hadn't been able to go since the divorce.

"I have something picked out too," Lori says. "And I rented a tux for the hubs. It's going to be so fun!"

All eyes fall on me. "I'm not sure if I can go."

Jillian shakes her head. "No. Not accepting that answer. Especially since you have a sexy date to bring with you."

"Oh, right." Part of not going last year might have been slightly related to being dateless, as much as it kills me to admit. "When is it?"

"It's the same weekend as always." Jillian looks baffled. "How did you forget about it? Haven't you seen the hideously designed flyers for it all over the office? This is the biggest social event of the summer. Early summer. Okay, May. The Literary Gala in February is the biggest."

I shrug. "Half the time, I don't know what day it is unless I check it on my phone. I kinda stopped going to events the last few years. And I like them, well the ones that serve free wine, but it's just not feasible as a single mom." The tickets might be free, but the dresses aren't. Neither is getting my hair and makeup done. I'm putting every spare penny toward a trip to Disney World. The smiles on the girls' faces will make it all worth it.

"Quinn Harlow is up for an award," Jillian reminds me. "You have to be there. She's going to thank you in her speech if she wins."

"When she wins," I correct. "When is it?"

"Next weekend. And I can get you a dress. My cousin is doing PR for an up-and-coming designer and is pretty much begging people to wear his stuff as long as you can be photographed and tagged on social media. And the gala is perfect for free exposure for a new designer."

Russell has the girls this weekend. Which means I have them next weekend, and don't want to lose a night with them. But...shit. Wearing a fancy dress, getting all dolled up, and stuffing my face with the free all-you-can-eat buffet catered by some of the finest chefs in New York City is tempting. Quinn is nominated for an award, and I should be there for her.

And Luke will be in a suit.

"I'll make it work," I say. Mom and Dad will gladly take the girls for a sleepover.

"And I snagged two rooms reserved on our block at the

hotel. Paid for by Black Ink, thank you very much." Jillian beams. "This was pre-Luke too. I was going to make you go and have a one-night stand with some aspiring author who'd do anything—and I mean *anything*—to get his, ahem, novel in the gentle yet rough hands of an experienced editor."

I raise an eyebrow. "You have issues."

She smiles again. "I know."

"Tell me more about Luke," Erin requests. "Do your kids like him?"

"They love him." I'm unable to hide my smile as I tell them about Luke playing with the girls over the weekend. "But for now, he's just a friend when we're around them. No handholding, no kissing...nothing like that in front of them. When he stayed the night this weekend, we made sure the kids didn't see him in my bedroom."

"How'd you swing that?"

"It's easy. They went to bed before us and Luke got up and moved to the couch in the morning. Well, Sunday. Saturday, Russell decided to play the role of decent human being for a change and came over to check on the girls."

"I bet that was fun." Erin shakes her head. "Did he give you hell?"

"Not enough. I'm sure I'll get an earful when I drop the girls off this weekend. He acted so appalled, like the thought of someone else wanting to be with me is wrong."

"Maybe he was jealous," Lori suggests. "Seeing you with another man might have upset him."

"That's his problem if it did," I say.

"So why'd Luke move here?" Erin opens her menu and skims over it. We're at the Salad Bar again, and she always orders the same thing. Why she even bothers to look at a menu is beyond me.

"I don't really know. He doesn't talk about his past. I've tried to get him to tell me about it and he changes the subject. I think something bad happened."

"What do you mean?" Jillian asks.

"He was a firefighter—"

Jillian's eyes go wide. "You're fucking with me right? You're dating this gorgeous guy who used to be a firefighter and you're just now telling me?"

"Yeah. Shoot me. Anyway, he has a burn on his shoulder and back, and I don't think it's an old scar. I thought about just asking him, but I either chicken out or the timing feels wrong."

"Interesting. Do you want me to try and get intel from Cole?" Jillian offers.

"No," I rush out. I haven't told anyone the extent of Cole's disdain for Luke, including how he took me out for a very inappropriate lunch and openly hit on me. "I'll talk to Luke about it when the time is right."

We order our food, and I text Luke to tell him about the gala.

Me: *So there's a fancy book party on the 19th. Want to be my date??*

Luke: *What's a fancy book party? And yes to being your date. I'll be your date anywhere, even a vaginal knitting live-action show.*

I laugh and start typing an explanation of what the event is.

"What's so funny?" Erin asks. "Did he send you a dick pic?"

"Ohh, let me see if he did!" Jillian leans over.

"I wouldn't laugh if he sent me a dick pic. Trust me. And he just makes me laugh."

"Awww," Lori swoons. "You're made for each other."

"Maybe." I put the phone down, trying not to think too much into it. Because every day, I see more and more promise of a future with Luke.

~

"Hey, Alexis," Cole says. I walk into the break room after lunch to refill my coffee mug, and Cole is standing at the counter, doing the same. He has a personal assistant. He really needs to start sending her to get his coffee for him like a proper asshole boss. "How are you?"

"I'm good. Finally feeling better, thanks. You?"

"Still dealing with that UK debacle, but we're making headway."

It's the first time Cole and I had a real conversation since Luke stormed the place and kissed me like he only had one kiss left to give. I wonder if it's weird for Cole to know that his brother is having sex with me, that Luke and I are getting naked and sweaty and doing bad things to each other. Bad things that feel so good. When he looks at me, does he remember my porn-star screams from that fateful night? Should I be embarrassed about it? Is he imagining me sans clothing, tangled up in Luke?

And now my mind jumps to wondering if Luke and Cole are alike in other aspects. They might not get along, but they are related, and most siblings have things in common, be it an allergy to fabric softener to a likeness in looks. Or dick size. Fuck. No. Don't go there.

God, I'm awkward even in my own head.

"Can I do anything to help?"

Cole laughs. "Be Emma's new editor?"

I laugh too, and then realize he's serious. "I don't know.

Those books border on horror, right? I don't think I'm right for the job."

"You've done a great job with Katie James' book, and that's paranormal."

"It's heavy on the romance and not very scary. Though she did say book two gets more intense."

"*The Fake Wife* is a thriller."

"It gave me nightmares months after I turned in the edits. And it wasn't about demons."

Cole laughs. "Well, if you change your mind, let me know. And, uh, don't mention this. I only asked you because I trust your judgment. With books," he adds quickly.

"I will."

Cole smiles, pops a top on his coffee, and goes back into his office. I let out the biggest sigh of relief. We had a normal exchange. Normal, and pleasant. Maybe, just maybe, things will work out.

Then again, if it seems too good to be true, it probably is.

"Are you still bleeding?" Kara leans over the sink, watching blood water swirl down the drain.

"Not really, but my finger stings like motherfucker." I don't like blood. Especially my own blood when it's outside of my body. "It's a tiny cut. Why is it hurting so much?"

"Maybe you hit a nerve?" my sister suggests. I turn off the water when the doorbell rings. "Can you get that, Jeff?"

"It's fine," I say and grab a towel, wrapping it around my hand. The Friday night date that was supposed to happen last week is happening now. Jillian and her boyfriend are meeting us. I feel bad making Luke drive all this way only to go back into the city, but we'd rather stay the night here—

alone—than hit the sheets at his place when Cole is home. I open the door for Luke, using my foot to hold Pluto back.

Luke slips inside, bending down to pet the excited pup, and then gives me a hug and a kiss. He's dressed in dark jeans and a black shirt, and looks like he walked off a GQ photo shoot featuring the bad boy your mother warned you about.

Only, Luke is a damn good man.

"What's this?" he asks, taking my hand in his and carefully peels the towel back.

"Nothing." I shake my head, smiling to cover up my embarrassment. "I cut my finger on the metal edge when I tore off a piece of cling-wrap. It's not bleeding anymore, but it stings."

Luke brings my hand closer to his face, inspecting the little wound. "That's because you have a piece of metal stuck under your skin."

I make a face and shudder. "Well, crap."

"Bring me tweezers and I'll get it out."

"You say that like it's not a big deal."

"It's not," he says. "I was an EMT before I was a firefighter, and the training is required anyway."

"Oh, lucky for me." I look up at Luke. The stubble on his face has grown out into a neatly trimmed beard, which looks incredibly sexy on him. His blue eyes sparkle like deep pools of water, and suddenly, I'm dying of thirst.

"Lexi," Kara calls from the kitchen. I know she's already creeped around the corner to get a look at Luke. "How's the finger? Should I call an ambulance?"

"She's dying to meet you," I warn Luke, and lead him through the living room and into the kitchen. We go through introductions, and then Luke and I sit at the table so he can perform minor surgery on my finger.

He holds an ice cube over the metal splinter for a minute before going in with the tweezers. I close my eyes and look away, and just seconds later he's done.

"I only have Disney Princess band aids," I say as he wraps one around the cut. "Life with little girls, right?"

He smiles. "It gets the job done, and I'm digging the pink."

The four of us pile into Kara and Jeff's SUV. Luke sits in the back next to me, and takes my hand in his as we head off to the city. Jeff and Luke talk sports most the way, with Jeff giving Luke a hard time about being a Bears fan, and talking about how awesome of an experience it was for Luke to go to two of the Cubs' games when they won the World Series.

An accident slows our trip into the city, and Jillian and Aaron are already at the table with drinks by the time we finally show up.

"Luke, this is my friend Jillian and her boyfriend Aaron," I introduce. Luke shakes Aaron's hand and pulls the chair out for me. "Jillian works with me."

"Ah, so you know my brother," Luke tells her and takes a seat next to me.

"That I do. And I have to say, you two look nothing alike," Jillian says.

Luke laughs. "I like her," he whisper-talks to me. The rest of the night goes by smooth as honey. We talk. We laugh. We all get along and Luke fits in with my little circle of friends.

Luke's phone rings right after dessert is put on the table. He pulls it from his pocket, looks at the screen, and frowns. He silences the call and slips his phone away, but his whole demeanor has changed. He doesn't pick up his fork. Doesn't reach for the beer the waitress just set in front of him. It's like he's been frozen, and he sits unmoving for a good minute. Slowly, he reaches to his right shoulder and touches the little patch of burned skin that's visible and not covered by his shirt. He stares forward, unblinking.

I put my hand on his thigh, and my touch is all it takes to thaw him. He puts his hand over mine and turns to me, stealing a kiss. Everyone else is still talking, not having noticed Luke's weird behavior. He goes back to talking to the guys, and Kara, Jillian, and I get up to use the bathroom.

"Please tell me you're still not wondering if this is going to work," Kara says as soon as we're away from the table. "I'd fight you for him if I believed in violence. And if I wasn't married."

"I know, right?" Jillian says. "He's a total catch and is crazy about you, Lex. I can tell just by the way he's looking at you."

"I agree. I think you guys have a good thing going. His energy is a bit chaotic, but yours is a total disaster, so it works."

"Hah, funny," I tell my sister. "And yes, of course I agree and want things to work out. I'm still not sure about his long-term goals, but we can worry about that later, right?"

"Right," they say in unison.

"Get to know him, let him get to know you, and take things slow," Jillian says. "And enjoy the sex."

"Oh, I am."

"I have a really good feeling about him," Kara assures me. "Taking care of you when you're sick and playing down your relationship for the sake of your kids says a lot about him."

We use the bathroom and head back to the table. Maybe it's the wine, or maybe everything my sister and Jillian said is true and a year from now Luke will still be in the picture. Thinking that far ahead is definitely from the wine.

The bill comes and Luke takes it before I have a chance to ask if he wants to split it. He sets his phone on the table and pulls a credit card from his wallet. Face up, I can see the screen of his phone when another call comes through. The name Caroline flashes across, and Luke hurries to decline the call and put the phone back in his pocket, but not before I see he has three missed calls from her already.

"Who was that?" I ask.

Luke shrugs and doesn't meet my eyes. "Wrong number, most likely."

My stomach flip-flops. Is Luke lying to me?

chapter twenty-six

LUKE

I grab my order and look around the busy coffeehouse for a table, finding one in the back. I sit, take a drink of hot coffee, and pull my laptop out of its case. It's sitting there on the table, mocking me. Opening it shouldn't be this hard.

I close my eyes for half a second, inhale, and open the damn thing. It boots up, has an issue connecting to the wifi, and then is good to go. I log onto the internet and move my fingers over the keyboard. I know what I need to type into the search bar.

But I'm not sure I want to.

My mind flashes to Lexi and I know I have to do this. I can't work at the bar forever, even though I have more than enough inheritance from my grandparents to live off of for the rest my life. I haven't touched a cent of it other than putting half into savings and the rest into different investments.

I like being a firefighter. The danger hasn't stopped me yet, and it's not going to stop me now. But applying for jobs means bringing up the past. It means asking my chief for a letter of recommendation. It means explaining why I moved away from the department I was with for nearly a decade. And I don't want to do that.

Not now. Not ever.

My vision blurs from staring at the computer screen, and I blink then force myself to at least see what's available in the city. I know it's competitive and the FDNY runs a tough hiring process. I have a degree in fire science and am still certified as an EMT, which I know will help.

I make a few notes and bookmark openings. I look over the application, mentally filling it out but don't go any farther. Not yet. I have this stupid notion if I wait long enough, everything bad from my past will disappear.

I pick up my paper cup of coffee and sigh. That's never going to happen. Unless I go into a different profession... though I don't know what else I'd do. I navigate away from job hunting and waste time looking shit up until Lexi texts me. We're meeting for lunch in twenty minutes, and Lexi promises she will be on time. I smile and tell her it's no big deal. I'm not working until tomorrow and have nothing but time. She already has enough going on, worrying about meeting me at a specific time isn't necessary.

I want to take her on a vacation. Away from the city. Away from her job. Away from anything stressful. Just for the weekend, and just the two of us. We can fuck and sleep and eat and not have a care in the world for a fleeting forty-eight hours.

I finish my coffee and pack up my shit so I can start walking downtown, meeting Lexi at the Black Ink Press building. She said she'd meet me in the lobby so I don't have to "go through the trouble" of an elevator ride. I know Lexi to be considerate, but I also know she doesn't want to risk any drama between Cole and me. While I'd rather empty bedpans at an old-folks home than hang out with my brother, I can be professional for Lexi's sake.

And Cole, well, I think he can too. But it would be for his own sake.

"Luke!" Lexi calls as soon as I step foot into the building. The constant chatter, the stomping and clicking of shoes on marble, the echoes of phones ringing...it all disappears. I look through the sea of people, eyes latching onto Lexi. She's wearing a pencil skirt, heels, and a black sweater over an ivory colored blouse. Professional. And sexy. I get a semi just looking at her.

She crosses the lobby and we embrace. Her breasts crush against me and now my cock is hard. It's been a full day since I last felt her touch, and I missed it so fucking much.

"Is there a room I can fuck you in?" I whisper, lips brushing her ear as I speak.

"Actually, yes."

I lean back to look into Lexi's eyes. "You're joking, right? Because that's not funny."

"I'm being serious. I haven't been in this room, but I've heard talk. Construction started on an office on the ninth floor, then stopped. It's been half-finished and abandoned for months. I didn't believe it until Christine from marketing pointed out the ninth floor button doesn't light up in the elevators anymore."

"Let's go."

Lexi's eyes widen and she smiles. "Really? We could get caught!"

"That's half the fun."

"I've never done this before."

I slip my hands to her waist. "I'll be gentle."

Her smile turns devious. "Okay. Let's go." She takes my

hand and leads me to the elevator. We ride up to the eight floor, then find the stairs to make it up one more. Lexi's source was right: this place was gutted and then all progress halted. Probably due to lack of funds, but I don't give a shit why. All I'm concerned about is spreading Lexi's legs wide and thrusting my cock inside of her.

Lexi looks around, biting her lip. She puts her hand on a desk and nods. "Is here good?" Her eyes land on a spot across the room. "What about there? Or over here? Over here is good. We can hear if someone comes up but makes it so they can't see us right away."

"Relax." I pull Lexi to me and kiss her. She melts against me, and sways her hips against mine. I take her hand and lead her though a jumble of crumbled drywall and discarded office furniture. "This," I say, picking her up and putting her on a desk that's just feet from the floor to ceiling window. "This is where I'll be fucking you."

Lexi looks out, down at the people milling below, and then at the high rise across from us. Her eyes are wide and I know she's worried about the risk. Her cheeks flush in the way that drives me crazy and I lose control.

I pick her up and lay her down on the desk, kissing her like I'm drowning and she's my last breath. I bunch her skirt up and then move down, putting my head between her legs. Lexi covers her face with her hand, biting her bottom lip. She flicks her eyes down and watches me. I'm kissing her thighs, sucking, biting at the skin. She's writhing against me and when I slip a finger inside her panties, she's already wet. I hook my arms under her thighs and pull her to the edge of the desk.

Her legs go over my shoulders and she crosses her ankles. Her heels dig into my back. It's so fucking hot. I cover her pussy with my mouth, feeling her heat through her panties. Lexi moans and I yank her panties to the side, exposing her, and go in, mouth open, tongue out, and alternate between licking and sucking. I don't let up until Lexi comes, and once that first orgasm rolls through her, I slip a finger inside her core, bringing on another.

Lexi presses her hands over her mouth, muffling her screams. I'm so fucking hard right now it hurts. I need to be inside her. I stand up and undo my pants, yanking them down as fast as I can. Lexi pushes herself back up on the desk and widens her legs. She's reaching for me, hands landing on my ass as I push inside. I kiss her hard and thrust even harder. I push in deep. Deeper. I can't get enough.

My orgasm comes on strong, so strong it makes me pitch forward, letting out a guttural groan as I fill Lexi. She's panting, clinging to me for dear life. I rest my head against her forehead. We stay like that a minute before I pull out and put my pants back on. Lexi tells me there are tissues in her purse, and I dig through and toss her a few so she can clean herself up.

"Saying that was fun would be a serious understatement," she says and stands only to perch on the edge of the desk. "My legs are still shaking."

I take her by the waist and put my lips to hers. Her arms fold over my shoulders and she lays her head against my chest, heart still racing. I kiss her once more.

"I'm going to come have lunch with you more often."

"I can't fucking believe it," Lexi mutters, angrily typing out a text message. She pounds her thumbs against her phone, taking her frustration out on the cell. "This is just fucking like him."

It's Saturday night, and we should be leaving to go to the Black Ink awards gala in just a few minutes. Except Russell hasn't picked up the kids from Lexi's house yet like he said he would.

"He's doing this on purpose just to piss me off." Lexi throws her phone on the bed and closes her eyes, letting out a deep breath. "I don't understand why he *still* hates me. We're done. Over with. Out of each other's lives as much as we can be. And he still pulls this shit after two years."

"Babe, relax," I say and then wish I could eat my words. Lexi has every right to be pissed and stressed. Wearing a dark purple evening gown and professionally styled hair and makeup, Lexi looks stunning. "It'll be okay. Can we drop the girls off? I'll gladly go to his house and have a nice chat with him."

"He's not home. He says he's working. On a Saturday. He's never worked on a fucking Saturday. He's not working. I know it."

I stride across the bedroom and put my hands on Lexi's arms. "We'll figure something out."

She nods, and then lets out a defeated sigh. "I can't bring them with, and I have no one to watch them in time. I'll let Quinn know I can't go."

"No," I say firmly. "I'll stay here with them and you go. You need to be there."

"Luke," she starts, shaking her head. "I can't ask you to do that."

I smile. "You didn't ask. I offered. You said your parents are at dinner right now."

"Yeah, they'll come over if I ask, but it's their anniversary so I can't do that."

"If they're eating now, they'll be done soon, right?"

Lexi's mouth opens and she nods, catching my train of thought. "Yeah, I'd guess in an hour or so."

"I'll stay here until they get here and will meet you at the gala. I know what you have on under that dress. I'm not missing the chance to have you all to myself in that paid-for hotel suite."

She laughs and puts her hands on my chest. "You sure you're okay with staying behind with the girls?"

"Positive. My toes need new polish anyway. And you can't be late."

"What would I do without you?"

"Let's hope you never have to find out."

Her eyes fill with tears and she looks away, blinking. "I can't mess up my makeup." We kiss, and then she texts her mom. The plan works, and her parents should be over here in no more than two hours.

"Luke!" Lexi exclaims. "I can't leave you here. You'll meet my mother. Without me! Oh my God. My dad will be here too. You'll meet my parents without me. They can be ruthless. And ask lots of questions. Personal questions. They pry and have no shame."

I laugh. "The thought already occurred to me. It's not ideal, but I'll be fine."

"But this isn't how it's supposed to happen. I need to be there to buffer, to make it less awkward and make you not feel like they're already writing our marriage vows."

"Lexi, it's fine. Nothing about us is conventional, so meeting your parents for the first time while I babysit your kids seems fitting, really."

She smiles and everything is worth it.

chapter
twenty-seven

LEXI

I've only been here for half an hour, and already I'm missing Luke and the girls. I check my phone for the millionth time, smiling when I see a picture Luke sent. The girls dressed him up like a princess, and Grace even put sparkly makeup on his cheeks. My heart flutters and I cannot wait until I get him alone tonight. I hold up my phone to show Jillian.

"He's a total keeper," she says. "Seriously, Lex. I'm not one to say that if I wasn't sure either."

"I know." I can't stop smiling. "He's incredible and I really think we're on the start of something good. No rushing, of course."

"Of course. Take it day by day. Enjoy it. Enjoy him. And know that I'm a little bit jealous of you."

"You're joking, right?" I say with a snort of laughter.

"Not at all. The beginning of relationships are the best. Everything is new and exciting...and Luke is so perfect."

"I thought Aaron was perfect?"

She rolls her eyes. "Please, you don't have to humor me. We both know he can be an ass."

"I thought that was part of why you liked him," I joke.

"Funny. And while Aaron treats me well, what Luke is doing for you is a whole new level of adorable." She loops her arm through mine. "Get drinks with me before the speeches start. I'll need a good buzz to get through all the boring chatter."

"We can take a shot every time someone complains about the 'changing tide in publishing'."

"We'd be on the floor before the night is over." Jillian laughs. "That's a challenge I just might accept."

We order glasses of wine from the bar and take our time going back to the table. The place is filled with authors, agents, and publicists, as well as the rest of the behind-the-scenes teams, like us editors. I've lost count of the number of hands I shook when the table comes into view. Aaron is talking to Cole, whose black suit is custom tailored and looks great on him. Aaron comes to almost every publishing function with Jillian, and is in that weird not-quite-an-acquaintance-yet-still-not-a-friend zone with Cole.

"Hey, Lexi," Aaron says. "Where's Luke? I thought he was coming with you tonight?"

Cole's eyebrows go up. "Yeah, where is he?"

I can feel Jillian's gaze on me. "He's watching my kids," I explain. "My ex bailed last minute, so Luke stayed behind to babysit until my parents can get over. He'll be here in a few hours."

"You trust my brother with your kids?" Cole shoots out.

"Wait," Aaron says loudly before I can tell Cole that I fully trust Luke. "He's your brother? Lexi is dating the boss's brother?" He laughs, earning a harsh glare from Jillian. "How'd that come about?"

"Uh, long story," I mumble, bringing my wine glass to my lips. I take a long drink.

"Hey, there's Quinn Harlow," Jillian says, saving me. I mumble a goodbye and turn away, hoping to God that Quinn catches my eye and waves me over. She's with a group of her friends, deep in conversation about something, and looks absolutely gorgeous. Her black hair is braided in neat rows and pulled into an elaborate side bun. The red dress she's wearing is designer and her makeup is sheer perfection.

Sometimes I want to be her.

"Lexi!" she squeals and breaks away from her group to give me a hug. "You look great!"

"Nowhere as good as you," I tell her. "How are you? Are you nervous? Don't be, because I've heard from a rather reliable source that you're getting that award."

Quinn waves her hand in the air. "I'm not worried. Do you have a minute? I have something I want to talk to you about."

I check the time on my phone—and okay, check to see how Luke is doing with the girls—and go with Quinn to the bar. She orders a Moscow Mule and angles her body toward mine.

"There's two parts to this, so don't freak out," she starts.

"Telling someone not to freak out makes them freak out," I say, raising an eyebrow. I take another drink of wine. "What's going on?"

"You know about my idea for the *Cold Water Bay* series, right?"

"Yes. I can't wait for it! I love friends to lovers, baby-daddy drama."

"Okay, this is the part I need you to not freak out about." She flashes a nervous smile. "I'm going to self-publish it."

I blink. "Oh. Wow. Did not expect that."

"I've been crunching numbers all month. Financially, it

makes sense. So many of my friends are indie authors, and they love it."

"I've seen a lot of authors say that, and I don't blame you for wanting to go that route. Honestly, I'm surprised you haven't taken the leap sooner."

"Part of it was not wanting to lose you. You get me and my books. Which is the second part..." She puts her hand on mine. "I want you to still edit for me. There are four books and at least two novellas in the series, and I'm willing and ready to sign a contract with you to prove I won't bail on this. Plus I'm kinda used to having deadlines. I don't know how well I'll work without them, and you're a good ball buster. So...what do you say, Lexi?"

I lean back. Blink. Replay her words in my head. Losing Quinn's series will be a blow to Black Ink. She's one of the biggest sellers right now. Me working with her on the series the Press *isn't* getting won't look good.

"Cole Winchester will hate me for this," I say. "But I'm already fucking his brother, so yes. Why the hell not?"

"Oh my God, yay! I'm so exci—wait, you're fucking who? Cole has a brother? Why did you not tell me this?"

I laugh and shake my head. "Luke, Cole's brother, is my boyfriend. He'll be here later actually. He stayed behind to babysit my kids until my parents could come by and watch them."

Quinn's eyes gloss over and she bites her bottom lip, staring at me. I know that look.

"You are not writing a book about this," I warn.

"Oh come on, Lex! It won't be you. And you know I love a good office romance. Plus brothers...threesomes are popular right now. In fiction at least. Have you...?"

"God, no!" We both laugh. "How'd your agent take it?"

"Super bummed," Quinn says. "But she understands too.

Oh, and before I forget…Kelley, my friend you did those last minute edits for, wants to know how to credit you and if you have time to do a second book."

"I get credit?" I don't mean to sound so excited.

"In indie books, most editors do."

"I'm already liking this new gig."

Quinn beams. "I'm so glad you do. Can you meet next week to go over details? I'm in the city until Wednesday."

"Yeah. Does Tuesday work?"

"Yes, just give me the time."

The lights dim, letting us know the speeches and awards ceremony is about to start. I go back to the table, a bit surprised to see Cole still sitting there. The table seats eight and is filled, and the only empty chair is between Cole and Jillian. The bigwigs from Black Ink—the guys who get the final say in what we publish or not—give speeches about books and publishing. Not even five minutes into it, Caitlin Black brings up the ever-changing tide of publishing. I look at Jillian and raise my glass of wine.

She shakes her head, silently laughing, and takes a drink too. My phone vibrates with a text, and I trade my wine for it, moving it down into my lap so it's less obvious I'm not paying attention.

It's another picture from Luke. The girls finished Luke's makeover, and put clips and bows in his hair, and are sitting in the selfie next to him beaming.

Luke: *They said I needed to get my hair done for the night too.*

Me: *I love it. So sexy. Are the girls being good?*

Luke: *Yeah. They're great kids. You did a good job with them. Paige told me you're the "best mama" and I have to say I agree. Also, it took me way too long to figure out that "girl-cheese" is really a grilled cheese sandwich.*

Me: *LOL I should have written you a cheat-sheet. You don't have to go out of your way and cook anything. Grace knows where the snacks are. You can tell her to get something from the pantry.*

Luke: *Already made it :-) Grilled cheese is easy, you know.*

I'm smiling like a fool. I scroll up to the photo of Luke with the girls. We *are* on the start of something good. I can't wait to see where this takes us. Applause breaks out around me, and I drop my phone onto my lap so I can clap. I look up just in time to see Cole looking away. Was he reading over my shoulder? It doesn't matter. I just hope things don't get weird. Again.

The formalities end—and Quinn did win that award—and now it's time for us to get up and mingle. It's the best and worst part of these functions. Best, because I can mingle my way over to the food. Worst, because I have to pretend I don't hate the human race. I'm glad I have Jillian to walk around with. I can throw her to the wolves and she'll thank me later. For real. She loves talking.

My mom texts me to let me know they just left the restaurant, so I can let Luke know they're on their way. I sneak away from the crowd to call Luke.

"Hey babe," he answers. "Miss me yet?"

"Not at all," I tell him. "Okay. Maybe just a little. How are my girls?"

"Still great. Grace is helping Paige in the bathroom, and I hear a lot of giggling. I'm not really sure what to do," he confesses, which makes me laugh.

"If they're not out in two minutes, you can tell them to get dressed and come out. They should listen to you. My parents are on their way too. I still feel terrible for leaving you alone with them."

"Don't. We're having fun here and I'm sure your parents will be just as charmed by me."

Now I'm laughing again. God—this man. "I don't see how they won't be. Oh, Quinn won."

"See? You needed to be there. Aren't you glad you went ahead?"

"Yes. It's very professional to be here for her, plus she's my friend. I've been editing for her since she started writing. Oh, and you'll never guess what she told me! Really, you'll never guess since you don't know anything about publishing."

Luke laughs. "What did she tell you?"

"She's going to self—" I cut off when Jillian rushes down the hallway, calling my name. "Hang on."

"Thank God," Jillian rushes out. "I've been looking for you. I need you. Now."

"Why? What's going on?"

"Cole," she says. "He's drunk. There are a lot of important people here and he's going to make a fool out of himself. I don't know what to do. I've never seen him like this. Lori and Christine tried to get him to go home already and it didn't work."

"Luke?" I say into the phone, following Jillian back towards the event room. "I'll call you back. Or will see you when you get here in a bit. Apparently your brother is wasted."

"Cole doesn't drink," Luke tells me. I look inside and see Cole at the bar.

"He is tonight." I sigh. "If I can find his assistant, I'll make her deal with this. But if the owners of Black Ink Press see him drunk in public, they'll throw a shit fit."

"Let them. It's his own damn fault."

"Luke, stop. I know you guys don't get along, but he's my

boss. And he's been my friend for the last few years. I'll just...uh...take him for a walk." I see Cole obviously checking out Jenny Rosita, a film agent. She's married and her husband is standing right next to her, about to notice Cole's wandering eyes.

"A walk? Like a dog?"

"He's acting like one," I say. "I have to go. Call me when you're here and I'll meet you at the door."

"Can't someone else deal with him?" Luke sounds annoyed. "Why does it have to be you?"

"Because I'm the nice one who can't say no."

"That's what I'm worried about," Luke grumbles and I'm not entirely sure I caught what he said. "I think your parents are here."

I stop in my tracks, mind checking out of the gala and going back home. I wish I were there, introducing Luke to Mom and Dad. And not because I want to save Luke from parental torture. But because I'm proud to say he's mine.

"Good luck. Feel free to use the girls as a distraction."

"I should probably wash the sparkly makeup off before I meet them. Shit."

"Nah, it'll make them like you more. Really."

"There's something I never thought I'd hear: wearing makeup will score bonus points with my girlfriend's parents."

I laugh. "Like you said. We're unconventional."

"I'll see you soon. Be careful around Cole. I don't trust him. I think he's up to something again."

Luke's words throw me. "Okay. Drive safe."

I hang up and rush into the event hall, making a beeline for Cole. I stand in front of him, blocking his line of sight from Jenny. To be fair, I'm having a hard time not staring too. I don't know how she can show that much cleavage with no nipple slippage. Double sided sticky tape? I mentally shake myself. It doesn't matter.

"Hey!" I say to Cole. "How ya feeling?"

"Alexis," he sighs and reaches out, tucking a curl behind my ear. The gesture is intimate and makes me shiver with discomfort. Luke touches me like that. "You look amazing tonight."

"You're not so bad either. How about we go get some fresh air." I put my hand on his back and turn him around. "And maybe a water."

"Nah, I'm good."

"Really you should—never mind." I remember Luke's words about water not helping like people think it does. "It's nice tonight. Come take a walk with me."

I checked my coat at the door, glad the late spring air only had a slight chill to it. I don't own a coat that looks good with this fancy-shmancy dress. I slip my arms through my hot pink Northface jacket and lead Cole to the doors.

"I'm sorry, Alexis," Cole says when we start down the sidewalk.

"Sorry for what?" We walk slowly, and Cole stays close to me. I can't tell just how far-gone he is, and I don't want to be responsible for him falling into oncoming traffic.

"For being an ass." I stop, turning toward him. "I didn't mean for things to get so dragged out. And I guess I...I just got a little jealous."

"Of Luke?"

"Yeah. He was talking about this great girl he met at the bar, going on and on, and I hated seeing him happy. Because I want to be happy. He took that from me, you know." His words slur a bit. "And I wanted to take it from him. And then I saw he called you and I knew I needed to not only get even but also protect you from him. Luke doesn't date. He's a love 'em and leave 'em kind of guy. I've never seen him commit to anything in his whole life."

My brow furrows. Is there any merit in Cole's drunk ramblings? Wait—saw he called? My mouth opens and an audible gasp escapes my lips. "The next day...that Monday... you were in my office when he called. You knew. You knew all along and were just waiting for us to get caught. That's why you took me to lunch!" I whirl around, staring down Cole.

"Yes," he admits. "And I'm sorry. All I wanted was to get even, and then I realized that everything he said was true. You *are* an amazing woman, and I want you too."

I stop walking and put my head in my hands. This is just too much.

"I'm so sorry, Lexi," he says again, despondent.

"You're my boss and Luke is my boyfriend and I'll be the first to admit that it's weird. But I really, *really* like him, so let's please just put this all behind us, okay? All is forgiven and move on with a clean slate? I don't want to have you mad at me forever." The words leave my mouth before I realize the implications.

"Forever?" he asks, the word slurring a bit. "You already want forever with...with *him*?"

I shake my head. "I don't know. It's too early to say, but I'm the happiest I have been in a long time. I just want us all to get along. Not that I expect to hang out or double date or anything, just not be at each other's throats. Please, Cole. This is making me really uncomfortable. I like Luke. I'm with Luke. We're happy. You're drunk and don't mean what you're saying. Can we drop this, please?"

Cole looks down at me. "Of course."

I let out a breath of relief, wishing so much Luke was

here right now. "Why don't you two get along? What happened to make you dislike him so much?"

"I don't dislike him. I hate him."

"Yeah, but why?"

Cole's eyes close and he stops walking. He lets out a huff and moves forward again, and I'm struggling to keep up. "He knows. Ask him. What he doesn't say speaks volumes."

"Fine. I will ask him."

"Though he's going to tell you he doesn't know what I'm talking about. That's how he is. Manipulative and a liar. Did he tell you why he left Chicago?"

I shake my head. "Not specifically. I know he got injured at work, so I assume it had to do with that."

"You need to ask him about that too. But be prepared for everything to change."

Is Drunk-Cole dramatic or has the booze shut off his filter and everything he's saying is true? We walk around the block and then go back inside. Caitlin Black, the granddaughter of Isaac Black, the founder of the publishing house, is making her way toward us.

"I fucking hate that woman," Cole mutters. "She's such a fucking bitch."

"Okay, and we're leaving," I say and take Cole's arm, spinning him around before he has a chance to say something nasty to Caitlin. I don't like her much either. She's one of those people that can find the smallest thing to criticize you for. Stress rises inside me. I don't want to be Cole's babysitter all night. I want to go back into the event hall, get another glass of wine, and talk to Quinn and Jillian until Luke gets here.

And then I want to take him up to our hotel room and fuck his brains out.

I flick my eyes to Cole. The best thing will be getting him

out of here. Once he's home, he can't do any damage. Once he's home, I can enjoy the night how I intended. With Luke, and Luke alone.

"I think it's time I take you home," I say to Cole.

He grins. "Yes, take me home."

LUKE

"*H*e looks beau-ful!" Paige says proudly to her grandparents, pointing to the sparkles on my face. "I did his hair."

"And I did his makeup," Grace adds. Lexi's parents just walked through the door and the girls are eager to show off their skills. The second that door closed, a wave of nerves went through me, and it had nothing to do with the princess makeover.

I like Lexi. A lot. And I want her parents to like me too. I've never met anyone's parents before, and never took anyone home to see mine. I'm meeting Lexi's mom and dad now out of necessity, but it's still just as nerve-wracking regardless.

"You girls did a great job!" Lexi's mother coos. She looks at me and smiles. "I'm Brenda. Nice to meet you."

"Richard," Lexi's father says and extends his hand. "I see my granddaughters gave you the star treatment. We want to thank you for what you did tonight for our Lexi."

"I'll do anything for her," I confess. "I'm a little crazy about your daughter."

Brenda beams. "How could you not be? Lexi is quite the catch."

I mirror her smile. "She really is."

"Papa!" Paige says and takes her grandfather's hand. "Come see Addy's new bedroom set! It has so many pieces!" Richard takes off after Paige and Grace, and Brenda says she's going to bring me makeup remover for the sparkles. I guess they're hard to come off sometimes. I take the bows from my hair and run my fingers through it, glad the messy look works for me.

"Lexi warned me not to ask too many questions," Brenda says, coming down the stairs from Lexi's room with a washcloth and bottle of makeup remover. "Or embarrass her. So I won't. Not this time." She gives me a wink and hands over the supplies. It takes a good five minutes of scrubbing to get my face clean, and now I have a new appreciation for women who do this daily. I go upstairs and change back into my suit, then head down to say bye to the kids before I drive into the city.

The girls are in the living room, playing with their dolls. "Thanks for hanging out with me tonight," I tell them. Paige runs over and throws her arms around me.

"Will you play with me again?"

"I'll definitely will play with you again."

"Yay!" Paige's little arms squeeze me as tight as she can. "Don't go! Stay one more minute!"

"Honey," Brenda says. "Luke has to go home and get in bed. It's late. And you two—and you, Pluto—are coming over to our house for a sleepover!"

Paige gets all excited and starts doing her "sleepover dance", which looks eerily similar to the pizza dance. Grace lets out a disappointed sigh.

"We're only going over because Dad didn't want us."

Grace isn't even my kid, and the comment hurts. I want to give her a hug, take her out for ice cream, and punch Russell in the fucking face.

"No," Richard quickly says. "Your father had to work tonight. He loves you very much."

Brenda's green eyes narrow and she's shaking her head. Grace's eyes fall on me. "I wish he was our dad. At least he plays with us. Dad just puts in a movie and gives Paige his phone to watch those stupid egg videos."

I move my gaze to Richard for help since I have no fucking idea how to respond to that.

"He's your friend," Brenda says. "And you heard Luke, he'll come over and play another day."

And now I get why Lexi was so hesitant in the first place to let her kids know that I'm in the picture. They get attached easily and disappointed even easier. Paige takes her arms from me and lets out a dramatic sigh.

"Okay, bye. See you later alligator. In a while crocodile. Too-da-lou, little shoe."

"That's not how you say it," Grace quips. We all laugh and I get up to leave. Richard walks me to the door while Brenda helps the girls gather up their stuff.

"I do hope to see you again, Luke," he says. "Though I have a feeling we will. You seem like a good man."

"I was raised to be one."

"Your father must have been a good role model."

I shake my head. "He was a terrible one. But my stepfather was great."

Richard smiles and opens the door for me, holding Pluto back. I call Lexi on the way and get her voicemail. Assuming she's busy talking to famous authors or something cool like that, I don't bother leaving a voicemail. My mind drifts to Lexi, to taking that gown off her and utilizing the oversized jetted tub in the hotel room. I'm looking forward to spoiling her, to doing everything I can to make her relax and feel good.

My phone rings a few minutes later. But it's not Lexi. It's Caroline again, and I can't decline the call fast enough. Doesn't she get it by now? I don't want to talk to her. I don't want any of her pointless updates. Nothing changes. Nothing will change.

You can't fix broken.

When I get close to the place the gala is held, I get an alert on my phone. The alarm at the house was triggered, and it took thirty-seven seconds to turn off via the keypad right inside the door. I call Lexi and get her voicemail again. I leave a quick message saying I'm going to check out the house and make sure things are okay.

The cleaning company Cole hired knows the code. I told Cole it was stupid to let anyone have the code, and he argued with me that the company was reputable and that "most people on this block allow their staff"—his words, not mine—to come in their house when no one is home. Cole wasn't home much anyway, so someone had to come in during the day.

The girls who came in and cleaned the house twice a week were college students, always very friendly and very nice. They didn't strike me as the breaking and entering type, but you never know. They could have given the key and the code to someone else.

Maybe I'm a little paranoid. Being a little never hurt anyone. I'm close to our house, but these damn one-way streets make it take twice as long to get there. I have to park several yards away down the street and walk to the house.

There is a light in the living room, its soft yellow glow lighting up one of the front windows. So someone *is* in there. I pull my keys from my pocket and sneak through the alley so I could enter the house from the other side. With silence that would impress a ninja, I open the backdoor and emerge into the kitchen.

I hear a voice. A voice I know. A voice I like. A voice that can get me hard with just a few dirty words.

"For the love of God, just lay down!" she exasperates. "I need to get back to the gala!"

My eyebrows push together. Who is she talking to? I walk through the kitchen, through the formal dining room, and emerge into the living room. Lexi and Cole are sitting on the couch. Cole's belt is on the floor, and his shirt is untucked. Lexi holds a blanket, and her shoes are lying discarded in the doorway.

"What the hell is this?" I demand. The sound of my voice causes Lexi to jump. Cole turns, eyes meeting mine for a millisecond before he turns around. He wraps his arms around Lexi and pulls her in for a kiss.

I freeze, knowing I'm going to blow at any second. Anger takes over, and all I want to do is beat the ever-living shit out of Cole. I want to punish him with my fists, hitting him until blood splatters the walls and the raging hurt inside me goes away.

And Lexi—what the fuck is she doing here? I told her Cole wasn't over his revenge. I don't even know what I supposedly did, but he's dead set on ruining the one thing I have that makes me happy.

Lexi tenses and pushes Cole away. She breaks away and reaches for me. I storm past her, grab Cole's shirt and shove him to the ground. I don't see anything but red. My fist smacks into his face. Once. Twice. Three times. Blood drips from his nose or maybe his lip. I don't know. I don't care. I'm so fucking mad.

"Luke!" Lexi screams and puts her hand on my shoulder. I stop, calmed by her gentle touch. I stand up and stare down at Cole, filled with so much rage. "Luke," Lexi says again, and I turn, eyes meeting hers. I want to hug her, hold her, tell her she's mine and is never to go near this fucker ever again.

Then I do something I never thought I'd do.

I turn and walk away.

I walk away, not because I don't want Lexi. I walk away because I do. It's not fair to stick her in the middle of this, to subject her to the petty game Cole insists on playing. She's not a pawn to be used in his revenge.

I can't do that to Lexi.

Because I'm in love with her.

I don't want to hurt her. To cause her more drama or pain. Being with me automatically puts her in the middle of something she shouldn't have to deal with.

"Luke!" Lexi calls, and I can feel the floor vibrating as she runs through the house. "Wait! Please, Luke!" I'm not thinking. I'm just moving. And now I'm back in my car, heading down the street. I make it two blocks before I slow down. This is what he wants, and I'll be damned if I give it to him.

I make an illegal U-turn and speed back to the house. Back to Lexi. I'm going to kiss her harder than I ever have before, and then I'm going to take her upstairs and fuck her so good she'll be screaming my name loud enough for the neighbors to hear.

And then finally, Cole will know he can't come between us.

My phone vibrates in my hand. I look down, expecting Lexi.

It's Caroline again, though this time she sent a text

message. I look down, and read the two words she sent me. Two words that change everything. Two words I never thought I'd read. Words that defy the very reason I left my life behind and moved halfway across the country. Because if I was wrong about this, then I'm wrong about everything.

Two.

Little.

Words.

He's awake.

∽

The story continues in book two of the Love is Messy Series, TWICE BURNED.

ABOUT THE AUTHOR

Emily Goodwin is the New York Times and USA Today Bestselling author of over a dozen of romantic titles. Emily writes the kind of books she likes to read, and is a sucker for a swoon-worthy bad boy and happily ever afters.

She lives in the midwest with her husband and two daughters. When she's not writing, you can find her riding her horses, hiking, reading, or drinking wine with friends.

Emily is represented by Julie Gwinn of the Seymour Agency.

STALK ME
www.emilygoodwinbooks.com
www.facebook.com/emilygoodwinbooks
Instagram: authoremilygoodwin
Email: emily@emilygoodwinbooks.com
Sign up for my mailing list here.

ACKNOWLEDGMENTS

There are so many people to thank, it's nearly impossible to name them all. But first and foremost, thank you Mimi for coming over during the day and watching my girls so I could write. This book would have taken twice as long to write if it weren't for your help. To my husband: thank you for going the extra mile to help me with this book from giving me kid-free evenings to your encouragement.

To my beta readers: you all rock! Your excitement over this book and early feedback are critical. Rose. Diane, Felicia, Theresa, Melanie, Michelle, Paige, and Debby...I cannot thank you enough.

Christine: you have the patience of a saint for putting up with me, for helping me, for encouraging me, and for being my friend.

TL Smith: my release sister! This has been one hell of a ride and I'm so glad you're on it with me!

ALSO BY EMILY GOODWIN

Standalone Novels

One Call Away

Never Say Never

Outside the Lines

First Comes Love

Then Comes Marriage

Stay

All I Need

Love is Messy Duet Series

Hot Mess (Luke & Lexi, book 1)

Twice Burned (Luke & Lexi, book 2)

Bad Things (Cole & Ana, book 3)

Battle Scars (Cole & Ana, book 4)

Dawson Family Series

Cheat Codes

End Game

Side Hustle (Releasing Dec 6th)